DRUMFIRE

The new and unusual case for
Detectives Brock and Poole

One Saturday night, a masked gunman walks into a jazz club and murders the drummer. Very soon, Detective Chief Inspector Brock and Detective Sergeant Poole find themselves taking an interest in the guests at a party in Surrey's stockbroker belt, which leads them to look again at a five-year-old robbery and to interview a dozen or so armed robbers. The killer is eventually arrested, but not before numerous extra-marital affairs come to light and a bullion van is attacked...

Graham Ison titles available from Severn House Large Print

Working Girl
Whispering Grass
Kicking the Air

DRUMFIRE

Graham Ison

Severn House Large Print
London & New York

This first large print edition published 2009
in Great Britain and the USA by
SEVERN HOUSE PUBLISHERS LTD of
9-15 High Street, Sutton, Surrey, SM1 1DF.
First world regular print edition published 2007 by
Severn House Publishers Ltd., London and New York.

British Library Cataloguing in Publication Data

Ison, Graham.
  Drumfire
  1. Brock, Harry (Fictitious character)--Fiction. 2. Poole,
  Dave (Fictitious character)--Fiction. 3. Police--England--
  London--Fiction. 4. Detective and mystery stories. 5. Large
  type books.
  I. Title
  823.9'14-dc22

  ISBN-13: 978-0-7278-7790-1

Printed and bound in Great Britain by
MPG Books Ltd, Bodmin, Cornwall.

One

It was a beautiful, warm summer's evening on a Saturday in early July. My girlfriend Gail Sutton, a gorgeous, leggy blonde and sometime actress and chorus girl, had just poured me a brandy. We'd enjoyed a very pleasant dinner *à deux* – she's an exceptionally good cook – at her town house in Kingston. Now we were relaxing in the sitting room on the first floor, gazing out through the open French windows and at peace with the world.

And at nine o'clock my mobile rang.

Gail shot me a glance that forbade me to answer it, but she knew that I couldn't ignore it; I was liable to get calls at any time of the day or night. That was one of the penalties of being a detective chief inspector on – are you ready for this? – one of the major investigation teams of Specialist Crime Directorate 1, in our case known as Homicide West. We used to be called Serious Crime Group West, but the Metropolitan Police takes great delight in changing everything from time to time. Not that it makes any difference. Same detectives, same job.

'Harry Brock,' I said into my little plastic box. I'm not exactly a dab hand with mobile phones, but I can just about manage to use one for the basics. Like receiving and sending calls. Sending text messages is, however, a foreign country. If I'm silly enough to try, I usually finish up sending an incomprehensible, misspelt message to someone I don't even know.

'It's Gavin Creasey, sir,' said the night-duty incident-room manager at Curtis Green, the headquarters of Homicide West. Curtis Green is a little-known turning off Whitehall in Westminster, although not many people know that, including the police. The CID officers of Homicide West have the misfortune to be responsible for investigating murders – murders that none of the elitist squads of the Metropolitan Police want to demean themselves to investigate – in that broad swathe of London that stretches from Westminster to Hillingdon in the west, Barnet in the north and Richmond in the south. And that includes Chelsea, a place where the poor naive taxpaying residents believe that they are immune from any such nastiness.

'What is it, Gavin?'

'You're not going to believe this, sir...' Gavin began.

'Try me,' I said.

'The Starlight Club, Fulham Palace Road.'

'What about it?' I began to feel disturbing

vibes already. Anything involving a club always turned out to be a problem. In my case, anyway.

'It's a jazz club, guv. At about eight-thirty, a guy wearing a mask entered the club with a sawn-off shotgun, and fired at the drummer. Completely destroyed the bass drum.' Creasey emitted a coarse laugh, but that is the sort of incident that will activate a policeman's black sense of humour. 'But then he lets off a second round and kills the drummer.'

'And?' I queried.

There was another laugh from Creasey. 'He escaped in the ensuing confusion, sir.'

'I presume you mean the gunman escaped, not the victim,' I said sarcastically, and made a wry face at Gail. Gail just sighed; she knew what was going to happen next. 'Get a car down here for me, Gavin. I'm not going to risk driving myself.' There is nothing the Black Rats, as we of the cognoscenti call the traffic police, like better than to catch a CID officer with a positive breathalyser reading.

'Right, sir,' said Gavin. 'Er, home address?' he queried archly.

'No,' I said, and gave him Gail's address. 'Have Dave Poole and the rest of the supporting cast been informed?' Dave Poole was my black sergeant bag-carrier, a term the Criminal Investigation Department uses to describe an investigating officer's assistant.

But in my case, Dave was probably more useful than my right arm. What I didn't think of, and that was a fairly long list, Dave certainly would.

'On their way to the scene as I speak, sir.'

Five minutes later, considerably quicker than if I'd been a civilian reporting an ongoing burglary, an immaculate traffic car drew up outside.

The driver, a white-capped constable, wound down his window. 'Understand you want a lift to Fulham, guv,' he said, and yawned.

'Yes. The Starlight Club in Fulham Palace Road.'

'Hop in, guv. Urgent, is it?'

'Yes,' I said, but not without some misgiving. A misgiving that proved to be fully justified. The car swung out of the mews and carved its way through the Saturday evening traffic with the aid of its siren and blue lights. Most other road users wisely avoided us, but one ageing Toyota driver stopped dead, right in front of us. My driver swore volubly, mounted the footway – policemen always call pavements 'the footway' – and suggested that Toyota man should buy a copy of the Highway Code and get someone to read it to him. Unfortunately this useful piece of advice was lost; the windows were closed and Toyota man didn't hear it.

Eventually, however, I was deposited,

somewhat shaken, at my destination. Eight miles in about as many minutes through London's dense traffic is enough to unnerve even the bravest, and I am definitely not in that category.

'Thank you,' I said as I staggered from the car.

'Any time, guv,' said the driver cheerfully.

I determined that there wouldn't be another time if I could possibly avoid it.

The usual blue-and-white tapes had been strung out around the building that, with any luck, contained the Starlight Club, where my latest investigation was about to begin.

Registering my arrival with the incident officer – a tired inspector who looked as though he'd rather be someplace else – I learned that Fulham's centre of hot jazz was in the basement. But where else would it be?

Descending a dark, uncarpeted staircase, I found that the Starlight Club comprised little more than a number of cellars knocked into one. There were tables with dirty check tablecloths, and candles in bottles that were, I supposed, intended to provide a subdued and intimate lighting. But the effect had been rather spoiled by the floodlights that the forensic-science team had brought with them and set up around the stage in order to take photographs of the scene.

Dave Poole was in earnest conversation with Henry Mortlock, the Home Office forensic pathologist. Although Henry and I are on separate call-out lists, we always seem to arrive at the scene of the same murders. Perhaps he likes my sense of humour, although I have to say that his perverted and cynical outlook on life would rival that of the most hard-bitten, long-serving detective.

'Harry, nice of you to come,' said Henry, as though he were welcoming me to a select soirée arranged especially to listen to the latest work of an obscure composer. 'Cause of death was a shotgun blast to the chest at close quarters. Time of death about eight-thirty.'

'You've been talking to the witnesses,' I said.

'No, I haven't, but Sergeant Poole has.' Henry waved a thermometer in Dave's direction. 'I'll let you have a report in due course.' And with that he departed. Obviously Henry was not an aficionado of jazz played in basements.

'Do we know who this guy is, Dave?' I asked, drawing closer to the stage and surveying the drummer's body. It was not a pretty sight: the chest area and the bottom half of the face were a mass of blood and torn shirt.

'Just as well he won't be needing that shirt again,' commented Dave, and glanced up. 'Goes by the name of Rod Skinner, guv,' he said. 'Or did.'

'Well, that's something, I suppose. Have the CSEs finished yet?' I asked, using the accepted abbreviation for crime-scene examiners.

'They're not called that any more,' said Dave, glancing up from his pocket book. 'They're now called forensic practitioners: senior forensic practitioner, forensic practitioner and assistant forensic practitioner, as applicable.' He gave me an owlish grin.

'Ye Gods!' I muttered. Obviously the boy superintendents in the funny names and total confusion squad at Scotland Yard had been at it again. 'I suppose I'm still a detective chief inspector,' I observed sarcastically.

'Probably depends on the outcome of this murder, guv,' said Dave drily.

'And have the *forensic practitioners* finished, by any chance?' I asked, repeating my original question, as amended, and laying emphasis on their new title.

'Here, Mr Brock.'

I turned to find Linda Mitchell standing behind me, the very picture of a sexy scientist in her fetching white coveralls and plastic overshoes.

'Dave's just been telling me you've got a new title, Linda,' I said.

Linda's pretty face adopted an expression of displeasure. 'Unfortunately, Mr Brock, it makes no difference to my pay,' she said. 'I don't know why they bothered.'

'Welcome to the club,' I said. I concluded that Linda had been working with case-hardened detectives for too long. It had left its mark and some of the scepticism had rubbed off.

We were joined by Kate Ebdon, attired as usual in jeans and a white shirt, her auburn hair tied back in a ponytail. Kate, an Australian, is the detective inspector in charge of the 'legwork' team that does all the day-to-day enquiries that are inevitably spawned by a murder. She was a useful addition if for no better reason than that she scared the life out of villains, and had been known to charm the pants off male detectives. Literally. Or so it was rumoured.

'I've got the surviving four-fifths of the band over there, guv'nor.' Kate waved a hand at a disconsolate and ageing group of musicians corralled at a table in a corner. I later discovered that they were a saxophonist, a double-bass player, a trumpeter and a pianist. But the demise of the drummer had clearly not blunted their thirst; each had a glass of beer in front of him. 'The missing fifth member, who only recently played his last paradiddle, is lying on the stage in amongst the wreckage of the bass drum, sundry snare drums, a tom-tom, cowbells, maracas and a hi-hat.'

'Yes, I've just had a look at him.'

As I approached the little group of musicians, the double-bass player – a man of at least fifty – told us he was called Les Roper and appointed himself spokesman.

'How much longer do we have to hang about here, chief?' he demanded.

'How long would you have been here otherwise?' asked Dave from behind me.

'Midnight at least,' said Roper.

'You've still got a couple of hours in hand, then,' said Dave dismissively. 'By the way, what d'you play?'

Roper was obviously mystified by that question. 'What do we play? Well, I play bass, and Jim—'

'What sort of music?' asked Dave patiently.

'Oh right. Jazz, of course.'

'Trad or modern?'

'Trad. There's a lot of people who don't like modern jazz.'

'Yeah, I know. I'm one of them,' said Dave. 'But that blows one motive out of the window,' he added, turning to me.

'What motive?'

'If they'd been playing modern, we could have been looking for a trad-loving killer.'

As I may have mentioned before, Dave Poole has a quirky sense of humour, but he's an outstandingly good detective. What's more, he's very well educated, which is pretty unusual in our trade. He has a good degree in English from London University, something that's obvious from his dislike of people

13

who bastardize the language. Mind you, he can speak the lingua franca of the criminal fraternity when it suits him.

'How long have you known Mr Skinner, Mr Roper?' I asked, determined to make a start on finding out who had killed the drummer and perpetrated an act of criminal damage on his drum kit.

'About three weeks, I suppose,' said Roper.

'And the rest of you?' I asked.

'The same,' said the trumpeter, whose name, Kate said, was Cyril Underwood. 'He only joined us three weeks ago. The last drummer did a runner and we rooted around until we found Rod. He reckoned he was a sessions musician. Well, we all are really, but the four of us have been together for about a year. That's right, isn't it, lads?' He looked around at his fellow bandsmen, and they nodded. 'We've been playing gigs here, off and on, for about six months. We call ourselves the Jazz Kittens.'

Kate Ebdon stifled a laugh. Anything less descriptive of this little group of geriatric jazz players as 'kittens' would have been hard to envisage. 'I've had the lads take brief statements from that lot, guv,' she said, waving a hand at the thirty or so jazz enthusiasts who were seated at various tables around the gloomy cavern. 'All right to let them go?'

'Anything useful, Kate?' I asked.

'Not really. The first that most of them

knew of anything was when this guy loosed off at the bass drum. Then he discharged his second cartridge and hit the drummer fair and square in the chest. People started screaming and leaping about, and while that was going on the guy with the shotgun took off.'

'Didn't anyone try to stop him?' I realized immediately that it was a stupid question. When a guy with a sawn-off shotgun decides to escape through a crowd of panic-stricken patrons they tend to afford him right of way.

'No,' said Kate. 'I don't think they tried.'

'Description?'

Kate laughed. 'Ah yes. Now let me see.' She glanced briefly at her pocket book. 'Between five-six and six-two. Slim to heavy build. Dressed in blue jeans or maybe khaki chinos, with a black T-shirt or possibly a light blue one or even a white one, with or without an anorak, thin or bulky. The one thing those who saw him were agreed on was that he was wearing a stocking mask over his head.'

'Terrific!' This was shaping up to be the usual sort of murder I investigated. 'Is there a bouncer on the door of this place?'

'No, guv,' said Dave. 'And if you want my opinion the management is breaching about twenty fire regulations and more Health and Safety laws than you can shake a stick at.'

'Make a note,' I said. 'It might be all we've got to go to court with.' I was joking of course, even though it might turn out to be true. 'Yes, Kate, you can let the so-called witnesses go. By the way, who called the police?'

'About six of them, guv,' said Kate. 'All on their mobiles, except for those who found they couldn't get a signal while lying face down underneath a table in a basement.'

Funny thing about CID officers, they all seem so terribly cynical. I can't think why.

Linda came back to me. 'We're about done here, Mr Brock. I'll let you know what we've found as soon as possible, and I'll run the fingerprint check as soon as I can.'

I returned to Cyril Underwood, the trumpeter. 'You said earlier that you found Mr Skinner about three weeks ago.'

'That's right.'

'How?'

'We put an ad in the local paper.'

'Which local paper?'

'The *Fulham Gazette*.'

'So he must live locally,' I mused.

'Dunno,' said Underwood. 'I don't know where he lived. It didn't matter. He turned up for a session here one afternoon when we were rehearsing, and we took him on.'

'What d'you know about him?' asked Dave.

'Nothing, except he was a good drummer. You see, chief, there's lots of people who think they can play drums, but when it comes down to it, they're just amateurs. But Rod was bloody good.'

'Did he ever say anything about his personal life? Or did he mention any enemies?'

Underwood laughed. 'No, he never said anything at all really. Kept himself to himself. But we didn't care, did we?' He glanced at the other three members of the group, and they shook their heads. 'See, we're only interested in playing jazz. It's a sort of passion, if you get my meaning. Just can't help doing it.'

'How old was Rod Skinner?' I asked. I had formed my own opinion when I viewed the body, but it's good to get confirmation.

Les Roper, the bass player, sucked through his teeth – presumably as an aid to thought – and eventually took a guess that Skinner had been about forty-five years old. Which was exactly what I'd thought.

'Have you got the Jazz Kittens' names and addresses, Kate?' I asked.

'Yes, guv,' said Kate, coughing to hide another outbreak of laughter, 'and brief statements. I've arranged for them to come to the local nick tomorrow and give detailed statements.'

'OK,' I said to the group of musicians, 'you can go now, but I may want to see you again in the near future.'

The band began to pack up their instruments. Their conversation seemed to lack any regret at the passing of Rod Skinner, other than the inconvenience it would cause them in having to find a replacement drummer.

17

'Happy bunch, aren't they, guv?' said Kate as the instrumentalists disappeared up the stairs and into the night.

'Is there a manager in this place?' I asked, having suddenly realized that we had yet to speak to anyone in authority.

'Yes, there's an office in the corner behind the bar,' said Dave. 'I told her to stay there until we had time to speak to her.'

'*Her*?' I don't know why – call it male chauvinism, if you like – but I always imagined that a place like this would have a man in charge. Doubtless, Gail would have had a few pithy words to say about that.

Erica Leech was in her late thirties or early forties, with short blonde hair cut in a mannish style. She wasn't slim, but all the bulges were the right shape and in the right place. Her yellow vest top revealed the sort of well-developed shoulders of someone who might have been a serious swimmer in her youth. When we entered her office she was sitting behind her desk nursing what looked like a large Scotch.

'I understand you're the manager, Ms Leech,' I said once introductions had been effected.

'I'm the owner,' said Erica. 'And this sort of palaver doesn't do my business any bloody good at all.' I rapidly came to the conclusion that Ms Leech wouldn't be laying a bunch of flowers at the front of the stage. 'Can I offer you a drink?' she asked.

'No thanks. The drummer is the man who was killed,' I began.

'Yeah, I heard. He was good, that boy.'

I was amused at her description of Skinner as a boy. We were fairly sure that Skinner was in his mid-forties and, therefore, older than Erica.

'What d'you know about him?' I asked.

Erica drained her glass and stood up to refill it from a whisky bottle on top of a filing cabinet. 'Nothing, really. All I do is to hire the complete package. If I get wind of a good group, I'll go and have a listen and if they're up to the mark, I'll take them on. This lot performs here twice a week. Fridays and Saturdays.'

'Did you ever get anyone here enquiring after him?' Dave asked, keen to discover if anyone had been sussing out the place in general and Skinner in particular.

'Not as far as I know. No one asked me, anyway. I've got a couple of waitresses working here. They might have been quizzed about him.'

'Waitresses?' I turned to Kate Ebdon. 'What d'you know about waitresses?' I asked.

'There were a couple of kids with big boobs and miniskirts here when I arrived, but the ambulance crew took them away. They had a touch of the vapours and were carted off to be treated for shock. I've got their pars, though,' Kate added, using the customary police shorthand for 'particulars'.

'So you know nothing about Rod Skinner then, Ms Leech?' I asked, returning my attention to the owner of the Starlight Club. 'Other than he was a good drummer.'

'Didn't even know that was his name until Cyril told me he'd been shot. And for goodness' sake call me Erica.'

'Where were you when the shooting took place, then?'

'In here, trying to do the books. If I don't keep up to date, I'm in a right bloody state by the time the tax return's due to go in. Then I'll have the Inland Revenue down here bending my ear and demanding to see everything.'

'Revenue and Customs,' said Dave, a stickler for accuracy in such matters.

'What?' Erica gazed at Dave as though he'd taken leave of his senses.

'It's called Her Majesty's Revenue and Customs now.'

'Frankly, I don't give a toss what they're called,' said Erica with a dismissive shrug. 'They're still a bloody nuisance.' She waved a hand towards the main part of the club. 'How much longer are you going to be messing about in there?'

'We're just about wrapped up now,' I said.

'And can I open tomorrow night?'

'As far as I'm concerned, Erica,' I said.

'You'll probably have the place full to overflowing with ghoulish rubberneckers,' said Dave. 'And we may even be here ourselves.'

'I've no doubt,' said Erica.

Two

It was getting on for midnight by the time we got back to Curtis Green. I brought my notes up to date, and handed Gavin Creasey the statements we'd acquired so that he could make a start on setting up the admin that goes with a major enquiry. Then I told the troops to go home. There was little else to be done at that time of night, and I wanted the team reasonably fresh for the morning. Even then our initial course of action would be governed largely by the reports I was awaiting from Henry Mortlock and Linda Mitchell.

Despite Gail's vain protestations, I was up at six on the Sunday morning, and arrived at the office at about eight-thirty. Detective Sergeant Colin Wilberforce, the day-duty incident-room manager, was already there, poring over the mountain of paperwork we'd assembled so far. Colin is the finest manager I've ever had working for me. His desk, along with everything else that goes with a murder enquiry, was immaculate. Even his pens were lined up, not daring to be otherwise. The crime-scene photographs had already arrived and were mounted on a board, and I knew that the names of all the witnesses would be recorded on Colin's computer together with any action that been taken, and notes about what was yet to be done.

'Anything come in yet, Colin?' I asked.

'Not yet, sir. Miss Ebdon's team is already out and about taking more detailed statements from witnesses.' Colin referred briefly to his daybook. Despite all this computerized gismo, he was a great believer in pen and paper. Bit like me, really. 'Dr Mortlock is doing the post-mortem this morning at nine-thirty, and I've had a message from Linda Mitchell to say that they've drawn a blank on Rod Skinner's fingerprints, and there's no trace of him in CRO.'

CRO is the term we real coppers still use for Criminal Records Office, although the wunderkinder at the Yard have probably called it something else by now. If they haven't, then they're falling down on their God-given crusade to bewilder us all.

For the moment we were stymied. We had a dead drummer in the mortuary whose name was Rod Skinner, and that was all we knew. It is well known that one of the incontrovertible facts of criminal investigation is that in order to find out who murdered someone, you have first to discover who were his friends and associates. Because one of the other incontrovertible facts of murder is that the vast majority of victims are killed by someone they knew. But so far we didn't even know where the damned man had lived.

Dave and I were at Horseferry Road mortuary at the appointed time. Henry Mortlock was waiting impatiently.

'Ah, you've got here, Harry,' he said, waving a scalpel.

'You said half-past nine, Henry.'

'Yes, yes, dear boy, but can we get on? I've got an important golf match this afternoon. No time to waste, no time to waste,' mumbled Henry and made the first incision while giving voice to some obscure aria from a Bizet opera. At least, that's what he said it was when I asked him.

An hour later we were no better informed than we had been the previous evening. Rod Skinner, deceased, had died as a result of a shotgun cartridge being discharged at his thorax. One of the few valuable pieces of evidence Kate Ebdon had obtained from witnesses was that the killer had been very close to his victim when he fired. Henry's assessment of the spread of shot, and the presence of wadding, confirmed what we had guessed anyway: the weapon had been a sawn-off shotgun. I say we had guessed because even in these days of widespread law-

24

lessness in London, one would be ill advised to walk the streets with a full-length shotgun; a sawn-off can be secreted beneath a coat. But thereby arose a problem. According to some of the witnesses, the killer had not been wearing a coat, although others had suggested an anorak of some description.

Leaving Henry to tidy up and rush off to his game of golf, we returned to Curtis Green.

A thought occurred to me: did the killer park a car right outside the Starlight Club?

'Dave, was there by any chance a CCTV camera outside the venue?' Coppers always call a murder scene the venue.

'No, guv.'

Well, so much for that idea.

I spent a few minutes sifting through the initial statements that Kate's team had obtained from the witnesses last night. They told us very little, but perhaps the more detailed ones her DCs were out taking now would reveal more. So far, though, all we knew was that a man wearing a stocking mask had entered the Starlight Club at about half-past eight on Saturday evening, walked up to the stage, fired a cartridge at the bass drum and a second at the drummer, thereby killing him. He then made good his escape. Wonderful!

How the hell is it that a man armed with a

shotgun can walk into a club, kill the drummer in front of about thirty people and then walk out again? And nobody knows who he was or where he went. And nobody knew very much about the dead drummer either.

'I suppose we'd better put Skinner's name on the PNC, Colin,' I said. If in doubt put the details of a victim on the Police National Computer. You never know, it might turn up something.

'Gavin Creasey did it last night, sir,' said Colin.

Incredibly it paid dividends almost immediately. Ten minutes later, the station officer at Esher police station, in the Surrey Police area, telephoned the incident room to tell us that a Mrs Barbara Skinner had reported that her husband Rod had not returned home the previous evening. It was, she had told the officer, most unusual, and she was 'a bit concerned' that something might have happened to him. Fortunately for us, the Surrey sergeant had interrogated the PNC and, bingo, there it was. Also fortunately, he had not told Mrs Skinner that the police had an interest in her husband, like they were investigating his murder. I always prefer to see the reaction of the nearest and dearest when the police arrive, because sometimes one of those nearest and dearest turns out to be the killer.

'Did Surrey give you an address, Colin?'

'Yes, sir. The Gables, Tunney Road, Cobham.'

Thanks to what Dave calls positive driving, we covered the twenty-five miles from Curtis Green to Cobham in just over half an hour. Dave doesn't like working on Sundays. But then neither do I.

The house Rod Skinner had shared with his wife Barbara was large, undoubtedly expensive and set in about an acre of grounds. On either side of the long drive there was a screen of leylandii, at least twelve feet in height, that must have pleased the neighbours no end.

Lying on the outskirts of Cobham, the house would probably have marketed at upwards of three-quarters of a million pounds. So what, I asked myself, was he doing playing drums in a jazz band at a sleazy club in Fulham? Surely he didn't need the money. But there are other reasons than money for playing in a jazz band. As Trumpeter Underwood had said, it's a sort of passion.

I pressed the bell push and was treated to a carillon of tuneful chimes that seemed to go on for some time.

Eventually the door was opened by a barefooted woman who was, I guessed, in her mid-forties, but who would undoubtedly claim to be forever thirty-nine. She was a brassy peroxide blonde attired in white cropped cargoes and an orange vest-top short enough to leave her midriff bare. Although she had a good figure, the ensemble was quite unsuitable for a woman of her age, but I was not here to discuss fashion.

'Mrs Skinner?'

'Yes, I'm Babs Skinner.'

'We're police officers, Mrs Skinner.'

In the circumstances, I was unable to give the usual assurance that there was nothing to worry about, like insensitive policemen do when they've come to serve you with a summons for causing death by dangerous driving. There clearly *was* something for this woman to worry about.

'It's about Rod, isn't it?' guessed Mrs Skinner, pulling open the door and stepping back: an unspoken invitation to enter.

'I'm afraid so,' I said as Skinner's widow – although she didn't know that yet – conducted us into a spacious sitting room furnished with a white carpet, two black leather settees and four ditto armchairs. On one wall was a fireplace large enough to walk into, and in a corner was the largest television set I had ever seen alongside a state-of-the-art sound system. A sofa table near the window was laden with bottles of just about every alcoholic drink available: a dipso's delight. There was money here; of that there was little doubt. 'I'm Detective Chief Inspector Brock and this is Detective Sergeant Poole.'

'Sounds serious,' said Babs, but she didn't sound serious; she actually sounded drunk.

'I'm sorry to have to tell you that your husband is dead, Mrs Skinner. He was murdered.' There's never an easy way of breaking news of that sort. And over the years I've found it's best just to come out with it.

Surprisingly this announcement was met with silence. Babs Skinner pushed a hand through her long hair and dislodged the sunglasses that she wore high on her head. They fell unnoticed onto the seat beside her. But there were no tears, no hysterics and no apparent anguish. 'How did the stupid sod get himself murdered, then?' she asked eventually.

Which was not the reaction I'd expected, nor had been accustomed to in the past. I told Mrs Skinner what we knew so far, which wasn't very much.

'I saw a bit about that on the telly last night,' said Babs Skinner, 'but I never knew it was Rod. They never mentioned who it was. What in hell's name was he doing playing drums in a jazz club in Fulham?' She stood up and walked across to the sofa table. 'D'you guys want a drink?' she asked over her shoulder. 'Because I'm going to have one.' Without waiting to hear our refusal, she prepared herself a very large gin and tonic, with much more gin than tonic. So full was the glass that when she added ice the liquid

29

overflowed onto the table. Looking once more at her somewhat raddled features – adorned with an excess of mascara and tangerine lipstick – I guessed that we'd been lucky enough to catch her in that narrow gap between the end of her hangover and her first serious drink of the day.

'Did you know he was a drummer?' I asked.

'It was news to me, love.'

'Did Mr Skinner have any connections with Fulham?' asked Dave.

'Not that I know of,' said Babs. 'But he might've had before we were married.'

'And how long have you been married?' Dave waggled his pen, eager to write down the answer.

'Eight years. And we weren't going to make nine, I can tell you.'

'Oh?' I contrived to look interested.

'We were on the point of divorce.' To my astonishment, hardened drinker that I am, Babs Skinner drained her glass and stood up to recharge it. 'He was running around with some woman. Mind you, that's how he picked up with me. We'd both been married before, you see.'

A motive, perhaps? Angry husband kills his wife's lover?

'Did he tell you he was seeing another woman?'

'Didn't have to,' said Babs scathingly. 'A

30

woman can always tell. When a middle-aged loser like Rod has a shower before he goes out of an evening and suddenly starts using aftershave, he's up to something.' She paused for a moment or two. 'So I thought, sod you, mate, and found a feller of my own. So now you know why I'm not too cut up about his death.'

But looking at the Skinner residence, I wouldn't have described Babs's late husband as a loser. 'An open marriage, then,' I said.

'Wide open,' Babs agreed with some fervour.

I knew all about open marriages. My former wife Helga and I had divorced a while back. When I met her all those years ago, she'd been an attractive twenty-one-year-old physiotherapist who'd treated me at Westminster Hospital after I'd been involved in a punch-up with a crowd of yobs in Whitehall. It was a whirlwind romance and we were married two months later. But, as the pessimists at the nick accurately forecast, it turned out to be a mistake.

Helga was German and the only thing I really derived from our marriage was that I learned fluent German. On balance, I think I'd've been better off going to evening classes.

However, Helga insisted on continuing to work even after our son Robert was born, and would leave him with a neighbour. It was

31

while this neighbour was minding him that he fell into her pond and drowned; Robert was only four. I blamed Helga for her selfishness and she blamed me for not providing enough money to enable her to stay at home.

Mind you, Helga's parents never approved of me, probably because I was a copper. But I didn't approve of her parents either, and made no secret of my dislike of them.

Things went from bad to worse after Robert's death. Helga started an affair with a doctor at the hospital where she was then working, and I had one with a forensic scientist at the Metropolitan laboratory. But my scientist married a major in the Hussars, and I heard that Helga married the doctor. Good luck to him; he'll need it. But I dare say her parents approve.

That, however, is all in the past, and I'm now in a relationship with Gail Sutton. I was fortunate enough to meet her while working on another case involving the murder of a chorus girl at the theatre where Gail was, to use her words, 'kicking the air for a pittance'.

'D'you happen to know the name of this woman your husband was seeing, Mrs Skinner?'

'No idea, love, and I couldn't care less. Probably some tart. That's the sort he usually goes for.'

That much was obvious; he appeared to have married one. 'And what's the name of this man you're having an affair with?'

'Why d'you want to know that?' demanded Babs.

'Just answer the question, please.' This was no time to suggest that he might have killed Rod Skinner in order to eliminate an impediment to the continuance of the affair.

'Charlie Hardy.'

'And where does Mr Hardy live?'

'In Esher. Fifteen, Little David Street.'

'And what is his occupation, Mrs Skinner?'

'He's an antiques restorer. Works a lot with his hands.'

I sensed, rather than heard, Dave stifling a laugh. 'Why did you report your husband missing, Mrs Skinner?' I asked. 'If, as you say, he was seeing another woman, isn't it possible that he might have spent the night with her?'

'I was pretty sure he *was* with her,' said Babs, and laughed sadistically. 'I just thought I'd put the bubble in for him. Teach him a bloody lesson.'

I didn't quite follow the logic of that, but I let it pass. As I did it occurred to me she might be guilty of wasting police time.

'Did your husband own a car?' Dave asked.

'Of course he did.' Babs Skinner gazed at Dave as though he had asked a fatuous question. Common tart though she clearly was, she gave the impression of not knowing anyone who didn't own a car. 'It's a BMW.

33

A big one.'

'D'you happen to know the number of it?' Dave persisted.

'Not offhand, but I'll see if I can find the logbook for you. It should be in the study somewhere. Despite his many faults, Rod was quite good at paperwork.' Babs continued to talk as she walked out of the room.

'Funny old set-up,' whispered Dave.

'And about to get funnier, I suspect,' I said.

A few moments later Babs Skinner returned and handed Dave the registration certificate of her husband's car.

Dave noted down the details and left the room, presumably to call Colin Wilberforce and ask him to arrange a search for the vehicle that, with any good fortune, was still languishing in some Fulham side street. But knowing my luck, it'd probably have been nicked.

'What did your husband do for a living, Mrs Skinner?' I asked.

'Do?' Babs gave a scornful laugh. 'He never did anything. Most of the time he lounged around the place watching that thing.' She pointed at the television. 'Sometimes he'd be out playing golf, but I haven't the faintest idea where he went in the evenings. Probably screwing that tart of his, I expect.'

'Did he have a private income, then?' I asked.

'A private income? Oh, very hoity-toity. If

you mean did he have to work, then the answer's no.' Babs stood up and walked, somewhat unsteadily, to the drinks table and poured herself yet another hefty gin and tonic. 'He had plenty of cash when I married him,' she said over her shoulder. 'That's why I married the sod. But I never asked where it came from.'

Waiting until she had sat down again, I tried a delicate question, even though I knew that Colin Wilberforce had told me that there was no trace of Rod Skinner in our criminal records. 'Had he ever been in trouble with the police?'

'Not that I know of, though I wouldn't be surprised if you told me he had. But you'd've known that anyway.' Babs frowned. 'So why ask me?'

Dave returned from making his phone call. 'D'you know the name of Mr Skinner's former wife?' he asked, and opened his pocket book.

Babs considered the question. 'It was either Sharon or Tracy, I think. I know it was some soap-opera name, but I can't really remember.'

'And I don't suppose you happen to know where she is now, Mrs Skinner?'

'No, love.' Babs gave Dave a smile and a lingering glance. Dave is six-foot tall and well built, and always manages to attract lingering glances from women. But Dave is happily married to Madeleine, a principal dancer with the Royal Ballet. Mind you, there is a bit of canteen scuttlebutt that suggests Madeleine occasionally attacks Dave, but I doubt it. She's five foot two. Mind you, ballet dancers are pretty strong.

'I suppose you'll have to sell up here now,' I suggested.

Babs scoffed. 'Not a bit of it.' She waved a hand around the room. 'This place is all paid for.'

'Is that your husband?' asked Dave, pointing to a framed photograph displayed on top of the television.

'Yes, darling, that's him.'

'I wonder if we may borrow it. It may help us when we're talking to people who might have known him.' Fortunately, Dave didn't have to explain why we really needed it: that the lower half of Rod Skinner's face was such a mess that he could not possibly be recognized from any scene-of-crime photograph we showed around.

'As far as I'm concerned, you can keep it,' said Babs, crossing the room and handing over the photograph.

'Well, thank you for your assistance, Mrs Skinner, and I'm sorry to have been the bearer of bad news,' I said.

'I'll get over it,' said Babs.

With a house worth about seven hundred and fifty grand and a boyfriend, I thought she probably would get over it.

'We may have to see you again,' I said. But there was no 'may' about it. It was a racing certainty. 'We'll see ourselves out.'

'Any time, love,' said Babs. 'And next time stay for a drink, eh?'

As we left, she was once more lurching towards the drinks table, empty glass in hand.

We stopped at a pub just outside Esher, but the car park was full of four-by-fours. The bar was overflowing with refugees from places like Chelsea and Notting Hill, drinking overpriced Pimm's and convincing themselves that they were having Sunday lunch in the depths of the country, and calling each other 'darling' at the tops of their voices. We decided not to bother fighting our way through the serried ranks of pseudo-upper-class yobbery, and eventually had a pie and a pint at an earthy boozer in Battersea.

'You used to have sawdust on the floor in here,' I said to the licensee.

'Had to get rid of it, guv'nor,' said the landlord. 'Used to get all the Hooray Henrys in here from across the river, thinking it was olde worlde.' He emphasized the last two words and flicked the air with two fingers of each hand to indicate quote marks. 'It got right up the locals' noses having them in here wah-wahing all over the place, and we had one or two punch-ups of a Saturday night.'

He sniffed and wiped the top of the bar. 'What's your pleasure, gents?'

'What d'you think of it so far, guv?' asked Dave when we were settled at a corner table with pints of bitter and a couple of Melton Mowbray pies.

'Apart from the fact that there's more than meets the eye with our Mr and Mrs Skinner, Dave, I'm not sure. Unless he's a genius at the stock market, I'm wondering where his money comes from.'

'He's got to be a villain, guv.' Dave always took the view that unexplained wealth could only be the result of some criminal enterprise.

'One that hasn't been caught,' I said gloomily. 'D'you reckon Babs is on the game?' I asked, tossing out the odd thought that was passing through my mind.

'She probably was once, but I shouldn't think so now, looking at her,' said Dave. 'She's not exactly a grand-a-night screw, is she? But she might have topped her old man. A drum worth three-quarters of a million looks like a good motive to me,' he added, echoing my earlier thoughts about Babs now inheriting the house.

'I don't exactly see a lush like her barging into a Fulham jazz club with a sawn-off, and blowing him away, Dave.'

'No, I suppose you're right, guv.' Dave drained his glass, took out his cigarettes and

tossed me one.

'I'm trying to give up, Dave.'

'Yeah, I know, guv. You keep telling me.'

It was true. I'd been trying to pack it in ever since a master at school had caught me having a drag behind the bike sheds, and told me about his brother who'd died from lung cancer as a result of smoking twenty a day. But despite that, I still smoke. And Dave's no help. Even the Commissioner's draconian ruling that there should be no smoking in police buildings hasn't stopped either of us.

Three

Monday morning brought good news. Miracle of miracles, Skinner's car had been found undamaged a couple of streets away from the Starlight Club. From there, on Kate Ebdon's instructions, it had been taken on a low-loader to Lambeth where it would be searched, and examined for some evidence that, I hoped, might lead me to Skinner's killer.

The vehicle had been locked, but then no one but a naive raving lunatic would leave an unlocked car in Fulham on a Saturday evening. Or for that matter at any time anywhere else in London.

Dave had made the necessary arrangements for a search team to meet us at Lambeth, and at nine o'clock we started.

I pointed out to the leader of the team that the vehicle was a top-of-the-range BMW and that it might take some time for him to get into it. He laughed and opened it in twenty seconds flat.

'How d'you want to play this, guv?' he asked.

'Let the fingerprint guys have a go at it,' I

said, 'and then we'll take it from there.'

It took the fingerprint officers an hour to declare themselves satisfied, and to announce that they had found quite a few marks. But then they would, wouldn't they? When people get in and out of cars, they tend to leave their fingerprints all over it. Whether any of these marks would be of any value, however, remained to be seen.

'What now, guv?' asked the search-team leader.

'Empty it,' I said.

The searchers started at the front of the vehicle and worked slowly and methodically towards the rear. Every item in the car was removed and placed on a bench, along with labels saying where the particular item had been found. The first haul was of little interest: a couple of unpaid parking tickets, receipts for petrol from a garage in Cobham, cigarette packets and a polystyrene box that had once contained a hamburger.

I gave the parking tickets to Dave knowing he would get someone to check where they were issued. That would tell us where Skinner's car was at a given time. Whether he was the driver, or if that information would be useful, remained to be seen, but you've got to try.

Then the search team found a briefcase in the boot of the car. The lock expert made short work of opening it.

'And what have we here?' said Dave, taking out a tatty little burgundy book that these days is supposed to be a British passport. 'Well, well, well. It's in the name of James Wright, guv, and guess whose photograph appears in it.'

I took the document and stared at a face that, when compared with the photograph of Rod Skinner that Babs had given us, was undoubtedly one and the same. 'Now I wonder what that's all about,' I mused.

But more was to come. After handing me a mobile phone, Dave unearthed a photograph of a laughing Erica Leech taken on a sunny beach somewhere. She was attired in just the bottom half of a bikini and was running out of the sea towards the photographer. 'If Erica didn't even know Rod Skinner's name, guv, how come he's got a snap of her in his brief-case?'

'Because she knew him as James Wright?' I suggested, pointing to the passport. And that turned out to be the truth. Very nearly.

'It doesn't matter what he was called,' said Dave. 'She reckoned she didn't know him ... sir.' He always calls me 'sir' when I make some sort of ludicrous comment. 'According to her it was Cyril Underwood, the trumpeter, who told her Rod Skinner's name. And not until after he was murdered.'

'Which means that we shall have to have another chat with Ms Leech.'

'I reckon she must be the bird that Babs Skinner was talking about,' Dave said.

'Or one of them, Dave. But I don't see Erica as a soap-opera name, which is what Babs Skinner said.'

'Babs Skinner wasn't talking about her husband's current screw, guv,' Dave explained patiently. 'She said she didn't know who she was. The soap-opera star was Rod Skinner's ex.'

As I have mentioned before, Dave thinks of the things I forget. And doesn't hesitate to point them out.

We arrived at the Starlight Club at about eight o'clock. I was not at all surprised to meet Kate Ebdon at the door, along with DC John Appleby. Next to them stood a blue-chinned thug with a shaven head and the obligatory earring who, presumably, had been hired by Erica Leech as some sort of access control to prevent the entry of any more killers.

'Looking for anything in particular, Kate?'

'Checking on the punters as they go in, guv,' said Kate. 'Just in case we missed anyone from the night before last. In my experience the minute a shooting goes down in a place like this, the customers tend to take off like their arses were on fire. We've already found three who scarpered before the Old Bill arrived on Saturday.'

As Dave had predicted, the jazz club was heaving with people who had heard about Rod Skinner's murder and just couldn't wait to see where it had happened. This evening, though, there was a different band playing. I presumed that Les Roper and company had yet to find a replacement drummer. But then I recalled that Erica Leech had said that the Jazz Kittens only appeared two nights a week.

We made our way to the office.

Erica was standing by the filing cabinet in her office, riffling through the contents of one of the drawers, presumably still struggling with her tax return. This evening she was wearing a black full-length stretch-jersey dress that left one suntanned shoulder bare.

'A full house tonight, Ms Leech,' I said.

Erica laughed, a dry, humourless laugh, and slammed the drawer of the cabinet. 'I doubt they'll be here next week,' she said, sitting down behind her desk. 'Anyway, what can I do for you?'

I produced the photograph of her that we'd found in Rod Skinner's briefcase, and placed it in front of her without comment.

'Where the hell did you get that from?' demanded Erica, blushing to the roots of her hair. Her alarmed reaction clearly demonstrated that we had caught her wrong-footed.

'We found it in the boot of Rod Skinner's car,' I said.

'D'you want to tell us how it got there, Ms Leech?' asked Dave.

'The last time you were here, I asked you to call me Erica,' said the woman, presumably while she gave herself time to think up an excuse for Rod Skinner having possessed a revealing photograph of her.

'D'you want to tell us how it got there, *Erica*?' Dave said.

The woman stood up and poured herself a whisky. She waggled the bottle in our direction, but I shook my head. I make it a rule never to drink with anyone who may turn out to be a suspect. And right now Ms Leech was heading in that direction. Supposing that Rod Skinner had done something to annoy Erica, really annoy her. Kate Ebdon had told me that there was a back entrance leading to a basement area, and it was feasible that the club's proprietress could have donned a disguise in her office, gone out that way and in through the front entrance. She could then have walked in and murdered Skinner before returning by the forward route reversed, as we coppers are fond of saying. There was certainly no point in searching the office for a shotgun now, not two days after the murder.

'OK, so we had an affair. So what?'

'Why then did you tell me that you didn't know Rod Skinner, and that you didn't even know his name until Cyril Underwood told you?' I asked.

'I didn't think it was relevant.'

'Really? Are you married?' That was the usual reason for a suspect denying having had an affair with a murder victim. And a very good reason it is too.

'Yes. Well, estranged now, I suppose you'd call it.'

'As a result of this affair with Rod Skinner?'

'No.' Erica broke eye contact with me and gazed at the opposite wall. 'Because of the one before it,' she added meekly.

'And is your husband's name Leech?'

'Yes, Howard Leech. Why? You don't need to speak to him, do you?'

'I don't know yet. Where does he live?'

Erica shot me a malevolent look and then, somewhat reluctantly, scribbled a Fulham address on a piece of paper and handed it to me.

'World's End,' I said. Perhaps I sounded sarcastic, but I received another hostile glance.

'And where do *you* live?' asked Dave.

'Same place,' said Erica curtly.

'But you're estranged, you said.'

'So we might be, but we're civilized about it. Howard lives in the top flat and I live in the bottom one.'

I understood estrangement. The marriage between Helga and me had been in a similar state of suspension for some time before the divorce was finalized.

'Where was this photograph taken, Erica?' asked Dave, picking up the print.

'Juan-les-Pins,' said Erica promptly. 'It's in the South of France.'

'I know where it is,' said Dave sharply. He was always irritated by people who thought he was uneducated simply because he was black. The irony being that he was undoubtedly much better educated than the average witness with whom he came into contact. 'When?'

'About a year ago, I suppose. Yes, it was July.'

'And how long were you there?'

'Three weeks.'

'And where did you stay?'

'The Royale. It's right on the seafront. But why all the questions?'

'And who picked up the tab, Erica?' I asked, ignoring her question about questions.

'Look, what the hell is all this?' Erica's temper had begun to shorten quite dramatically. 'What's this got to do with Jimmy's murder?'

'Who's Jimmy?' I asked innocently. This was not the time to tell Erica that we'd found a passport in the name of James Wright in the boot of Skinner's car, and that the passport had Skinner's photograph in it. Anyway, I had yet to confirm that it was a legitimately issued passport and not a skilful forgery.

'It's Rod's real name,' admitted Erica, but

her expression told me that she had slipped up in revealing Skinner's other identity, and had instantly regretted it. But then she didn't know what we knew. 'He's Jimmy Wright.'

'Why does he call himself Skinner, then?'

'It's his stage name,' said Erica, making a ridiculous attempt to cover her mistake.

'Yes, and Detective Chief Inspector Harry Brock's *my* stage name.' I laughed. 'You don't expect me to believe that, do you?'

'I'm only telling you what he told me, *Chief Inspector*,' said Erica, with a touch more sarcasm than I thought necessary. 'And I really don't see what my spending three weeks on the Riviera with Jimmy has to do with you.'

'Did you know that Mr Skinner, or Wright, was married?'

'Yes, of course I knew. So what? I'm not the first woman to have an affair with a married man, and he wasn't the first man to have an affair with a married woman. But there's no need to shout it from the rooftops, is there? That's why I didn't mention any of this when you were here on Saturday. You know what the newspapers are like. Before you know where you are, it's plastered all over the front page of the tabloids. I can almost write their headline for them: "Jazz club owner in love nest with murdered drummer." And no doubt they'd get hold of that somehow.' She gestured at the photograph. 'That would look great, wouldn't it? A picture of me half naked plastered all over the front page. Anyway I didn't want Jimmy's wife finding out.'

'Mrs Skinner knows already,' volunteered Dave who, like me, is always annoyed when witnesses waste our time.

That statement shocked Erica, and her complexion lost a little of its colour. 'But how on earth did she find out?' she asked, clearly worried. 'We were very discreet.'

'I dare say Mr Skinner told her.' Dave was obviously intent on repaying this woman for her original deceit. 'You see, the Skinners had an open marriage too, and he was probably boasting about you just to annoy his missus. Probably showed her your photograph too.'

'To get back to my question about your three weeks in Juan-les-Pins, Erica. Who paid for it all?'

'Jimmy did.'

'And how much did it cost?'

'I've no idea,' said Erica haughtily. 'When your boyfriend takes you on a luxury holiday, you don't ask how much it cost. All I know is that he produced a platinum credit card and the bill was settled without question. In fact the manager was fawning all over him. Quite sickening, it was.'

'What was the name on the credit card?' asked Dave.

'I don't know. I never saw it,' replied Erica tersely.

49

'How long before you and he went on this holiday did you meet Mr Skinner?' I was determined to keep using the name that Babs Skinner believed was her husband's name, despite the contradictory evidence of the passport.

'About three weeks.'

'Didn't take him long to carry you off to the fleshpots of the South of France, then.' I didn't altogether blame the deceased Mr Skinner alias Wright. Although Erica was a well-built woman, she exuded sexual attraction and, no doubt, was a good performer. Being the cynic I am, I could think of no other reason than sex for Skinner having spent a large sum of money on her.

'So what?' Erica was getting annoyed at our continuous probing into her private life.

'What did Mr Skinner do for a living, Erica?' asked Dave.

'I don't know, but whatever it was it must have paid well. We always went to the best restaurants, had the finest wines and stayed in the best hotels.'

'Did you stay in hotels often?' I asked, assuming she meant that they had stayed in hotels together.

'You wouldn't expect him to screw me in my grotty little flat in World's End, would you?' demanded Erica, injecting a little coarseness into the conversation. But if it was intended to shock Dave and me it failed lamentably; detectives are accustomed to that sort of language and often use it themselves. 'And now, I've got some work to do,' she said. 'If you've quite finished intruding into my affairs.' But then she realized that that was entirely the wrong word to have used, and blushed again.

'Whether you like it or not, Erica, I'm afraid your private life has become public,' I said. 'Your boyfriend has been murdered, and it's my job to find out who was responsible.'

'Well, it wasn't me,' said Erica defiantly.

'You said just now that the break-up between you and your husband was due to the affair *before* the one you had with Rod Skinner.'

'So?'

'Who was that with?'

'Why d'you want to know that?' Our intrusiveness was starting to get on Erica's nerves.

'Was he the jealous sort?' I asked.

'I suppose he was,' said Erica thoughtfully. 'He slapped my face once when he thought I'd been chatting up another man. But he regretted it because I can take care of myself.'

Looking at her shoulders and upper arms I could quite believe that; I suspected that she could land a hefty punch if necessary.

'Yes, he was jealous,' continued Erica, 'and the irony of it is that that was the very reason

I chucked him over. Anyway, why d'you ask?'

'It might have been a reason for him to kill Rod Skinner,' I said quietly.

Erica stared at me; she obviously hadn't thought of that. But it didn't take her long to dismiss the idea. She laughed. 'I think you might change your mind once you've met him,' she said.

'Maybe so, Erica, but I'll still need to see him. Perhaps you'd tell me who he is and where I can find him.'

She didn't hesitate. Grabbing another piece of paper, she quickly wrote down a name and address. It seemed that her cast-off lover was called Frank Seaton and he lived at 27 Hendy Road, Putney.

'And what's Mr Seaton's occupation, Erica?'

'He runs an art gallery in Chelsea.' And she wrote down that address too.

We drove down to Cobham the following morning, mainly to get to the bottom of why Rod Skinner was also known as Jimmy Wright. But I determined that we would call on Charlie Hardy before we spoke to Babs Skinner again.

'If this Hardy guy's an antiques restorer, guv, he didn't do a very good job on his bed-mate,' commented Dave on the way down the Portsmouth Road from Curtis Green.

But as I've said before, Dave has a perverted sense of humour.

The address that Skinner's widow had given us for Charlie Hardy proved to be a mews garage converted into a workshop, its front doors open to the street. Inside was a young man wearing a white T-shirt, jeans and an apron, and working at some sort of noisy machinery. He was a good six foot tall, and his muscular forearms bore a thin covering of blond hair, matching the equally blond hair of his head. He looked to be in his late twenties, and I could quite see why Babs Skinner would have been attracted to him. But I wondered what it was about Babs that attracted Hardy to her. It wasn't long before I found out.

'Mr Hardy?' I shouted.

'That's me.' Hardy shut off the lathe and turned to face us. 'What can I do for you?' He looked expectant, like we'd got a roomful of precious antiques that were in need of his specialized treatment.

'We're police officers,' I said. 'I understand you know Babs Skinner.'

'That's right. I suppose you've come about Rod's murder. Babs phoned me on Sunday afternoon. She said you'd been to see her. Terrible thing to have happened. Poor Babs.'

This was an enigma. Here was a man who was at least eighteen years younger than his paramour, and yet he was sympathizing over the death of her husband.

'I understand from Mrs Skinner that you're her boyfriend.'

'You could say that, but I'm more of a toyboy really.' Hardy grinned. It was an ingenuous grin with no trace of embarrassment. 'It's only about sex. She wants it and I provide it.'

It's odd how many people are prepared to talk quite openly to complete strangers about their sex lives. 'How long have you known her?'

Hardy reached across to his bench and picked up a tin. 'About a year, I suppose,' he said, and began to roll a cigarette.

'And how did you meet?'

Hardy didn't seem at all surprised that I was asking these questions and was very frank with his answers. 'A village hop down at Cobham one Saturday night. She asked me for a dance, and then another, and then another.' This was accompanied by a further open grin. He turned and absent-mindedly caressed a Windsor wheelback chair standing on the bench. At least that's what Dave later told me it was. 'Then she asked me what I was doing on the following Monday morning,' he said, facing me once more. 'I guessed what was coming, and I told her there was nothing that couldn't wait. Right, she said, come down to The Gables at ten o'clock. When I got there she was wearing a flimsy sort of robe, and it was obvious that she wasn't going to waste any time. There was no offer of coffee or anything like that. She just took me straight up to her bedroom. Since then I've been a regular visitor.' And he grinned his candid grin again.

'I take it you never met Mr Skinner,' said Dave.

'Yes I did. A couple of times. The first time was when I turned up one Friday morning to service Babs, and I met him on his way out. It was a bit of an embarrassment and I was trying to think up some excuse for being there, like I'd come to look at an antique that needed some loving care.'

Dave turned away, and once more I sensed that he was smothering a laugh.

'What did Skinner say?' I asked.

'He shook hands and asked if I was the guy who was shafting his missus. I didn't know what to say. It reminded me of the old joke.'

'What old joke?' Dave asked.

'You know. The one where a husband asks his wife's lover if she's a good screw. So the lover says she is because he doesn't want to offend his bird's husband.' Hardy chuckled at that. 'Anyhow he said he was off to play a round of golf and wouldn't be back until after lunch. Then he laughed and got into his car.'

'Did Mrs Skinner ever tell you what her husband did for a living, Mr Hardy?' Dave asked.

Hardy shook his head. 'No. We never talked about anything. There was only one reason for me being there, and when I arrived we'd get on with it. Then I'd go home.' He paused. 'Until the next time.'

'You said that you'd seen Rod Skinner a couple of times,' I said. 'Tell me about the other.'

'Babs invited me to a drinks party one Saturday, and he was there, along with a lot of other people. I must say that the men looked a dodgy lot, bit like second-hand car dealers, all talking out of the corner of their mouths. They were like something out of *Guys and Dolls*. The girls were obviously on offer and two or three times one of them made a beeline for me. Quite blatant about it they were, too: saying things like they fancied me, and what about it. One twenty-something chick told me, quite openly, that there was a spare bedroom upstairs and suggested that she and I used it, but I was quite happy with Babs and I didn't want to rock the boat. Anyhow, Babs spotted what was going on and had a few quiet words in the girl's ear.' Hardy smiled. 'Come to think of it, it wasn't all that quiet. I was across the other side of the room by then, but I heard Babs say that I belonged to her and that the other girl'd better steer clear if she knew what was good for her. I think she did it loudly enough so that all the other women would hear.'

Four

After leaving Charlie Hardy's workshop, we'd stopped for a sandwich and a cup of coffee, and arrived at The Gables in Cobham at about half-past two. It was a sweltering hot day and humid with it, and the temperature must have been in the high eighties.

This time there was an Audi TT on the drive. I presumed it belonged to Babs and had probably been in the garage the last time we'd called. There certainly seemed to be plenty of money in the Skinner household; Rod's BMW hadn't come cheap, and the Audi TT kicked off at about twenty-two grand at the bottom end of the range. Dave took a note of the Audi's registration mark. He collects things like that.

After a lengthy pause, during which time I was beginning to think that Babs was out, she answered the door. With a glass in her hand. 'Oh, it's you,' she said brightly. 'Sorry to have kept you waiting, but I was sunbathing on the patio. By the pool,' she added, presumably to make sure that we were suitably impressed by her wealth. I imagined that the delay had been caused by her need to find the bright orange kaftan she was wearing. 'Let's sit outside.' We followed her through the house, and out of the French windows on the far side of the room where we had interviewed her on the previous Sunday morning.

Fortunately the table and chairs to which she directed us were beneath a huge open-sided gazebo. The pool, a good fifteen yards long, was tranquil, blue and very inviting.

Babs saw me eyeing it. 'You're welcome to take a dip,' she said, and glanced at Dave Poole. Doubtless his physique attracted her and she was hoping for an excuse to see more of it.

But we were here on business, and many a policeman has fallen foul of a femme fatale and wrecked his career as a result. And I can think of few things better guaranteed to cast doubt on an officer's professional reputation than cavorting in a swimming pool with a suspect of the opposite sex. And everyone we were interviewing was a suspect until proved otherwise.

'Would you like a drink, Mr Brock, Mr Poole?'

'Thanks. Something non-alcoholic, if you have it,' I said, answering for both of us.

'Of course.' She made a rather unsuccessful attempt to sashay sexily into the house, and returned minutes later with a tray on which were two glasses and a jug of lemon juice.

And a large gin and tonic.

'We spoke to Mr Hardy this morning,' I began.

She did not express any surprise that we had talked to her boyfriend. 'Dishy, isn't he?' she said.

But I wasn't going to be drawn into discussing Charlie Hardy's physical attributes. 'He tells me that he met your late husband on a couple of occasions.'

'Yes, that's right, he did.' Babs did not seem to find this at all out of the ordinary.

'And on one of those occasions at a party you held here, he told me.'

She gave that some thought. 'Yes, he was here. It was about two months ago.'

'I gathered from him that most of the guests were friends of your husband.'

Babs nodded, and made a wry face. 'All of them, except for Charlie,' she said. 'Awful people. I don't know where he met them, but they weren't my cup of tea. As for the tarts they brought with them, well, they were quite unspeakable. No morals at all. One of them even tried to get Charlie into bed with her. And by the time the party was over, most of them were naked and in there.' She waved at the pool. 'It was a disgusting orgy, Mr Brock. Quite disgusting.' She tossed her head. 'I mean to say, having sex on the patio in full view of everyone else is not the done thing, is it?'

I was fascinated by this woman's stance on moral behaviour. Not only did she openly admit to an affair with a man much younger than herself, but she had invited him to a party where her husband and his friends were present along with women she condemned for adopting the same attitude to sex as her own appeared to be.

'Did you know these friends of your husband?' I asked.

'No. I'd no idea where he'd picked them up. I don't think they were from his golf club,' she said with sarcastic emphasis. 'We had a row about it afterwards and I told him I didn't want to see them here again. I said that if they were the sort of people he mixed with, he could entertain them somewhere else.'

'But he didn't mind Mr Hardy being here?'

'Not at all. He knew that I was getting laid by Charlie, but he couldn't have cared less. Anyway, he had a bird on the side. I told you that the last time you were here, didn't I?'

'Was she at this party?'

'No.'

'Why? Because you'd told him not to invite her?'

'On the contrary, I told him she'd be welcome – what's good for the goose and all that – but he said that she couldn't make it.'

'Does the name Erica Leech mean anything to you, Mrs Skinner?'

'No. Should it? I suppose that's one of his women.'

'*One* of them?'

'Oh yes. He played the field. Rod was a good name for him, wasn't it?' she said, and gave an unladylike guffaw of coarse laughter.

'As a matter of fact, we interviewed her last night,' I said. 'And she admitted to being a friend of your late husband.'

'Really?' said Babs, but it was only polite interest. 'How did you find her?'

'She owns the jazz club where Mr Skinner was playing when he was murdered.'

'Really? How interesting.' Babs sounded surprised at this. 'But I still can't work out what he was doing playing the drums there. I didn't even know he had a drum kit, let alone play them.' She paused in thought for a moment or two. 'Was she butch, this woman? That's the sort he usually goes for. And if they were bisexual, so much the better. As far as he was concerned, I mean,' she added hurriedly. 'Personally I'm not into that sort of thing. It's men only for me, all the way.' She afforded Dave an impish smile and glanced at our glasses. 'More lemonade?'

'Thank you,' I said. 'There's one other thing, Mrs Wright...'

'And what might that be?' Babs had just picked up the jug, but she started quite noticeably and put it down again with a crash. 'What did you call me?' she asked,

61

immediately realizing that she had slipped up in responding to the name in the passport we had found in Rod Skinner's car. 'What on earth made you call me that?'

'Sorry,' I said. 'There are so many names cropping up in this enquiry that I tend to lose track of who's who.' Well, that was one way out of it, and it did no harm to give the impression that I wasn't really on top of my job. I concluded from her quick recovery that there would be no profit in pursuing that line of enquiry. Doubtless any questions about Rod Skinner's alter ego would be met with a flat denial that she'd ever known him by any other name.

'Did you know the names of any of these people who came to this party, Mrs Skinner?' I asked.

'I do wish you'd call me Babs, darling.' The error she had made in responding to the name of Wright had clearly disturbed her, and I suspected she didn't want to slip up again.

'Well, did you?'

Babs took a sip of her gin and tonic and gazed thoughtfully at the swimming pool. 'I didn't know any of their surnames, but there was an Eric, a Brian and a guy who called himself Fruity. Oh, and one of the tarts was called Roxy. She was one who went after Charlie, but finished up getting laid by Fruity on the patio.' She laughed again; she laughed readily. 'Apt name for him. Not that she'd arrived with him. I tell you, Mr Brock, it was an orgy. But never again,' she said, apparently overlooking the fact that her husband was now dead and would not, therefore, be inviting any more of these friends.

'It's possible his name was Metcalfe,' I mused. 'People called Metcalfe are usually known as Fruity.'

'Is that so?'

'Well, I don't think we need to bother you any more, Babs,' I said. 'Thank you for the drink. We'll see ourselves out.'

'Do pop in any time you're passing,' she said. She stood up and stretched. Then she tottered a little before regaining her balance. 'I think I'll have a swim.'

I'd no idea how many gins she'd consumed before we'd arrived, but I thought it was extremely dangerous to swim in the half-drunken state she was in. However, I consoled myself with the fact that if she did drown it would be the Surrey Police who investigated it.

I just hoped she wouldn't drown before I'd completed my enquiries.

Back at the 'factory', as CID officers call their office, the report from Linda Mitchell was awaiting me. Like the result of the post-mortem, it didn't tell me much that I didn't already know. However, among the items recovered from Rod Skinner's car was his mobile phone, and I set DC John Appleby to checking all the numbers in its directory. It's often surprising what useful information can be found in a cellphone directory these days.

'Anything on the passport we found in Skinner's car, John?' I asked.

'Yes and no, sir,' said Appleby. 'I went round to the Passport Office in Petty France and spoke to one of the supervisors there. He took details and said he'd ring me.'

'Right. Well, let me know when you've got something.'

The result of DC Appleby's enquiry at the Passport Office was not what I had antici- pated. In fact, it was one hell of a surprise.

On the Wednesday morning I was sum- moned to the commander's office. It had to come sooner or later, but fortunately he'd been on leave since the murder.

The problem with the commander was that he had spent his entire career in the Uniform Branch and hadn't got a clue, literally, about the investigation of murder. However, some bright spark in what the hierarchy is now pleased to call the Human Resources Direc- torate had made the momentous decision that he was ideally suited to command Homicide West. This ill-advised posting had had an unfortunate effect on the comman- der: he now thought that he was a detective.

And that meant that he'd persuaded himself that he knew all about the intricacies of criminal investigation, and demanded all the details of a current enquiry. Consequently the likes of us had to explain what progress we'd made in words of one syllable. And even then he often failed to grasp what we were talking about.

'You wanted to see me, sir?'

'Ah, Mr Brock.' Unlike real CID commanders, our man never addressed me by my first name. I imagined that he was afraid I would reply in kind, and he wouldn't have been able to cope with that. 'This is Detective Chief Superintendent Drew.'

'Good morning, sir,' I said politely. I had not met the sharp-suited character who was relaxed in one of the commander's armchairs, and something about him told me that this was no bad thing. In fact, I wondered briefly if he might be from the Directorate of Professional Standards, what we ordinary coppers call 'the rubber-heel squad', but I couldn't think of any transgression of mine that might have incurred that department's interest. You never know, though.

'The commander tells me you're doing the Skinner topping, Harry,' said Drew.

Ah, a real detective.

'Yes, sir.'

'The Chief Passport Officer tipped me the wink that one of your lads was making enquiries about a passport in the name of James Wright.'

'That's correct, sir.'

Drew stood up. 'I don't think I need take up any more of your time, guv'nor,' he said to the commander. 'We'll adjourn to Harry's office and sort this out. Let you get on, eh?'

The commander blinked a few times and primped his pocket handkerchief. I don't think anyone had ever called him 'guv'nor' in his life, but Drew had obviously sussed him out as being of no great assistance.

'As you wish, Mr Drew.' The commander seemed disappointed that he was being excluded from further discussions, but, as I later learned, Drew was an officer who wielded considerable power, and because of the arcane matters with which he dealt was the sole arbiter of who should be told what.

'I could do with a cup of coffee, Harry,' said Drew, once he was ensconced in my small office. 'I know that the powers-that-be have decreed that no one's allowed to smoke in police buildings any more, but d'you mind?'

'Not at all, guv,' I said, and tossed him one of my Marlboros. 'I'll get one of the lads to drum up some coffee.' I picked up the phone.

A few minutes later, Dave Poole came in with a tray of coffee and put it on my desk. As he turned he caught sight of Drew. 'Hallo, guv,' he said, with a look on his face that expressed both surprise and delight. 'Long time no see, as the Pope said to the Archbishop of Canterbury.'

'Mr Brock looking after you, Dave?' asked Drew.

'More or less, guv,' said Dave. 'But he's a hard man to work for.'

Drew laughed. 'Bugger off, Poole, you cheeky bastard, and leave us in peace.' He glanced at me as the door closed behind Dave. 'Don't bother to run after him to find out who and what I am, Harry,' he said. 'I'm about to tell you.'

'I have to admit I've been wondering what this is all about, guv.'

'Well, I wasn't going to give you the spiel in front of your commander. I get the impression he's full of piss and importance, but hasn't got a clue what the Job's all about.'

I thought it impolitic to comment on that truism, and stirred my coffee.

'Right,' said Drew, 'let's get down to business. Jimmy Wright, known as "Shiner" Wright and also, it seems, as Rod Skinner, is a villain.'

'But his fingerprints turned up "No trace", guv,' I said. 'So did a search of CRO.'

'They would have done,' said Drew. 'He was in the witness-protection programme. His dabs and his record were taken out of the system when he turned supergrass.'

'So how come he turns up dead in the Starlight Club?' I asked.

'I was hoping you'd tell me, Harry. Not that it matters any more. You see, Wright, whose real name is Dennis Miller, was involved in the Wembley heist about five years ago.'

'Christ!' I said. 'So he was one of that team. I remember that.' There were very few detectives who didn't remember it. On the Friday night of a Bank Holiday weekend, a team of six forced their way into a shop next to a safety deposit, and held the Pakistani shop-keeper hostage. They cut through the wall and 'arced' the vault. Among the team were an alarms expert, a computer man and a CCTV engineer. They took the security guards hostage, and when the relief guards came on duty, they got captured too. Between them this little team of robbers managed to fix the computer-controlled alarm system so that the distant control centre at the security company headquarters wasn't alerted. Indeed, they'd even forced the captive guards to send the periodic 'All OK' message.

'The upshot,' Drew continued, 'was that they got away with jewellery and diamonds worth about ten million pounds. If they'd been able to fence all of it, the take would have worked out to about eight hundred grand apiece. Anyway, that was the Miller's tale, so to speak, but they'd chosen well.

There was a rumour that a lot of cash was in there as well, laundered cash that certain dishonest punters had stashed away rather than let the Inland Revenue lay its hands on it. Naturally enough, the aforementioned punters didn't report their losses and the guess is that the villains' haul was a damned sight more than the security company's honest clients claimed had been nicked.'

'So how was it that Miller came to grass up the rest, guv? I presume that's what he did.'

'Someone on the team made a mistake.'

'Ah, the Leatherslade syndrome,' I said. The Great Train Robbers of over forty years ago had made one mistake. Even though they had meticulously cleaned their hide-out, Leatherslade Farm, of fingerprints, they overlooked just one. But it was enough, and eventually the entire team was arrested.

'That's about the strength of it,' said Drew. 'One of the security guards heard one of the villains call one of his mates "Dusty". It was bloody tenuous, and it was time-consuming. But the Flying Squad did a protracted search of all the Dusty's with the sort of form and professionalism who could have been in-volved.' He laughed. 'And I reckon that one or two snouts got leaned on. Eventually they homed in on Dennis Miller. He was on parole, had the expertise and he ran with a top-class team of villains. It fitted, so the Squad nicked him. And he couldn't sing loud enough. With his form, he could see himself facing a bloody long time in the nick, and he promptly turned supergrass. He yielded up his share of the loot, so he said, and fingered the other five who'd been with him on the heist.'

'Nice one,' I said. 'What about the tomfoolery?'

'Some of the jewellery was recovered shortly afterwards,' said Drew, 'but not much. It took the Squad quite a while to track Miller down, and it gave him and his mates plenty of time to knock the gear out. Mind you, some of it still occasionally rises to the surface. The net result was that that little team all went down for upwards of twenty years. And I don't have to tell you, Harry, that they all swore vengeance on Miller.'

'You do surprise me, guv,' I said with a laugh.

Drew laughed too, and threw me a cigarette. 'So Miller was fixed up with a new ID as James Wright and was settled in a nice little house at Hatfield in Hertfordshire with his wife, Daphne Miller, who became Ann Wright. Then, about three years ago, lo and behold, he disappeared off the screen. When we checked up on him, as we do from time to time, we found that the house in Hatfield had been abandoned. None of the neighbours knew a damned thing. It was the usual story:

he was a nice man, kept himself to himself, no loud parties, and all that sort of guff. And now he turns up in Fulham. Dead.'

All of which explained why Erica Leech knew Skinner as Jimmy Wright. He had a legit passport in that name, and that name would not have appeared in any of the suspect indexes held by Special Branch officers or the Immigration Service people at ports. And it would have been too risky for him to try for a duff passport in the name of Skinner. So he used the Wright passport when he took Erica to France.

'What's happened to the house in Hatfield now?' I asked.

'Once it was obvious that Miller'd done a runner, we put it on the market and flogged it. We couldn't put another supergrass in there, for obvious reasons.'

'So where does that leave me, guv?' I asked. But somehow I knew.

'He's of no interest to us now, Harry. I'm afraid he's just become what looks like yet another gangland topping. And sorting that, I gather from your esteemed commander, is down to you.'

'Thanks a bundle,' I said. 'What about the team he helped to send down?' It was a hopeful question, but I knew the answer before I asked it.

'All still in the nick, Harry, with at least another ten to do before they're eligible for parole. If they're lucky.'

'I thought you'd say that, guv,' I said gloomily. 'Any chance of the names?'

Drew opened his briefcase, and withdrew a secret registry docket. 'Copies of their records, Harry, and details of the heist, for what that's worth,' he said, handing over the docket. 'There's also a full case history of Miller there, but I'd ask you to keep it under lock and key until you can return it to me.'

'It's got to be something to do with the team he grassed on,' I said.

'Racing certainty, Harry. At a calculated guess, I'd say that one or more of them hired a hitman to top Miller alias Wright alias Skinner. But I don't know how this hired gun found him. And before you ask, those five are all in different nicks.' He pointed at the file.

'If the guy's stupid enough to play drums in a jazz club in Fulham on a Saturday night, I wouldn't've thought it would have been too difficult to find him,' I said. 'Was there any evidence that he was a drummer in his past life?'

'Not that I know of,' said Drew, 'but I don't think we looked into that too deeply.'

'And I presume he didn't have a facial.'

'No, the vain bastard was offered cosmetic surgery, but turned it down. I reckon he was too squeamish. Funny that, when you think about it. Doesn't mind the sight of blood so long as it's not his own.'

'Is it OK if I share all this with Dave, guv?' I asked, and as an afterthought added, 'And is it all right to make enquiries at the Hatfield place?'

'Sure, Harry. It's all dead and buried now. Just like Miller will be in a day or two's time.' Drew grinned, stubbed out his cigarette and stood up. 'I'll leave you to get on with it, then. And the best of luck. If there's anything you think I might be able to help you with, give me a bell.' And with that he wrote his telephone number on my pad. He paused at the door. 'I shouldn't mention any of this to the commander, Harry. It'll only worry him, and you can quote the Assistant Commissioner as authority if you want to stay shtum.'

Five

It was predictable that the moment Detective Chief Superintendent Drew left Curtis Green, the commander would send for me.

'Anything I should know about, Mr Brock?' he asked airily.

'No, sir.'

'Well, what did Mr Drew want exactly?' There was a touch more tetchiness in the commander's voice this time.

I had no intention of playing the trump card Drew had handed me by referring the commander to the Assistant Commissioner. That would only succeed in making my life a misery, and I am nothing if not someone who enjoys an uncomplicated life. From a disciplinary point of view, that is.

'He had some knowledge of Skinner's associates, sir,' I said. 'Just the useful helpful snippet that tends to pass between CID officers. As I'm sure you know from your own experience, sir.' I was chancing my arm with that sarcastic comment, but the commander seemed to take it as a compliment.

'Quite so, Mr Brock, quite so,' he said, and then frowned. 'But I thought you told me

that this man Skinner had no previous convictions.'

'Neither had he, sir,' I lied. 'Lucky not to have been caught, I suppose.'

'I see. Very well, Mr Brock,' said the commander, and waved a hand of dismissal.

I spent the rest of the morning perusing the file that Frank Drew had left with me, and discussing its contents, and its implications, with Dave and Kate Ebdon.

'Blimey, guv,' said Dave. 'It's a bloody dog's dinner. Is there any point in interviewing these fingers that Skinner succeeded in getting banged up?' We had decided early on that we would continue to refer to our victim as Skinner. Otherwise we'd finish up confusing ourselves. And in my case that wouldn't be difficult.

'They got sent down for twenty-five years, Dave,' I said, tapping the file with a forefinger, 'and they've got at least another ten to do, if not more, before anyone mentions the word parole. Sure as hell they're not going to admit to any involvement in Skinner's topping. They've nothing to gain and everything to lose. The only way to go right now is to start checking on who they've run with in the past. And that's going to be a long and probably futile business.'

'So what do we do now?' asked Dave.

'A trip to Hatfield.'

'We're not likely to learn anything up there,

guv. From what you were saying, he's been gone from there for three years.'

'I know that, Dave, but we shan't know for certain until we've done it.'

Dave was absolutely right and it hadn't needed him to tell me. But one of the ground rules of murder investigation is that every avenue must be explored until it turns out to be a cul-de-sac. Then you go back to the crossroads and start over.

And that is exactly how it turned out. We were fortunate enough to find women at home in the houses on either side of the one once occupied by the Skinners in their guise as the Wrights. That in itself was unusual. In these days of working mothers, police usually have to make such visits in the evenings, after put-upon grandmothers have returned their grandchildren to the parental home.

But it was to no avail.

The consensus among the residents on either side of the Wrights' former home, and beyond, was that the Wrights had been perfect neighbours. They had never been known to fight with each other, they'd never played their TV or their hi-fi too loudly, never held noisy parties, always passed the time of day pleasantly enough, but kept themselves to themselves.

Questioned about Mr Wright's occupation, none of the neighbours was able to assist us, and certainly none of them knew he had been a drummer. One woman volunteered the suggestion that Mr Wright had been injured in an industrial accident and was living on disability benefit. But that snippet of information was negated by the woman's next statement that she hadn't heard it from the Wrights. Her husband, she told us, had picked it up from someone else in the local pub.

The Wrights, we were told by those who had lived nearest, appeared to be of modest means. They ran a small car, probably about six years old, and never seemed to go out. The only note of dissent came from one neighbour who felt sorry for Mrs Wright who, she assured us, was a sober and rather dowdy woman. 'Her husband never seemed to take her out, poor dear,' she had said. 'I think she spent most of her time watching telly.'

Finally, we tried the woman now living in the house formerly occupied by the Wrights, but predictably she knew nothing. She and her husband had bought the property through a local estate agent some eighteen months ago and didn't even know the previous occupants' names.

We returned to Curtis Green to ponder our next move. But I decided against pondering too long. I rang Gail and suggested that she join me for a bite of dinner in town.

★   ★   ★

As usual I met her at Waterloo Station. And, as usual, the home-going crowds parted for her much as the waters of the Red Sea are said to have parted for Moses. Gail's father George is a millionaire property developer, drives a Rolls-Royce and talks incessantly about Formula One motor racing and the history of the land speed record. As she is his only child, he dotes on her and sends her a substantial allowance when she's 'resting' from the acting profession. Which is why she's able to live to a standard that I could never hope to equal.

As testimony to her expensive lifestyle, she was wearing a sleeveless pink-and-white polka-dot dress and pink sandals, and carried a pink Italian handbag, all of which must have cost a fortune. But I noticed that the dress had what appeared to me to be an unfinished, uneven hem, and made the mistake of commenting on it.

'That, darling, is called a handkerchief hem,' she said, assuming an air of condescending pity for my ignorance in matters of haute couture. 'It's the latest fashion.'

'Oh,' I said, and lapsed into banal small talk until we arrived at one of our favourite restaurants.

The head waiter, as obsequious as ever, conducted us to a secluded table. A past admirer, sitting alone on the far side of the room, waved discreetly at Gail. But I'm accustomed to this now; it seems to happen every time we go to a London restaurant. I waved back.

'Well, darling, and how's your day been?' asked Gail, leaning back slightly so that the waiter could flick a napkin across her lap.

'Lousy,' I said, but I wasn't about to tell her of the complication that had arisen that morning. There are some things one can never tell a girlfriend, or even a wife. 'How about you? Found anything?'

This was a standard conversation between us. Following the murder of a dancer who had been appearing in the chorus line alongside Gail in a production of *Scatterbrain*, the show had closed. The latter, however, was not the result of the former. Gail had taken the opportunity to 'rest' for a while, but I had detected of late an impatience to return to the theatre, preferably in an acting role rather than as a dancer.

However, she was convinced that her ex-husband Gerald Andrews, a theatrical director, had put the 'black' on her with producers and other directors. And all because she had divorced him after finding him in bed with a nude dancer. But she was more annoyed, she said, that it had been *their* bed in which she found them. Funny creatures, women.

'There's not a great deal on offer,' said Gail, as the first course arrived, 'and the latest terrorist outrages haven't exactly encouraged foreigners to come here. Let's face it, they're the ones who keep London's theatres alive.'

'Perhaps it would help if producers were to put on shows that people wanted to see,' I said, which was also part of our routine chats. But it was a view with which I knew Gail agreed.

'As a matter of fact, I'm thinking of looking for something entirely different.'

'Like what?'

'I was thinking of setting up a casting agency.'

'Really? But if, as you say, there's not much around, you wouldn't be very successful, would you?'

Gail took a sip of her wine. 'You know your trouble, don't you, darling?' she said sweetly. 'You're a cynical old copper.'

'Not so much of the old,' I said.

On the train back to Surbiton, Gail asked the question that one or other of us always asked at the end of a pleasant evening. 'Your place or mine, darling?'

'Let's make it mine,' I said, hoping that Gladys Gurney, my super-efficient cleaning lady, had been in and done the business.

And, thank God, she had. But she had left an acerbic note prominently displayed on the hall table. It read: *Dear Mr Brock, I have put all the clothes I found on your bedroom floor into the washing machine. I'll leave it to you to switch it on. Yours faithfully, Gladys Gurney (Mrs).*

'Your Mrs Gurney seems to be a treasure,' said Gail, kicking off her sandals.

But it was apparent that Gladys was trying to teach me a lesson. The washing machine contained, among other things, one of my suits and a pair of trainers.

Gail laughed. 'Got the message, darling?' she asked.

Thursday morning. Five days since Skinner's murder.

The reports had started to come in. The fingerprints found in Skinner's car had been identified. At least, those capable of identification had been.

One set belonged to Skinner, verified by those taken from his body by Linda Mitchell and, of course, by those in the file that Drew had handed me. Another set had been identified as belonging to Babs Skinner – Linda had taken elimination prints from her shortly after we had visited her – but she had no previous convictions recorded against her.

There was, however, a more interesting ID than that of Rod Skinner. A convicted armed robber who had served five years and had been released some three years ago had also been in Skinner's car. His name was Albert Metcalfe; it was a good chance that he was the 'Fruity' whom Babs Skinner had seen romping with Roxy on the patio down at The

Gables.

DC John Appleby also had something to report. His search of the directory on Skinner's cellphone had revealed a number against the name 'Fruity'. Fortunately it was a landline number – not all mobile numbers are easy to trace these days – and a subscriber check proved that it belonged to Albert Metcalfe.

Interestingly enough, there was also a mobile number against the name 'Roxy', but we were in luck. Appleby had spoken to the service provider and they had come up with an address in Richmond. And even better, it was Richmond in Surrey rather than Richmond in Yorkshire. It's not often I get that lucky.

Also in Skinner's directory were an Eric and a Brian. Whether they were the same Eric and Brian that Babs Skinner had said had been at the notorious party remained to be seen, but the chances are they were.

However, there were three other names: Charlene, Vicky and Samantha. Was this trio part of the 'field' that Babs Skinner claimed her late husband had played, I wondered?

I was determined to ask Rod Skinner's widow some very searching questions. But not until I'd done a hell of a lot of homework on what we'd got so far.

'Get someone on to checking out those names on Skinner's phone, Kate,' I said to

DI Ebdon. 'You never know, we might just find the answer there.'

'Being done already, guv,' said Kate, with a smug grin.

Yesterday had been a day of intense activity on the part of DI Kate Ebdon's team. On Friday morning she was able to give me something to work on.

'We checked out the numbers that were on Skinner's mobile, guv,' she began, and handed me a list of the full names of those who had interested us, together with their addresses. 'I got the team working late, and they interviewed Eric Groves, Brian Baker and Roxy Peters. They all admitted having been at Skinner's party at The Gables. But we couldn't get hold of Albert Metcalfe. Of the other three women – Charlene Allen, Vicky James and Samantha Mount – only Charlene Allen was at home. She said she was at this party too. The Allen girl's an enigma. Good-looking, well educated and lives with her parents in a nice house in a decent neighbourhood in Thames Ditton.'

'So that leaves Metcalfe, Vicky James and Samantha Mount,' I said, running a finger down the list.

'I'll get the team out again today to check on them,' said Kate.

'What about form?' I asked.

'We knew already that Metcalfe has previous, but so do Groves and Baker. All three for armed robbery. Seems they were a team.' Kate smiled. 'Perhaps they were planning a job, guv,' she said.

'What did Roxy and Charlene have to say, Kate?'

'There's no doubt they sleep around, guv, and both admitted to having had a fling with Rod Skinner as well as with Metcalfe, Groves and Baker.' Kate shot me one of her lascivious grins. 'And I've no doubt Skinner had the other two as well.'

'What d'you think, Dave?' I asked.

'I reckon we're on a wild-goose chase with that lot, guv,' said Dave, waving at the list in my hand. 'I think we've got to divide this enquiry into two parts. First there's the little harem that provided entertainment for Skinner and his mates, and then there's another lot who were after him for grassing them up. I know they're still in the nick, but as you said the other day, they'll have had contacts who could have done the job. From their form, they're all good professionals.'

As usual, Dave had summed up the complex investigation with which we were faced.

'Nevertheless, we'll still have to interview them all,' I said with a sigh. 'It might just have been a lovers' squabble between Rod Skinner and one of the women that went seriously wrong. Or even a fight between Skinner and one of the other men over one of the girls.' But then I changed my mind.

'Kate, give me an assessment of those you think I should talk to and we'll tackle them first. By the way, did you mention Skinner's murder to the ones you saw?'

'Didn't have to,' said Kate. 'They all knew about it. Just goes to prove some of them read the papers, and don't only watch sport on the television.'

'More likely Babs Skinner's been on the phone to them, despite saying how much she hated these so-called friends of her late husband,' said Dave. 'Being a sober, dowdy woman with nothing else to do,' he added, laughing as he echoed the view expressed by one of the Skinners' former neighbours at Hatfield.

Despite Dave's summary of the situation, I decided that it was time we started to check out some alibis. And we started with Frank Seaton, who had been Erica Leech's boyfriend until, she told us, he had been supplanted by Rod Skinner.

The Chelsea art gallery was devoid of customers, and I wondered how people like Frank Seaton made any money. Dave Poole, however, was in no doubt at all. He was convinced that anyone who didn't do what he described as an honest day's work must be involved in villainy.

A willowy brunette of about twenty rose

85

from behind a reproduction antique desk the moment we were through the door. 'May I help you?' she asked in the modulated tones that seemed to be an essential qualification for young ladies working in the art world. She glanced suspiciously at Dave Poole.

'I'm looking for a Mr Frank Seaton,' I said.

'May I ask what it's about?' asked the girl.

'We're police officers,' I began, but got no further.

The girl turned towards an open door at the rear of the gallery. 'Daddy, the police want to talk to you.'

The man who emerged from what proved to be his office was tall, forty-ish, and had greying wavy hair. He wore an Armani two-piece linen suit with a watered-silk waistcoat, and sported the spotted bow tie and yellow buttonhole rose that seemed to be de rigueur for the arty-crafty world he inhabited.

'I'm Frank Seaton,' he said gushingly, approaching us with outstretched hand. 'Are you from the Arts and Antiques Squad?'

'No,' said Dave. 'Expecting them, were you?' He glanced around at the paintings that hung on the walls of the gallery as if searching for stolen masterpieces.

'We're investigating the murder of Rod Skinner at the Starlight Club in Fulham last Saturday evening, Mr Seaton,' I said.

'Really?' Seaton contrived an expression of helpless bafflement. 'Well, I don't see how I can possibly help you, gentlemen. I don't know this club you mentioned, and I've never heard of anyone called ... what did you say his name was?'

'Rod Skinner – or maybe Jimmy Wright?' I knew that Seaton was into denial straight away. He'd've known about the murder all right, unless he had no television and didn't read the papers. Furthermore, he'd've made the connection between the Starlight Club and Erica Leech, and he'd've known that we were here because she had told us where to find him.

'I'm sorry, but why should you think I could help in any way?'

'Because you are one of Erica Leech's cast-off boyfriends.' I spoke quietly, nevertheless managing to inject an element of menace.

'You'd better come into the office,' said Seaton hurriedly. 'Keep an eye on the shop, Jane, there's a dear. Just a little problem about a former customer.'

Closing the door firmly, Seaton sat down behind his desk, and waved us into two arm-chairs. This was obviously where business with more affluent clients was conducted.

'I know nothing about this murder, and quite frankly, I see no reason why you should come here pestering *me* about it,' said Seaton, going on to the offensive straight away.

'I understand that there was some acrimony between you and Mrs Leech when you broke up,' I said.

'*Mrs* Leech?' That appeared to have disturbed Seaton.

'Oh yes. She's married. As a matter of fact she lives with her husband in World's End somewhere.' I decided it was unnecessary to go into the details of the estranged Leeches' living arrangements, particularly as I'd now got Seaton on the run.

'Good God! I never knew that. What does he do, this husband of hers?'

'We don't know,' said Dave, 'although someone did suggest he was a Royal Marines commando.' But then Dave's a malicious bastard.

'Christ!' Dave's throwaway comment had knocked the stuffing out of Seaton. 'Look, I had nothing to do with this fellow's murder.'

'But you are not above using violence, are you?' I fixed Seaton with what I hoped was a penetrating stare.

'What d'you mean by that?'

'I am told that, in a fit of jealous rage, you assaulted Mrs Leech, after which she broke off the relationship.'

Seaton scoffed. 'It was rather the other way around, old boy. She assaulted me. Kneed me in the crutch, as a matter of fact, and then floored me with a vicious right hook. Bloody painful it was too. It was agony to pee for days afterwards.'

'Was the argument because Mrs Leech had

taken up with a new boyfriend?' I asked.

'In a way, I suppose it was,' agreed Seaton. 'But it was over a year ago now. What on earth she saw in that wastrel, I really don't know. The man was a drummer, for God's sake, a common musician. But then all Erica wanted was rough sex, not the sort of suave man who knows decent restaurants to take her to, and what wines to order with what dishes, eh?'

'Where were you last Saturday evening, Mr Seaton?' asked Dave, opening his pocket book and feeling for his pen.

'For God's sake, man, I had nothing to do with this sordid business.'

'Just answer the question, Mr Seaton.' Dave waggled his pen in a menacing manner.

'I was at home, as a matter of fact.'

'Is there anyone who can verify that?' persisted Dave.

'My wife Fiona,' said Seaton quietly.

'Ah!' said Dave and wrote down this vital piece of information. 'At twenty-seven Hendy Road, Putney, I presume.'

'How did you know that?' demanded Seaton. He was clearly alarmed that we knew where he lived.

'When we're conducting a murder investigation,' I said mildly, 'we tend to find out things.'

'Look, you don't have to speak to Fiona, do you? She doesn't know that I—'

'I'll bet she does,' said Dave, which did little to comfort Seaton.

'Don't worry, Mr Seaton,' I said. 'We're very discreet about these matters.' I didn't think that Seaton was anything more than a philandering husband. And having seen the well-built Erica Leech, I was more inclined to believe Seaton's account of the assault that had brought about the termination of his relationship with the jazz-club owner.

Seaton sighed. 'I suppose I'd better tell you the truth,' he said.

I couldn't believe he was about to confess to Skinner's murder. Which was just as well, because he didn't.

'I spent the evening with a young lady.'

'I see,' I said. 'Who?'

'Oh God!' Seaton ran a hand through his hair. 'Is this really necessary?'

I'd had enough of this vain fool. 'Yes, it is, Mr Seaton, unless you want to continue this interview at Chelsea police station. Your prevarication is leading me to believe you might have had something to do with Skinner's murder.'

Dave smiled approvingly, presumably at my use of the word 'prevarication'.

'Well, I didn't,' said the shaken Seaton. 'The girl's name is Inge Beck. She's a model. Here, I'll give you her address.' He wrote down the details on a slip of paper and handed it to me.

Six

As we were in the Chelsea area, I decided to take a chance on finding Frank Seaton's current girlfriend at home. And she was.

'Miss Beck?'

Inge Beck was tall and slender, with a good figure and expensively styled short black hair but, that said, my expectation of what a model should look like finished there. Devoid of make-up, she wore a pair of ragged old jeans ripped at the knees, mules and a loose white T-shirt that had slipped, either deliberately or accidentally, from her right shoulder. Even so, her high cheekbones and almond-shaped eyes lent her face a classical beauty.

'Yes, what is it that you want?' As I had anticipated from her name, the woman's accent was either German or Austrian.

'We're police officers, Miss Beck.'

'Really? How do I know this?' The woman gazed at us with an expression of doubt on her face.

I produced my warrant card. 'Detective Chief Inspector Brock of Homicide West, and this is Detective Sergeant Poole.'

'And what do you want with me?' she asked haughtily.

'It's about Frank Seaton,' I said.

'Oh, dear Frank, yes. What has he done? Been a naughty boy?' She laughed and led us into the sitting room of her luxury flat and gestured at two of several armchairs. The carpet was a thick black pile and the furniture, although not to my taste, was very Chelsea in style. Which means very expensive. Miss Beck was clearly in the high-earning bracket of fashion models. There were some paintings on the wall and I wondered whether they had come from Seaton's art gallery. And if they had, whether they were only on loan until this particular relationship came to its inevitable end.

'Mr Seaton has told us that he was with you last Saturday evening, Miss Beck.'

Inge Beck sat down on a leather settee opposite us and kicked off her mules. 'And why should you be checking on what Frank was doing last Saturday?' she asked, a mocking half-smile on her face.

'There was a murder at the Starlight Club in Fulham that night,' I said.

'Yes, I know this. It was on the TV. But what has that to do with Frank? Do you think he did this murder?'

'I don't know who did it, but if you can confirm that he was with you, then that will clear up the matter as far as he's concerned.'

'Frank wouldn't kill a fly. He is too squeamish.'

I thought that was a fair assessment of the man I'd met just over an hour earlier. 'Maybe, but was he with you?'

'Yes, he was.'

'From what time, Miss Beck?'

The woman gave that some thought. 'From about nine o'clock, I think.'

'Are you sure about that?'

'Oh yes, I think so. He came then and stayed for an hour. He said he had to go home to his wife, otherwise she would become suspicious.'

'You knew that he was married, then.'

'Of course.'

At that point Inge Beck's cordless telephone rang. She leaned across from where she was sitting, picked it up, and clicked it to 'receive'. The next few minutes were taken up with an animated conversation in German, every word of which I understood. Well, her half of it, anyway. As I mentioned previously, one of the few advantages of my marriage to Helga was that I'd learned to speak fluent German.

'I'm sorry for that,' said Inge, returning her attention to us as she replaced the phone on the side table. 'Now, what was it you were saying?'

'I said that you knew Mr Seaton was married.'

93

'Yes, of course I did. But if an old man like Frank wants to take me out and spend money on me, I am happy to let him.'

Even though Inge Beck must have been nearing thirty, I wasn't too impressed by her description of Seaton as an old man. He could only have been a year or two older than me. And he must have spent a hell of a lot of money to persuade this nubile young woman into bed. 'You're quite certain about the time, Miss Beck?'

'Yes. Positive.' But then she contradicted herself by adding, 'I *think* it was about nine o'clock.'

'Did he seem excited or nervous?' I asked, imagining that if he'd just shot someone and made a rapid escape, he would have arrived at the woman's flat in a muck sweat.

Inge laughed. 'No, he was not excited when he got here, but he was very soon afterwards,' she said. 'But he wouldn't have been at the Starlight Club, not after Erica Leech beat him up and threw him out. He never went near the place after that.'

'Oh, you know about that, do you?'

'Of course. I know all about all of my boy-friends.'

Inge Beck was a very strong-minded, per-sonable woman, and I was not surprised that she had more than one boyfriend. But I was glad that I wasn't one of them.

'What was Mr Seaton wearing when he

arrived here?' asked Dave.

'Chinos and a sleeveless lime-green T-shirt. Oh, and he had a gold medallion round his neck. I told him I didn't like it. I told him it looked quite ridiculous on a man of his age. Old men look better in a tuxedo.'

'You seem very certain about what he was wearing, Miss Beck,' said Dave.

'Of course. I'm in the fashion business. I notice what people are wearing.'

'Did Mr Seaton ever mention anyone called Rod Skinner or Jimmy Wright, Miss Beck?' I asked.

'Not to me, no. Skinner was the man who was murdered?'

'Yes, he was. And he was Erica Leech's current boyfriend.'

'Poor man,' said Inge, but I wasn't sure whether her sympathy was for Skinner being in that relationship or for having been murdered.

Although it wasn't far from the Starlight Club to Inge Beck's flat, it seemed unlikely that Seaton could have murdered Skinner at eight-thirty, changed his clothes and disposed of the shotgun and the stocking mask, and arrived there by *about* nine. Particularly as Inge had said that he had shown no signs of agitation when he arrived. And so we left it. For the time being.

'*Auf wiedersehen, gnädiges Fräulein,*' I said, out of sheer devilment, and was pleased to see that Inge Beck's haughty reserve slipped. Just for a brief moment.

'What was the telephone conversation about, guv?' asked Dave as we drove back to Curtis Green.

It was my turn to laugh. 'If only Seaton knew,' I said. 'She was fixing up to meet her German boyfriend this evening. And very intimate the chat was too. I think old arty-crafty Seaton's days in Inge's bed are numbered.'

'D'you think she was expecting us?' asked Dave. 'Seaton had time to ring her before we arrived, and it might just be that's she's deliberately dropping him in the mire in an attempt to ditch him. She was a bit vague about the time. Purposely, I think. Maybe he's done something to upset her.' He thought about that for a moment. 'Sure as hell, I wouldn't like to upset her.'

'We'll check, Dave,' I said, 'but I don't think he's got the guts to walk into a jazz club with a sawn-off shotgun and murder the drummer. And I don't think that Miss Beck would pussyfoot about if she decided to dump him. She'd just tell him his time was up and show him the door.'

'Yes,' said Dave thoughtfully, 'I reckon she would, guv.'

The address that Kate Ebdon had obtained for Albert Metcalfe was near Kew Bridge railway station, not very far from where Roxy Peters lived across the river in Richmond. Not that that meant anything.

The problem with villains of Metcalfe's calibre is that you never know when they are likely to be at home. It is a fallacy that burglaries only take place during the night-time hours. In fact, most of them occur during the day when householders are at work and are foolish enough to have left a window open, or a door unlocked. And there's always one. A skilled 'breaker' will go down a street ignoring secure premises until he finds one that is easy to enter. And he doesn't have to search for very long.

But all of that is irrelevant. From his record, we knew that Metcalfe was an armed robber, and such professionals will rarely demean themselves by joining the ranks of 'drummers', as housebreakers are known to those in the trade. Nevertheless, the same rule applied; he could have been out doing a robbery right now. We called at six o'clock that evening, and as luck would have it, he was at home.

Albert 'Fruity' Metcalfe was stocky and muscular, probably from working out in the prison gymnasium, and wore jeans and a dirty singlet.

'You must be the Old Bill,' he announced, surveying Dave and me. 'Fruity Metcalfe at your service, gents. I've been expecting you ever since I heard someone topped Rod Skinner. Come on in, guv'nor.'

A woman, careworn and dowdy, whom I presumed to be Metcalfe's wife, appeared in the hall.

'Get them kids out of here, Lil,' said Metcalfe at the doorway to the sitting room. 'We've got visitors.'

The woman glanced at us, undoubtedly recognized us for what we were, and ushered two children out of the room and escorted them away. She was probably wondering whether her husband was about to depart in handcuffs.

'Have a seat, gents.' Metcalfe closed the door, turned off the television and sat down. 'From the Bladder, are you?' he asked in rich Cockney tones.

'Yes, Homicide West,' I said, and introduced Dave and myself. The 'Bladder of Lard' was old, and now rarely used, rhyming slang for Scotland Yard, and I guessed that Metcalfe was trying to impress me with his credentials as an old-fashioned 'honest' criminal. The sort who wouldn't hold a grudge against the police when he'd been nicked 'bang to rights'.

'So, what can I do for you, Mr Brock?' Metcalfe paused, and waved at a table well stocked with alcohol. 'Can I offer you gents a wet?'

'No thanks,' I said. 'I understand that you

knew Rod Skinner quite well.'

'Yeah, we was great mates, him and me. First met in the nick, must've been, what, a good ten years ago? Wandsworth, that was. Bloody awful nick an' all. Still it wasn't too far for Lil – that's the missus – when she come visiting. Done a few jobs together after that, me and Rod.'

'Well, let's kick off with the routine question. Where were you last Saturday evening at around half-past eight?'

'Clubbing, up west.'

'Anyone verify that?'

'Yeah.' Metcalfe lowered his voice. 'A bird called Roxy Peters.'

'Would that be the same Roxy Peters you were screwing on the patio down at Rod Skinner's place a couple of months ago?' asked Dave.

Metcalfe threw back his head and roared with laughter. 'Your sergeant don't mince his words, do he, Mr Brock? Yeah, that's the one, Sarge. Been chatting to Babs Skinner, then, have you?'

'What's your wife think about that?' I asked. Not that I cared.

'She can please herself,' said Metcalfe. 'We don't exactly get on with each other these days. Go our separate ways, if you get my drift.'

'Which clubs did you and Roxy Peters visit, Mr Metcalfe?'

'I knew you'd be asking that, so I've written 'em down for you.' Metcalfe pulled a wallet from the back pocket of his jeans and took out a slip of paper. 'I knew you'd want to know, see, so I thought I'd save you a bit of time.'

'Thanks,' said Dave, a sour note to his voice. 'Very kind of you, I'm sure.' He knew, as did I, that Metcalfe might or might not have been at the clubs he'd listed, and might or might not have been with Roxy Peters. But, sure as hell, he'd've squared it with a mate to say they'd seen him there. It was also a racing certainty that Roxy Peters would be in possession of a similar list and had probably committed it to memory. On the other hand it was likely that no one *working* at those clubs would remember seeing Metcalfe. But that wouldn't mean he *wasn't* there.

'So you and Skinner did a few jobs together,' I said.

'Well, it's no secret, is it, Mr Brock? You've only got to have a dekko in your rogues' gallery. It's all there.'

'What was he calling himself then?' I asked.

'Dennis Miller, but he changed his name later on. Perhaps he was going straight.' Metcalfe chuckled.

'Did he say why he'd changed his name?'

'No. And it don't do to ask, do it?'

Either Metcalfe didn't know that Skinner had grassed and as a result had been placed

100

in a witness-protection programme, or he thought it wiser to keep quiet. But my instinct told me that Metcalfe, being a villain, would have known. So would a lot of other people. And that didn't make my job any easier.

'We won't waste any more of your time, Mr Metcalfe,' I said rising from my chair. 'We'll probably have to see you again.'

'I've no doubt you will, Mr Brock. Any idea when the funeral is? I'd like to go and pay me last respects, like. I dare say a few of Rod's other mates would an' all.'

'The coroner hasn't released the body yet, but it shouldn't be long. But who are these other mates of his?'

'Don't know their names. It don't do to ask too many questions in our line of work, if you take my meaning.' Metcalfe paused to scratch his chest. 'I s'pose you're off to see Roxy now, then.'

'No, there'll be no need to see her,' I said, attempting to give the impression that I'd believed his alibi, but knowing full well that Metcalfe would be on the phone to Roxy Peters the moment Dave and I had left.

Despite having told Metcalfe that I didn't intend interviewing Roxy Peters, we drove straight across Kew Bridge to her address in Richmond.

'Are we going to talk to all these people,

101

guv?' asked Dave. 'You know, the partygoers and hangers-on?' He sounded weary about the whole business.

'No, Dave. I think we'll concentrate on the villains. DI Ebdon's turned up form on Eric Groves and Brian Baker, and it's them we'll concentrate on.'

'So why are we seeing Roxy Peters?'

'Because I haven't finished with Metcalfe yet, and I'm bloody sure he's fixed up for her to provide him with an alibi. And I don't take kindly to villains who try to have me over.'

'D'you think he might've topped Skinner, guv?' asked Dave, as we pulled up outside the tall Edwardian house where Roxy had a flat.

'He might've done, Dave. On the other hand, he might've been involved in a bit of villainy elsewhere. In either case, we'll have him. And this time you can do the talking. Don't pull any punches.'

Roxy Peters was not what I'd expected of a good-time girl. Aged about twenty-five, she was demurely dressed in a smart grey suit – admittedly the skirt of which was above the knee – sheer black tights and high-heeled black shoes.

'Hello,' she said, gazing at us through a pair of black horn-rimmed spectacles, and spending more time looking at Dave.

'Miss Peters, we're police officers,' I said.

'Oh, Fruity told me you'd be coming to see me. Come in.' Roxy primped her short brown hair and held the door open. 'I'm afraid I'm in a bit of a mess, but I've only just got in from work,' she said.

We waited while she cleared newspapers, magazines and various other bits and pieces from chairs in her small and cluttered sitting room, and then sat down.

'Is it about Rod Skinner?' asked Roxy, sitting in an armchair, crossing her legs and arranging her skirt.

'Yes,' said Dave. 'Can I start by asking where you were last Saturday evening?'

Nice one, Dave. Instead of asking if she had been with Metcalfe on that occasion, he'd put the question the other way round. And from the bewildered expression on her face, it had obviously thrown her.

'I, er, I was out.'

'Where?'

She reached for her handbag. 'I've got a note of it here somewhere.'

'Don't bother with the names that Mr Metcalfe gave you,' said Dave. 'It was only last Saturday. You can't have forgotten.'

'We were in the West End.' Roxy was obviously discomfited at having to rely on her memory.

'The West End's a big place. Where exactly?'

'It was a club.'

'There are lots of them,' continued Dave relentlessly. 'Which one?'

'Er, I can't remember the name exactly.'

'Well, where was it?'

'Rupert Street, I think. Yes, I'm sure.'

'The Flamingo?'

'Yes, that's it.' Roxy looked relieved.

'The Flamingo's in Brewer Street,' said Dave. 'Try again.'

The look of relief vanished, and Roxy dissolved into tears. She reached for her handbag again and took out a tissue. Taking off her glasses, she dabbed at her eyes, trying not to smudge her mascara.

'Shall we start again, Miss Peters? You weren't with Metcalfe at all last Saturday evening, but he told you what to say to us when we asked you. I must warn you that it's a serious matter to lie under oath, and I suppose you'll be prepared to do that at the Old Bailey.'

The tears were replaced by sobs, the mascara now running unchecked down the girl's cheeks. 'I'm sorry,' she mumbled, 'but he said it was important.'

'Did he say why it was important? Was it that he'd murdered Rod Skinner and wanted you to cover for him?'

'I don't know. He just said that he had to have an alibi, otherwise the police would arrest him because he'd got a record.' Roxy looked up imploringly. 'But he's going straight now. He promised.'

Having demolished Metcalfe's alibi, Dave

moved on. 'How often did you have sexual intercourse with Rod Skinner, Miss Peters?'

Roxy stared at Dave angrily, the sort of scandalized expression that a woman adopts when she is accused of sexual impropriety. Particularly when it's true.

Dave just smiled. 'Well?'

But Roxy knew that he knew. 'Once or twice,' she said, her voice muffled by the tissue with which she was now dabbing her lipstick.

'Was that down at Skinner's place at Cobham?'

'Yes.'

'Where else?'

'Here.'

'And did you succeed in getting Charlie Hardy into bed at that party?'

'Who?' She replaced her glasses and stared at Dave once again.

'Babs Skinner's toyboy.'

'No,' admitted Roxy. 'Babs warned me off.'

Dave laughed. 'Who else did you hop into bed with at that party? Or into the pool with.'

'I was drunk. I don't remember what happened.'

'Who else have you slept with?' Dave's tone sharpened; he wasn't going to be messed around. 'Eric Groves? Or Brian Baker?'

'Certainly not.' But it was obvious that she was lying. I didn't know why, either; she'd admitted it when Kate Ebdon had interviewed her.

'Do you specialize in bedding armed robbers?' demanded Dave brutally.

'I'm not that sort of girl. I don't sleep around.' Roxy's pathetic, tear-stained face peered at me, as if hoping that I would come to her rescue.

But Dave was doing fine, and I had no intention of taking over the questioning.

'You were Rod Skinner's arm candy for quite a while, weren't you?'

'Yes.'

'Didn't his wife mind?'

'Rod said that she was sleeping with Charlie and that it was only fair that he should have some fun.'

'Where did he get his money from, Roxy?' Dave had decided to use the girl's first name to soften the harshness of his interview technique. He was doing the good-cop-bad-cop routine all on his own. And doing it very well.

'I don't know.'

'But he spent quite a lot on you, didn't he?'

'He took me out to some nice restaurants, yes.'

'And to good hotels for the night?'

The girl said nothing, but just nodded and looked down.

'And how long has Metcalfe been shafting you?'

Roxy wrinkled her nose at Dave's coarseness. 'A couple of months,' she whispered.

'Ever since the party at Rod's.'

'So you abandoned Rod Skinner in favour of Fruity Metcalfe. Why was that?'

'I found out that Rod was making love to another girl.'

Dave laughed at the girl's euphemism. 'Who was she?'

'Er...' Roxy furrowed her brow, searching her mind for the name. 'Charlene something.'

'Charlene Allen?' asked Dave.

'Possibly. I don't know.'

'How did you find out?'

'She told me at the party. She said that Rod was hers now and if I knew what was good for me, I'd clear off and leave him alone.'

'But luck was on your side, wasn't it, Roxy? You'd already had a bit of fun on the patio with Metcalfe, so you just switched your allegiance.'

'You make it sound very sordid,' said Roxy, for once showing a flash of spirit.

'Well, it is, isn't it?' said Dave. 'And what does Metcalfe do for a living?'

'I don't know. I didn't ask.'

'But he spent money on you, too. Why is it that a nice young girl like you goes in for middle-aged villains? Seem exciting, does it? I suppose you see yourself as Bonnie to his Clyde. Going to do a few robberies with him, were you?'

'No, it's not like that.' Roxy denied the

accusation spiritedly. 'Men of Fruity's age know how to give a girl a good time, and they're much more interesting than the silly youngsters I work with. All they're interested in are sport, fast cars and getting girls into bed.'

'Well, just remember that Bonnie and Clyde finished up getting shot dead by the police in Louisiana in nineteen thirty-four,' said Dave, displaying a detailed knowledge of the criminal history of the United States. But then he never ceases to amaze me. 'You spoke of the young men you work with. Where do you work?'

'In a bank,' said Roxy miserably. It might have been the fact that she worked in a bank that caused the misery, or it might have been having to admit it.

But whichever it was didn't matter. Both Dave and I realized that we had perhaps stumbled on something interesting. Roxy Peters had been bedded by Skinner and Metcalfe and, according to Kate, by Eric Groves and Brian Baker. And they were all armed robbers. So why did four robbers spend money on a fairly plain girl who worked in a bank? Well, you don't have to be an Einstein to work that out. Perhaps at last we were getting near a motive for Skinner's murder. When thieves fall out, you just never know what's going to happen next. Particularly if they fall out over a woman.

Seven

On Monday morning Kate Ebdon briefed me on the outcome of the interviews that she and her team had been conducting over the weekend.

I had telephoned her on Friday evening and told her not to speak to either Eric Groves or Brian Baker again. In view of what we had learned about Roxy Peters's employment, I decided that I would interview Groves and Baker when the time was right, and that wasn't just yet.

In my view it had now become a strong possibility that the three surviving robbers were planning a heist of some sort. That in turn could provide a motive for Skinner's murder, particularly if he'd found out about the heist and they'd found out he was a grass. But I had to accept that Dave and I were charting muddy waters. I said as much to him and he accused me of mixing my metaphors. I should worry. He knew what I meant.

Kate had not managed to speak to either Vicky James or Samantha Mount – two of the girls in Skinner's cellphone directory –

but was able to confirm that they lived in Wandsworth and Teddington respectively. Consequently, she was unable to say whether they had had affairs with Skinner, Metcalfe, Groves and Baker, or to tell me what the two girls did for a living. But my gut feeling was that they worked in either a bank or somewhere where large amounts of ready cash were held. I decided that Dave and I would have to have a word with them, sooner rather than later.

After a little persuasion, and a veiled threat, Roxy Peters had eventually told us the name of the bank where she worked, and I got Colin Wilberforce to make an appointment with the director of security at the group head office. And to give him Roxy Peters's name so that he could make a few enquiries about her before we saw him.

Alec Pearson was a retired deputy assistant commissioner and had spent all but his two years' foot duty in the CID, much of it with the Flying Squad. I didn't know him all that well; during his service, he had been near the top of the hierarchy and I had been close to the bottom.

'This is a pleasant surprise, Harry,' said Pearson as he ushered us into his well-appointed office. He noticed my appraising glance. 'Done all right for myself, haven't I?'

'This is DS Dave Poole, guv,' I said.

'You can cut out the "guv", Harry. It's Alec. I'm not in the Job any more, thank God. Take a word of advice. As soon as you've got your time in, take your pension and get out. The grass is definitely greener on the other side.' He glanced at the clock above the door of his office. 'I reckon the sun's over the yardarm, Harry. What's your poison? It's all paid for by the bank,' he added with a laugh.

'A Scotch, Alec, please.'

'And you, Dave?' asked Pearson.

'The same, please,' said Dave.

Once we were settled in Alec Pearson's plush armchairs with a drink in our hands, I started to tell him why we were there.

'I remember Dennis Miller,' said Pearson reflectively. 'A good villain in his day. And he used to run with the others you mentioned. You reckon they're planning a job?'

I explained what we knew of Miller and how he'd done a runner from the witness-protection programme and changed his name to Skinner. And went on to tell him a little more about the plain-looking Roxy Peters who worked in one of the branches of his bank.

Pearson shook his head slowly. 'The days of the big bank robberies are as good as over, Harry,' he said. 'So much of it's done electronically now – credit and debit cards – that we don't issue many chequebooks any more. I can't really see that these guys are hoping to

111

relive the good old days. There's not that much cash about. It wouldn't be worth the risk for what they'd be likely to get out of it.'

'What about bullion, Alec?' I asked.

'Now that, Harry, is a different ballgame altogether.' Pearson crossed to the safe in the corner of his office and extracted a file. Returning to his desk, he skimmed quickly through it. 'Interesting,' he said, looking up. 'We've got a consignment going to South America on the nineteenth.' He glanced at his desk calendar. 'Christ, that's this coming Friday.'

'How's it getting there?'

'Via Thiefrow,' said Pearson. Heathrow Airport had long been known to the police as 'Thiefrow', a name derived from its reputation for what the Americans call grand larceny.

'I doubt they'd try a heist at the airport, Alec,' I said. 'What with the terrorist threat, the place is crawling with armed police these days. They'd be stupid to try anything there. It's not like it was in the days of the Great Bullion Robbery.' Capturing the eight robbers who'd attempted to steal a quarter of a million pounds' worth of bullion in 1948 was one of the Flying Squad's 'battle honours'.

'So that leaves the route between the bank's vault and the airport, Harry,' said Pearson thoughtfully.

112

'Usual armoured bullion van?' I asked.

Pearson nodded. 'Yes.'

'And escort?'

'Only me in a follow-up car. Security vans look much of a muchness these days, Harry. Unless you're in the business you can't really tell the difference between one that's transporting bullion and one that's collecting electronic bank records.'

'But villains like this little team would make it their business to find out, wouldn't they?'

'Oh, sure.'

'And is that where little Miss Roxy Peters comes in?'

'I doubt it, Harry. I've checked our personnel records and she works as a teller in our Richmond branch.' Pearson laughed. 'If you were planning to nick someone's pension on the day they regularly paid it in, she might help, but she wouldn't know the first thing about bullion shipments.'

'But she might know someone who did, Alec. She's not above hopping into bed with anyone who might spend a few quid on her. If one of the villains she's been sleeping with paid her enough, she might be prepared to offer herself to someone who's got inside knowledge. Someone working in the bank, perhaps.'

'True,' said Pearson. He leaned over and refilled our glasses with whisky. 'But we're speculating here, aren't we? We don't know that's what this team have got their eyes on, if they've got their eyes on anything. Could be that they're just taking advantage of a bit of available skirt. You know what it's like, Harry. Pull off a good job and then spend, spend, spend. Usually on women and booze. And that's what brings them down more often than not.'

'Do these women mean anything to you, Alec?' I asked, and gave him a list of the names and addresses of the girls whose numbers we'd found in Skinner's cellphone.

'Soon find out.' Pearson summoned his secretary. 'Liz, see if personnel have got any trace of these three girls, will you?'

Minutes later, the secretary was back. 'There's a Charlene Allen working here at head office, Mr Pearson,' she said. 'It's the same address, and she's in the transport department. But we don't have a Vicky James or a Samantha Mount on the payroll.'

'Does the transport department deal with the movement of bullion vans, Alec?' I asked.

'Yes, it bloody well does, Harry.' Pearson leaned back in his executive leather chair and let out a sigh. 'It looks as though we're going to have to take this seriously,' he said. And then he smiled. 'Well, Harry, you're the copper. What are you going to do about it?'

'Nothing to do with me, Alec,' I said. 'I only deal with mundane things like murder. This is obviously a job for the Flying Squad.'

★ ★ ★

I decided to take a chance and go straight to the head of the Flying Squad. I knew that if I went through the normal chain of command by telling my commander first, something would inevitably be lost in the translation.

'Yes, I know Alec Pearson,' said the Flying Squad DCS, whose name was Robinson. 'He was the governor here when I was a DI. So what's the SP, Harry?' he asked, using a handy bit of terminology the police had appropriated from the racing fraternity. To the aficionados of the turf it means 'starting price', but to coppers 'what's the SP?' means 'tell me the tale'. Useful, this shorthand, isn't it?

I outlined all that we knew, starting with Rod Skinner's killing, down through his known associates, and finally telling him about Roxy Peters and Charlene Allen.

'Sounds like a runner, Harry.' Robinson made a few notes. 'I'll go and see Alec, and then I'll assemble a team. Might even get involved myself,' he said, rubbing his hands together. 'I do like an excuse to get away from bloody paperwork. In the meantime, can I ask you to lay off interviewing Groves, Metcalfe and Baker? Might be as well not to talk to Roxy Peters again, or this Charlene Allen.'

'How about I have a chat to the other two,

guv? Vicky James and Samantha Mount. We've no idea what they do for a living, and it might be relevant. Particularly if they're working somewhere that's even more attractive to this little team than your bullion.'

'Good idea, Harry. Can't have too much intelligence in this game. Why don't you take Kate Ebdon with you? She's very good at persuading people to talk when they don't really want to.'

There was no time to waste. I briefed Kate Ebdon on what I had learned from Alec Pearson, and told her that the Flying Squad was looking into the possibility of a bullion-van robbery on Friday. A robbery that could well involve Albert Metcalfe, Eric Groves and Brian Baker. And, indirectly, Roxy Peters and Charlene Allen.

We went to Wandsworth first, which is where Vicky James lived. And on the basis of Robinson's advice, I decided to let Kate do the talking.

'I'm Detective Inspector Ebdon of New Scotland Yard,' said Kate to the brunette who answered the door. She could never be bothered with explaining she was attached to Homicide West. It wouldn't mean anything to most people anyway, and technically she was correct in saying she came from the Yard. 'This is Detective Chief Inspector Brock.'

'What's it about?'

'I think we'd better come in, don't you?' said Kate, and pushed open the door.

'It's not really convenient,' said Vicky in a half-hearted attempt to abort the interview before it had even started.

'Might not be convenient for you, love, but it is for us,' said Kate, walking into the small sitting room cum dining room. She glanced at the young man watching television, but he didn't look up.

'It's the police, Gavin,' said Vicky nervously.

'Really?' said Gavin, but his eyes remained glued to the coverage of some athletics meeting that was appearing on the TV.

'What's this about?' Vicky seemed to sense why we were here, and the presence of Gavin, whom we presumed to be her boyfriend, was causing her some embarrassment.

'Rod Skinner,' said Kate.

Vicky blushed and put a hand to her mouth. 'What about him?' she whispered. She nodded towards Gavin, implying that she wasn't prepared to talk in front of him.

Kate crossed the room and tapped Gavin on the shoulder. 'D'you want to leave us alone for a while, mate?' she said. 'What I want to talk about to Miss James is confidential.'

'Why should I? I live here.' At last Gavin turned his head. But then he saw the determined look on Kate's face and capitulated.

'Oh, all right,' he mumbled, and slouched from the room, banging the door loudly behind him.

'Bit of a wimp, is he, your boyfriend?' Kate asked.

'He's OK,' said Vicky, but was clearly relieved that her live-in lover had been summarily banished by Kate.

'How long did your affair with Rod Skinner last?' Kate went on the offensive straight away.

'How did you know that I—?' Again Vicky's hand went to her mouth and she glanced nervously at the door.

'Let's not mess about, Miss James. We know that he was screwing you, and we know that you were at a party at his place in Cobham a couple of months ago. And no doubt you were one of the naked nymphs who finished up getting thrown into the swimming pool.'

'Oh God! Gavin will kill me if he finds out.'

'Well, he won't find out from us.' Kate paused. 'Unless you finish up at the Old Bailey giving evidence, that is. Then the whole world will know.'

'I don't know what to say.'

'When did you last see Skinner?'

'At that party. I was drunk, otherwise I wouldn't have let Rod...' The girl broke off and looked down at the floor.

'Otherwise you wouldn't have let him screw

you. Is that it?' asked Kate brutally.

Vicky nodded, but remained silent.

'Pull the other one, mate,' said Kate, her Australian accent becoming more marked as she got into her stride. 'You had it off with him quite regularly. But what puzzles me is why.'

'He was very generous. He knew how to look after a girl.' There was almost a note of defiance in Vicky's voice. Almost, but not quite.

'And there were three other girls there, called Roxy Peters, Charlene Allen and Samantha Mount.'

Vicky's eyes opened in surprise. 'How did you know that?' The way in which the police garnered evidence had clearly come as a revelation to this young lady.

'Where d'you work, Vicky?' demanded Kate, ignoring the girl's question.

'At the haulage company at the bottom of the road. You must have passed it if you came up from the station end.'

'And what exactly do you do there?'

'I'm a wages clerk.'

'Is that a fact?' Kate shot me a glance that said she wasn't in the least surprised. 'And when d'you pay out?'

'Oh we don't, not in cash anyway. We make up the wages and the overtime, but the drivers all have their money paid direct to their banks.'

'So you don't handle any cash?'

'Not really. Only small amounts, like when we have to pay drivers an advance for expenses. And sometimes we get foreign currency for them, when they have to go abroad.'

'What sort of stuff does this outfit carry?' Kate was determined to get as much information as possible from the girl.

'All sorts of things. Whisky is one of the regular loads.'

'How often do loads of whisky go out, and where do they go?'

'I'm not supposed to say. It's all confidential. In case there's a robbery.'

'Where and when?' Kate was not going to take no for an answer.

'The Continent, mainly. About once a fortnight.'

'Any particular day?'

'Fridays, usually.'

'Three guys called Eric Groves, Brian Baker and Albert Metcalfe were at this party. Apart from screwing you from time to time, did they ask questions about these loads?'

This time Vicky did not deny Kate's allegation that she was anybody's. 'Sometimes, but they were only taking a polite interest in what I did. Like I said, they knew how to treat a girl.'

'Did they ask specifics?' Kate demanded, not believing a word of what the James girl had just said. 'Like how much whisky and what dates.'

'They might've done.' Vicky began to fidget with her skirt, all the time avoiding Kate's incisive stare.

'I'm going to give you a word of warning, mate,' said Kate, 'and if you know what's good for you, you'll heed what I say. Do not get in touch with Metcalfe, Groves or Baker, and if they telephone you, hang up on them. If you don't, you could well find yourself standing in the dock at the Bailey alongside them. And if you're stupid enough to ring either of them now and tell them about our visit, we shall come back and arrest you. Got that?'

Vicky James, now close to tears, nodded. 'Yes,' she whispered.

'Silly little bitch,' said Kate as we got into the car and drove towards Teddington, where we hoped to find Samantha Mount.

The young woman who responded to our knocking was wearing an airline uniform of some sort.

'Are you Samantha Mount?' asked Kate.

'No.' The woman appraised Kate disdainfully, carefully examining her jeans and her white shirt, and her auburn hair tied back in a ponytail. Then she looked at me – I always pride myself on being smartly dressed – and must have wondered who we were and what we wanted. Or perhaps what we were selling. 'Did you wish to speak to her?'

'That's the general idea,' said Kate.

'I'll see if she's in. Who shall I say it is?'

'Police.'

'Oh!' The woman turned from the door. 'Sam,' she shouted, 'the police are here to see you.' And with that she walked away, leaving the front door wide open.

A petite, curvaceous blonde emerged from one of the rooms off the hall. 'I'm Sam Mount,' she said. 'Can I help you?' She was wearing a navy blue skirt and a white shirt with a name badge on it.

'We'd like to talk to you, Miss Mount,' said Kate. 'It is *Miss* Mount, is it?'

'Yes, it is. What d'you want to talk to me about?'

'Rod Skinner.'

'I don't think I know anyone of that name.'

'Yes you do, and your telephone number was in the directory of Skinner's mobile phone. Look, Miss Mount, we don't have time to mess about, so we'll either talk to you here or at Twickenham police station. Please yourself.'

'Oh God! You'd better come in, then.' Samantha Mount was clearly taken aback by Kate's aggressive threat to arrest her, and moved quickly to lead us into a bed-sitting room. 'There are three of us living here,' she explained. 'We each have a room of our own, but we share the lounge. The other two are in there now, watching television.'

'I take it you all work for an airline,' said Kate.

'Yes.'

'Have any of your flatmates been screwed by Skinner?'

'I don't know,' responded Samantha, faltering over her reply. 'I shouldn't think so.'

'Wise girls,' commented Kate. 'So what d'you do at this airline of yours? D'you fly?'

'No,' said Samantha, 'I'm a passenger-services supervisor. Ground staff.'

'Where is this?'

'Heathrow.'

'And how long have you worked there?'

'About three years.'

'So you've got to know the airport pretty well.'

'Of course. Look, what's this all about?'

'Well,' said Kate, adopting a conversational tone, 'it all started with Rod Skinner getting himself murdered in Fulham, a week ago last Saturday. And then we learned that he held riotous parties at his place in Cobham.'

'Why should any of this interest me?' Samantha pretended haughtiness, but she was no actress.

'Because, love, you were there and finished up in the pool. Starkers. And that was after you'd been laid by at least three of the guests, apart from Skinner.'

'Now look here,' began Samantha angrily. 'You can't just come in here making baseless accusations like that.'

Kate gave a derisive laugh. 'I don't give a damn what you did down there, mate,' she said. 'If you want to get yourself screwed, that's your business. How did you meet these guys?'

It had taken some time for Samantha to realize that we knew all about her social life, and that little would be gained by trying to pretend that none of it had happened. 'A friend rang me and said that there was this party down at Cobham and would I like to go,' she replied softly.

'Who was this friend?'

'A girl called Roxy.'

'Roxy Peters?' asked Kate.

'How did you know that?' asked Sam, her eyes opening wide.

'What interests me,' said Kate, ignoring the girl's question, 'is what you were asked by Rod Skinner, Albert Metcalfe, Eric Groves and Brian Baker, the four guys who had you. We know there was more to it than sex.'

'I don't know what you mean.'

'Look, love, this is serious. We haven't come all the way down here to talk to some empty-headed sheila who likes flaunting herself naked in front of men twice her age. I'm talking about a serious crime. Pumped you for details about the airport, did they?'

124

'Well, yes,' said Samantha softly, finally yielding in the face of Kate's unremitting onslaught.

'What did they want to know?'

'They were just interested. They wanted to know where different buildings were, and if the security had been tightened up. Rod and Eric both said they'd not been to Heathrow for a long time, and wondered how it had changed. Brian said he used to work there, but was glad he didn't any more. He said he used to work in one of the warehouses there, a long time ago. But he changed his job and never went back.'

And that was probably because he'd spent the next few years in one of Her Majesty's prisons, I thought.

'And you answered all their questions like a good, helpful little girl, did you?' asked Kate. 'Tell them about all the coppers bristling with guns, did you?'

'Yes.'

'And what did they have to say about that?'

'They seemed to lose interest.'

'I'll bet they did,' said Kate.

If these villains were planning to rob the bullion van, they'd obviously done their homework. And done it without having to bother with a visit to the airport. But they could have found out how heavily guarded Heathrow was just by watching the television news.

'We were really only making conversation until—'

'Until you got your kit off and jumped in the pool with them, I suppose,' said Kate dismissively. She turned to me. 'I think we're about done here, sir.' Finally she gave Samantha Mount the same caution that she'd given Vicky James about not speaking to the three villains who had deliberately made her acquaintance.

On the basis of what we had learned from Samantha Mount, I concluded that, so far, there was insufficient evidence to charge her with anything. But that rather depended on whether or not Metcalfe and company actually hit the airport.

Back at Curtis Green there was a message awaiting me.

'Mr Robinson rang from the Flying Squad, sir,' said Gavin Creasey, the night-duty incident-room manager. 'He said to tell you that DI Naylor of the Tower Bridge unit would be taking charge of the Friday bullion job. Does that make sense, sir?'

'Yes, it does, Gavin, thanks.' DI Brad Naylor and I had met before over an immigrant-smuggling racket. He was a good officer and if Metcalfe, Groves and Baker were planning a heist, they were in trouble already.

Eight

The fact that we'd stumbled on what could be a bullion robbery had rather put the mockers on further enquiries into Rod Skinner's murder. At least until after Friday. But Skinner would keep; he was in the mortuary, so he wasn't going anywhere, and I had a suspicion that one of our trio of suspects would eventually be convicted of his murder. Whether they carried out the robbery or not. Proving it, of course, would be another matter.

On Thursday, Alec Pearson and I met in Brad Naylor's office at Tower Bridge Road to discuss tactics. I took Dave Poole along too.

'By some miracle, we managed to get a Home Office warrant on the hurry-up to put intercepts on the landlines of our three suspects,' said Naylor, 'but the only product was their wives indulging in a load of chitchat with other women, or making appointments to have their hair done. That sort of thing. But there was no conversation between the targets at all. If they did talk then they did it on their mobiles.'

'What about an observation, Brad?' asked

127

Pearson.

'Thought about that, guv, and—' Naylor began, but was immediately interrupted by Pearson.

'I told you before, Brad, it's Alec.'

'Yeah, I know,' said Naylor, grinning at his former boss, 'but old habits die hard ... *guv*.'

Alec Pearson shrugged and then laughed. 'Go on, then.'

'I thought that if we put an obo on before Friday they might spot it, no matter how discreet it was,' said Naylor. 'After all, they're hardened criminals and are always on the lookout for a tail. I reckon if we start eyeballing them from very early on Friday, there's less of a chance of them sussing out that we're on to them. Plus,' he added, 'it gives us time to set up decent OPs on their respective drums.'

'Fair enough,' said Pearson. 'It's a chance we have to take, and it's your operation.' He grinned again. 'So long as you don't lose my gold, Brad.' What Naylor didn't know – and neither did I – was that Pearson had an ace up his sleeve that he was to reveal a few minutes later.

'You can always sue the Commissioner if I do,' said Brad. 'What about the route?'

Pearson took some papers from his briefcase and spread them on the table. 'The van will leave the Minories in the City at nine-fifteen with a crew of three, and go by way of

Hammersmith and Brentford and onto the M4 motorway. This is a copy of the detailed route.' He handed each of us a sheet of paper to which was appended a large-scale map. A red line on the map indicated the exact route that the bullion van would take. Leaning back in his chair, he took a minute or two filling and lighting his pipe. 'you remember the attempted Securicor heist back in 1990, Brad?'

'Yeah, sure. A little team tried to hijack a million quid when the crew stopped for tea at some place in Surrey.'

'It was at Woodhatch,' said Pearson. 'It was an unscheduled stop at a cafe behind a garage. But the crew had done it a couple of times before and the villains had clocked them pulling in for tea on those occasions.'

'How does that help us, Alec?' I asked.

'I thought that if this lot are planning a heist, it might be a good idea to lead them into a venue that would be of advantage to us. Strategically, I mean.'

'How are we going to do that?'

'I've done it,' said Pearson, blowing a plume of pipe smoke into the air. 'As usual the van will be in constant radio contact with our control room, so I got the driver to pop in there yesterday, at a time when Charlene Allen was there, and tell the controller that his crew would be stopping for a quick cup of tea at Heston Services on the M4, but to do him a favour and not to make a note of it in the log.'

Naylor nodded approvingly. 'Nice one, guv, but d'you think it'll work?'

'I hope so, Brad,' said Pearson. 'In my experience villains aren't very imaginative, and will always go for the tried and trusted routine. I know the Woodhatch job was a blow-out as far as the robbers were concerned, but I reckon this lot won't be able to resist the idea of having a pop at our bullion van at the service area. Look at it this way: at that point, the crew'll be out of the van and vulnerable. Heston Services is right on the motorway and that gives our team of robbers a much better chance of escape than if they were to try it on at, say, well, anywhere before they reach the M4.'

'I like it,' said Naylor. 'Bear with me a moment, guv.' Grabbing his phone, he made a call and ordered an immediate survey of Heston Services to determine the best place to secrete police vehicles and marksmen. He turned back to Pearson. 'What time d'you reckon your van will be at Heston, guv?'

'Difficult to say, Brad. Depending on traffic, I reckon between nine forty-five and ten. Certainly no earlier, but if there's a pile-up somewhere on the motorway your guess is as good as mine.'

'And just how much bullion will your van be carrying, guv?'

It was then that Alec Pearson sprung his surprise on us. 'It won't be carrying any, Brad. We secretly rearranged the whole programme. It was delivered to the airport yesterday and is already in South America.'

Naylor slapped the top of his desk and laughed. 'I'll say this for you, guv, you haven't lost your touch.'

Pearson joined in the laughter. 'Jack Capstick wasn't the only one to be called "Charlie Artful", Brad.'

'Who?' said Naylor, frowning.

'Never mind, Brad.' Pearson sighed. 'Capstick was one of the best detectives the Yard ever had, but a bit before your time. And mine,' he added.

We all met up at Tower Bridge Road at eight o'clock on the Friday morning. Alec Pearson was there too, claiming that he missed 'the good old days' and wanted to see the fun.

Brad Naylor told us that a covert surveillance on Metcalfe, Groves and Baker had been set up at five that morning. All three had left their respective homes at half-past seven and made their way separately to a lock-up garage in Lambeth. There they were joined by a fourth unidentified man. Carelessly, they left the doors of the lock-up open while they changed into painters' dirty white overalls. The surveillance team had laughingly reported that they looked like decorators going off on a job, but were satisfied that it was a job of a different kind to that implied by their outfits.

A few minutes later, the four climbed into a Chevrolet truck, and drove towards the Hammersmith flyover. Under constant surveillance.

'So I reckon it's on,' said Naylor cheerfully.

'What about a helicopter, Brad?' asked Pearson.

'I've got India Nine-Nine on standby,' said Naylor. 'But villains are getting wise to choppers now. If they catch sight of it circling they'll likely abort the whole operation. But I thought it'd be a good idea to have it waiting just in case, God forbid, they run for it.' He chuckled. 'Mind you, that would be a bit unwise. With the trigger-happy lot we've got with us today, they'd probably get shot if they try to leg it.'

At a quarter past nine, the armoured bullion van set off from the bank's vault near the Minories in the City of London.

I had decided to involve myself in the operation and joined DI Brad Naylor in his car. If I was going to get information about Skinner's murder from one of the robbers, it was more likely to come at the moment they were arrested. Particularly if any of them thought that by grassing on the killer there'd be a few years off the sentence they were likely to receive for today's blagging. It's wonderful when thieves fall out. On the other hand, of course, they would almost certainly be advised to clam up once they had had the benefit of consulting a solicitor.

Naylor's team of Flying Squad officers, augmented by some detectives borrowed from other teams of the Squad, were in several unmarked cars. Accompanying them were officers from CO19, the Yard's specialist firearms unit, two of whom had been secreted in the back of the bullion van, just in case things went wrong. And in my experience they frequently did. Other vehicles were stationed at points along the route that Alec Pearson had planned. Altogether there were some one hundred officers involved in the operation.

Dave Poole had hitched a ride in one of the Squad's cars, claiming that he enjoyed a good punch-up.

A team of police motorcyclists in civilian gear were playing leapfrog, one or other of them always keeping the van in sight. Another group of motorcyclists was doing the same with the Chevrolet. From time to time, Naylor received reports on their progress.

The bullion van wound its way past the Tower of London, into Lower Thames Street and under Cannon Street Station. So far, everything seemed normal and no unusual vehicles were seen to be following it. But we had come to the conclusion that any attempt to attack the van in heavy traffic would be doomed to failure.

When Naylor heard that Metcalfe and company had passed through Brentford, *ahead of the bullion van*, and were entering the motorway, he gave a shout of triumph.

'It's looking good,' he said.

He now received a further report that the Chevrolet had arrived at Heston Services, but acknowledged that it was inadvisable to be complacent. Although generally speaking criminals are none too bright, it was always possible that the Chevrolet with our suspects on board was a feint. If this was a meticulously planned robbery, the mere fact that Dave and I had interviewed Metcalfe might have caused him and the rest of his team to suspect that they were under surveillance. On the other hand, they might be part of a larger operation, and other members of the team might just be doing a blagging elsewhere that we knew nothing about. Come to that, they might even have planned it that way all along.

But we were in luck, and all those worrying thoughts were negated in the next few minutes as the robbers fell into the trap Naylor had set for them.

In accordance with Pearson's instructions, the bullion van pulled off the motorway at Heston Services and stopped in the car park.

The next few seconds were a blur of activity and noise. Revving madly, the Chevrolet raced out from behind the petrol station, screeching to a halt in front of the bullion van as the three bank employees alighted, stretched, and started to amble towards the self-service restaurant, laughing and joking among themselves.

They had gone no more than two or three paces, when three of the robbers leaped from the Chevrolet brandishing handguns. Each was wearing a Tony Blair mask and a blond wig. One of them seized the driver of the armoured van and pushed a gun into his ribs, while another warned the other two members of the crew that the driver would be shot if they didn't do as they were told. The fourth robber stayed in the truck with the engine running.

It was at that point that their plan fell apart.

At a radioed instruction from Brad Naylor, police cars broke cover and came in from all directions. One pulled up in front of the Chevrolet, while another stopped inches behind it, blocking its escape. A third stopped immediately to the rear of the bullion van. Both the robbers and their target were now securely boxed in.

An armed-response vehicle appeared from behind the petrol station and its three officers leaped out. Using their vehicle as cover, they levelled their Glock 17s at the robbers. Another ARV stopped near the bullion van, and in seconds its crew were out, their Heckler & Koch 33s at the ready.

Suddenly Brad Naylor's ethereal voice, transmitted through one of the police car's sound system, blared across the car park: 'Armed police. Throw down your weapons *now*.' The three villains promptly complied and looked around to see where the voice was coming from. A second order followed: 'Get down on the ground flat on your faces, arms and legs spread.'

Officers sprinted to the prone would-be robbers and handcuffed them. At the same time other armed officers yanked open the door of the Chevrolet, disarming the fourth 'Tony Blair' and motioning him to get out and join his colleagues flat on the ground. He too was handcuffed. All four were dragged into an upright position and had their masks and wigs removed by grinning Squad officers.

DI Naylor, hands in pockets, ambled across and surveyed his prisoners. 'Goodness gracious me! Messrs Metcalfe, Groves and Baker. *And* "Soapy" Hudson. Nice to see you again, gents. By the way, you're nicked. I don't have to caution you, do I? You all know it off by heart, so take it as read.' He turned to the inspector in charge of the Territorial Support Group. 'Get rid of that lot, mate, will you,' he said, indicating a crowd that had emerged from the service area and were now gawping at the police activity. 'They probably think we're making a TV cop show.'

'Which nick, guv?' asked one of Naylor's sergeants. 'Uxbridge or Hounslow?'

Naylor thought for only a moment. 'Hounslow, Ted.'

'What about Charlene Allen, Brad?' I asked as the four robbers were placed in a police van. 'D'you reckon she *was* involved? Given that she was in earshot when the bullion-van driver told the controller about the stop at Heston Services.'

Naylor grinned. 'We'll be able to ask her soon, guv,' he said. 'A couple of my women officers felt her collar at eight o'clock this morning. She's being brought down here from Surbiton nick as I speak.'

The four robbers made a sorrowful quartet, seated in the custody suite at Hounslow police station. But they were quickly moved into separate interview rooms.

It was, of course, Brad Naylor's job, and he would be responsible for seeing it through all its stages to the Old Bailey. Or at whichever crown court the case was to be heard. However, he had agreed to allow me to sit in on the interviews because of my interest in the Skinner murder.

At Naylor's suggestion, I had sent for DI Kate Ebdon. His view was that if anyone was going to get an admission of complicity from Charlene Allen, Kate was the officer to do it.

Naylor started with Albert Metcalfe, ostensibly the ringleader of this little gang of villains. It came as no surprise that he was his usual upbeat, confident self.

'Hello, Mr Brock, fancy seeing you again,' he said as we walked in.

'Never mind the socializing, Fruity,' Naylor began. 'You realize that we've got you bang to rights for this job, don't you?'

Metcalfe spread his hands, palms uppermost. 'What can I say, Mr Naylor? I was there and you nicked me. But how did you know it was coming off?' He was clearly puzzled that what he'd thought was so well planned an operation should have met with disaster in the form of the Heavy Mob, as robbers call the Flying Squad.

'That'd be telling, Fruity,' said Naylor, 'but Mr Brock here wants to ask you a few questions.'

Metcalfe turned to face me and folded his arms. 'I'm all ears, Mr Brock,' he said.

'Was Rod Skinner supposed to be in on this job, Fruity?' I asked.

'I don't want to speak ill of the dead, Mr Brock, but you can't nick him now, can you? Yes, he was s'posed to be one of the team, but some bastard topped him.'

'Is that why you brought Soapy Hudson in, then?' asked Naylor.

'Well, we had to have a fourth.'

'Why, playing bridge, were you?'

Metcalfe laughed. 'Playing bridge? That's very good, Mr Naylor.'

'So when did Soapy get pulled in?' persisted Naylor.

'The day after Rod got his comeuppance.' Metcalfe thought about that for a moment or two. 'That'd be a fortnight ago tomorrow. Don't time fly, eh?'

'Was he keen to come along?' asked Naylor.

'Not at first. Reckoned he was going straight.' Metcalfe scoffed. 'But we sort of persuaded him.'

'How?'

'Told him how much was on offer, and how we'd got a place set up to—' Metcalfe stopped suddenly, realizing that he was in danger of saying too much.

'A place set up where?'

Metcalfe laughed. 'You can't expect me to answer that, Mr Naylor.'

Naylor waved a hand. 'No need for you to, Fruity. We know already.' In fact, Naylor hadn't the faintest idea where the gang had intended to take the bullion. 'D'you trust these other guys you did this job with? Like Soapy Hudson, for instance?'

Metcalfe's brow creased into a tight frown. 'Did he grass?' he demanded. 'Is that how you knew we was going for a hit at Heston Services?' The thought had clearly worried him. 'I had me doubts about him right from the start.'

Having achieved his object of putting a wedge between Metcalfe and one of his co-conspirators, Naylor smiled beatifically. 'We never disclose our sources of information, Fruity,' he said.

'The bastard,' muttered Metcalfe angrily, now firmly believing that Hudson had sold out to the law.

'Who propped him for this job?' asked Naylor.

'Eric Groves.'

'Ah, I thought as much,' lied Naylor. He was beginning to enjoy reinforcing Metcalfe's misgivings about his partners.

'D'you mean that Eric—?' Metcalfe was too shaken to put his suspicions into words. It was becoming evident to him that he could trust no one.

'It looks as though you've fallen among thieves, Fruity,' said Naylor jocularly.

'That ain't funny, Mr Naylor.' Metcalfe shook his head over and over again. 'It wouldn't never have happened in the old days,' he added mournfully.

But Brad Naylor wasn't particularly interested in casting doubt on the loyalties of Metcalfe's gang. He was actually doing me a favour, a tactic that we'd agreed upon before the interview began.

'So who topped Skinner and let Hudson in,

Fruity?' I asked.

'I'm buggered if I know, Mr Brock,' said Metcalfe, 'and that's the God's honest truth. But I know that Grovesy and Rod never got on too well.'

'And that was about a woman, I suppose,' I said, taking a guess that turned out to be right.

'Strikes me you know everything, Mr Brock. Yeah, as a matter of fact it was.'

'Which one? Roxy, Charlene, Vicky or Sam?'

Metcalfe's eyes opened wide in surprise. 'How the bloody hell did you know about them?' he demanded.

'Like Mr Naylor said just now, Fruity, we never disclose our sources. I suppose it was at the party down at Rod's place in Cobham.'

'Yeah, as a matter of fact, it was. See, Charlene come with Grovesy, but Rod took her off of him. He said it was his house and his party, and if he wanted to screw Charlene, then he'd screw her. And he did. Mind you, I didn't blame him. She's some looker, is Charlene.'

'So it could have been Eric Groves who topped Rod Skinner,' I mused.

'Beginning to look that way,' agreed Metcalfe grudgingly, having decided that he no longer owed any allegiance to Eric Groves.

'Did Skinner and Groves have words about

141

Charlene?'

'Not 'alf.' Metcalfe laughed scornfully. 'This was in the summerhouse, see. It's on the other side of the swimming pool from the house, like. We heard voices that sounded like a punch-up was brewing, and me and Baker went in. Rod was in there with Charlene. Both of 'em were bollock naked and about to do the business when it seems Grovesy had charged in. Well, him and Rod was squaring up and it was starting to get a bit tasty, but we stepped in and told 'em to grow up. After all, it was only a bird, and there was plenty more of 'em at the do. Half of 'em naked by that time, an' all. But I know Grovesy of old, and he harbours grudges.'

'Did anyone else witness this confrontation, Fruity?'

'What? D'you mean did anyone else see it?'

'Yes,' I said with a sigh.

'Nah, not as I know of. But I do know that after we'd got Grovesy out of it, Rod *did* screw Charlene. And that really got up Grovesy's nose. Well, it would, wouldn't it? As a matter of fact, I heard Grovesy say he was going to give Rod a smacking.' Metcalfe had decided to throw Eric Groves to the wolves.

All of which might or might not be true, and I wondered if Brad Naylor had over-egged the pudding to the extent that Metcalfe was now convinced that Groves was a

142

grass. And having planted that seed in his mind, he was determined 'to do Groves's legs for him', as criminal parlance has it.

Nevertheless, Brad Naylor and I intended to capitalize on it if we could. We interviewed Groves next.

'Fruity Metcalfe doesn't think much of you, Eric.' Naylor went on the offensive immediately. 'He reckons you're a grass.'

Groves half rose in his chair. 'I've never grassed up no one,' he protested loudly, his face working with anger.

'I know that, Eric,' said Naylor soothingly, 'because I know where the information came from that enabled us to meet you at Heston Services, and it wasn't from you.'

Groves relaxed. The police were on his side, he thought. Poor fool. 'I might be a villain, Mr Naylor, but I ain't no grass.' Then he realized what Naylor had said. 'Then who did grass us up? That's what you're saying, ain't it? Someone put the finger on us.'

But Naylor just smiled. 'Now let me put my cards on the table, Eric. Today's little tickle is going to earn you, Fruity, Brian Baker and Soapy Hudson a fair old whack of porridge. And nothing you can say will make any difference.'

Groves nodded sadly. 'Yeah, I reckon so,' he said, resigned to a lengthy prison sentence.

'But what interests me, and interests Mr

Brock here even more, is who topped Rod Skinner.'

'No good asking me,' said Groves. 'I ain't got a clue, and that's a fact.'

'Fruity Metcalfe said that you propped Soapy Hudson for this job after Skinner was murdered. Is that right?'

'Yeah. So what?'

'Known him long, have you?'

'About ten years, I s'pose.'

'Reliable, is he?' asked Naylor, grinning.

'Always has been,' said Groves hesitantly. But the way in which the Flying Squad DI had posed the question caused a nagging doubt to enter Groves's mind. ' 'Ere, you don't mean it was him what grassed us up, do you, Mr Naylor?'

'You don't expect me to answer that, do you, Eric?' It was a cunning reply and one that did nothing to bolster Groves's confidence in his fellow robbers' trustworthiness. Doubtless he was well aware that there was no honour among thieves when the chips were down.

'It's obvious to me,' I said, 'that someone topped Skinner so that Soapy Hudson could have a piece of what would have been a profitable heist. But someone grassed and the Flying Squad was waiting at Heston Services for you all to show up.' More fiction, but it might work.

'Who was it?' demanded Groves. 'Who

squealed?'

'Never mind that, Eric,' I said. 'I want to know who topped Skinner.'

'I don't know, Mr Brock,' whined Groves. 'If I did, I'd tell you.'

'Now about this argument you had down at Cobham.'

'What argument?'

'Oh, come off it, Eric. You and Rod Skinner had a barney over a bird. Charlene Allen, to be precise.'

'Oh, that. Yeah, well, I'd brought Charlene to the party and Rod took her off of me. There was plenty of other skirt there for him to get his end away with, but he hit on Charlene.'

'And you were so angry about it that you went to the Starlight Club a fortnight ago and blew him away with a sawn-off.'

'Leave it out, Mr Brock. An argy-bargy about a bird's one thing, but it don't call for no topping.'

'Really?' I looked pensive. 'According to someone else who was at that party, you were heard to say you were going to give Rod Skinner a smacking.'

'Then they was telling you lies, Mr Brock,' said Groves unconvincingly.

So far, Eric Groves seemed to be our front-runner for the murder of Skinner, but mere suspicion is a long way from positive proof. Although, as Groves had said, a tiff over a girl

145

is hardly reason for murder, it is not unknown in the annals of crime. There have been quite a few cases where a dispute over a woman's affections has caused the knives to come out. Literally.

Nine

Brad Naylor decided that no further information would be gleaned about the robbery by talking to Baker and Hudson. The evidence was overwhelming and they and the other two were going on the sheet for armed robbery, possession of illegal firearms, and anything else that came to light in the course of Naylor's enquiries.

'I'm going to get my team searching each of their drums, guv,' he said. 'I've got a good skipper who's a dab hand at paperwork, so he can make a start on the report for the Crown Prosecution Service. I tell you, the bloody paper's more difficult than nicking these bastards.'

'I've noticed, Brad.' The preparation of the reports for the Crown Prosecution Service was the bane of a detective's life. 'In the meantime, I'll have a word with the other two.'

'D'you reckon Skinner's murder is down to any one of this team?' Naylor asked.

I shrugged. 'Damned if I know, Brad, but I'll keep trying. Let me know if you find anything interesting when you do the searches.

Like a sawn-off shotgun.' Not that that would help. Armed robbers were expected to have a sawn-off somewhere in their arsenal, and in any case the ballistics experts had told me that it was one hell of a job – if not impossible – to marry one up to a particular shooting.

But as I was about to tackle Baker and Hudson, Kate Ebdon swanned into the CID office where we'd set up our temporary headquarters.

'Charlene Allen coughed straight away, guv.'

'Well done, Kate.'

'Nothing to it. She was a pushover, the silly little cow.'

'Where is she now, Kate?'

'Crying her bloody eyes out in a cell,' said Kate.

'I want to have a word with her,' I said, and explained about the argument Skinner and Groves had had about her down at Cobham.

Charlene Allen made a pathetic figure sitting on the bed. Her make-up was smeared, her face tear-stained, and her worn-out jeans and polo shirt did nothing to support her reputation as a good-time girl. But unlike Roxy Peters, she was an exceptionally attractive girl with long, natural blonde hair and big boobs; an asset that Dave, had he seen her, would have described as a prominent 'quarterdeck'. It was probably her voluptuous figure that had attracted Groves to her in the first place.

She looked up as we entered the cell. 'What d'you want now?' she asked in a defeated tone of voice. Her arrest must have come as a great shock, particularly as, I later learned, she'd been detained at her parents' home in Thames Ditton. No doubt those respectable parents were now wondering how to explain it all away to their equally respectable neighbours. There was no way in which the neighbours could have missed that morning's flurry of heavy-handed police activity. Or would have wanted to.

'You're still under caution, Charlene,' said Kate. 'And my chief inspector wants to have a few words with you.'

'I want to talk to you about the murder of Rod Skinner,' I said.

'I don't know anything about it.' Charlene spoke in a cultured voice that, as Kate had said, suggested she'd been the beneficiary of a good education. I wondered how on earth she had become involved with a set of toe-rags like the four robbers now in custody.

'There was an argument between Skinner and Eric Groves down at Cobham a couple of months back,' I said. 'An argument over you.'

'I don't know what you're talking about,' she said churlishly.

'Listen to me, you dumb sheila,' put in

149

Kate. 'You're in quite enough trouble as it is. You've already admitted passing information to Groves about the bullion van's route, and that it was going to stop at Heston Services, and there's no doubt you'll be going to prison. So there's no point in lying any more. Just answer my chief inspector's questions truthfully.'

I tried again. 'Eric Groves took you to Rod Skinner's party down at The Gables in Cobham. But later on, he found you and Rod Skinner in the summerhouse. You'd both got your kit off and Rod was about to get across you when Groves came bursting in. Then two other guys came in and separated him and Rod. Nevertheless, after Groves had gone, Rod did have sex with you. D'you remember now?'

'Yes,' mumbled Charlene. She looked down and toyed with an emerald ring on the little finger of her left hand.

'Did you see Eric Groves again after that incident?'

'Once or twice.'

'And what did he have to say about it?'

'He said he'd forgiven me.'

That didn't surprise me. If Groves wanted information about the bullion-van run, then he would've been well advised not to fall out with the very girl who was in a position to supply it.

'But had he forgiven Rod Skinner?'

Charlene stared down at the bright red nail varnish on her toenails, peeping out from her sandals. 'He said he was going to get even with him. He said that no one took a girl off him without paying for it.'

'Did he say how he was going to get even?'

'No.'

'How did you meet Groves?'

'At a nightclub in Wimbledon. I'd gone there with a girlfriend one night. We'd often been there in the past. Eric happened to be there and offered to buy me a drink, and we got talking.'

'Who was this girlfriend?'

'Roxy Peters.'

'How soon was it that Groves asked you where you worked?' I asked.

'Almost straight away.'

'And what did you tell him?'

'I told him I worked in a bank, and he said that that was very interesting. He asked me what I did exactly and when I told him, he said it must be a very responsible job.'

Oh, you poor naive little girl.

'So you continued to see him after that, did you?'

'Yes.'

'But why? Groves is a rough diamond, and at least twice your age. In fact, old enough to be your father. What are you, twenty?'

'Twenty-one.' Charlene stared at me defiantly. 'Because he took me out and spent

151

money on me, that's why. He knew how to look after a girl. Much better than the silly sort of boys you usually get at these clubs with their stupid hairstyles and their earrings and bracelets and stuff. All trying to be jack the lad with their silly talk. All they ever want to do is get drunk. But Eric was different, he was a gentleman.'

For all her sophistication, I was surprised that Charlene Allen imagined that a convicted villain like Groves was a gentleman.

'How often did he take you to the Starlight Club? It's a jazz club in Fulham.' I floated that idea, not believing for one moment that I'd get a positive response.

'Two or three times.'

'Did he show any signs of knowing anyone there?'

'He seemed to be well known, yes.'

'Did he know anyone in the band?'

'Not that I remember.'

That didn't necessarily mean much. Erica Leech had said that the Jazz Kittens were only there twice a week.

'And then a couple of months ago he took you to this party down at Cobham. And that's where you met Rod Skinner and Brian Baker and the others.'

'Yes,' mumbled Charlene.

'And what did Mrs Skinner think about you having it off with Rod in the summer-house?'

'I don't think she knew, or if she did, she didn't care. There was a young guy there called Charlie somebody, and very early on he and Babs disappeared into the house somewhere. I never saw them again for an hour or two.' Charlene gave a wan smile. 'But I think I know what they were doing.'

'Did anyone mention that Rod Skinner was a drummer in a jazz band?'

Charlene looked surprised. 'No.'

'So you didn't see him at the Starlight Club.'

'No, I didn't know anyone there.'

'Did Rod tell you what he did for a living?' I asked. 'Or did anyone else tell you what he did?'

'No. All I can say is that he seemed to have plenty of money. Well, they all did. Eric had a big car and was always taking me to the best places. He even took me to Le Caprice once, the restaurant near the Ritz where all the celebrities go. And we went into the Ritz afterwards and Eric bought champagne. I'd never been to the Ritz before.'

'So when you learned that the bullion van was going to stop at Heston Services, you couldn't resist ringing him and telling him what you'd overheard.'

'Yes.'

'And that was because he'd been so generous towards you, and you felt you owed him a debt, was it?'

153

'Yes,' said Charlene with a convulsive sob.

'Well, your Eric is going to prison for a long time, Charlene, but I'll tell you this much: if their robbery had been successful, you'd never have seen him again. Not that you will anyway. Because, my girl, you've served your purpose. You've been taken for a ride. His only interest in you was that you were in a position at the bank to give him what he wanted to know. The fact that you were willing to spread your legs for him as well was a bonus. For him, I mean.'

Slowly it was beginning to dawn on Charlene Allen that Eric Groves had taken cruel advantage of her. In more ways than one.

'Whether you like it or not, Charlene,' said Kate, 'you're just a gangster's moll.'

We left Charlene, in tears once more, to contemplate the prospect of a few years in Holloway, the modern red-brick women's prison in North London.

'So, Eric Groves took Charlene Allen to the Starlight Club on two or three occasions,' I said, when DI Ebdon and I were back in the CID office on the first floor of the police station. 'Perhaps we're getting nearer to finding out who topped Rod Skinner.'

'It's bound to be one of the four robbers we've got banged up downstairs, guv,' said Kate, 'and I wouldn't be surprised if they all knew that jazz club. But one thing's certain:

it wasn't Charlene who topped Skinner. And I doubt it was Roxy Peters either.'

'I wonder where Groves got his money from, Kate.'

'Jobs he'd done in the past, guv,' said Kate. 'Where else? I don't somehow see him working on a building site.'

'What d'you know about the Starlight Club, Brian?' Dave asked. I'd decided to let Dave kick off the interview.

Brian Baker was an armed robber very similar to many others we'd interviewed, but he proved to be less communicative.

'Nothing.'

'Are you telling me you didn't know that that was where your mate Rod Skinner was murdered?' persisted Dave.

'I've got nothing to say about anything to you, copper.' I got the impression that Dave's black face did not exactly encourage Baker to be helpful. Although villains will often happily take a black man on to their team, they seem to object strongly to black detectives. Bad luck!

The other problem was that Baker had been caught bang to rights and knew he was going down for a lengthy stretch. Thus there was no profit for him in talking to the police. But I had to try.

'I'm not interested in this stunt you pulled this morning,' I said. 'I'm investigating

Skinner's murder.'

'Well, it's no good talking to me. I don't know who topped him.'

'Was it Eric Groves?' I persisted.

'Why would Eric want to top Rod?'

Well, at least I'd got beyond the flat denial stage. 'Perhaps it had something to do with Charlene Allen and the argument he had with Rod about her.'

'Don't know anything about that.'

'Really? Well, your mate Fruity Metcalfe says that you and he came across Groves having words with Skinner in the summer-house just as he was about to screw Charlene Allen. And apparently Groves was later heard to say that he was going to give Skinner a smacking.'

'So what?'

'How well did you know Charlene?'

'Didn't know her at all. She was Groves's bird.'

'How come that Groves was lucky enough to find a girl who was in a position to tell you all you needed to know about the bullion van's movements? Because it seems to me that he was the kingpin in this little tickle of yours.'

'He bloody wasn't,' said Baker vehemently. 'Rod set this job up, and he started planning it months ago.'

'So it was just fortunate that Groves found this girl Charlene at some night club in

Wimbledon, was it?'

'Is that what he told you?' Baker gave a derisive laugh.

'Your mates have been singing away like canaries,' I said, pushing the wedge deeper between them. I thought it unwise to tell Baker that it was Charlene who'd told me.

'Rod met this bird Roxy Peters and started screwing her. She worked in a bank at Richmond, but used to go to this nightclub in Wimbledon.' Baker had finally decided that if his cohorts were talking, so would he. 'She told Rod that Charlene was a mate of hers and that she worked for the bank an' all, but at head office. So Rod steers Eric Groves in her direction and he took it from there. But you could see that Rod fancied her. Who wouldn't?'

Which is near enough what I thought had happened. 'You said just now that Rod started planning this heist months ago.'

'Yeah.'

'So how did he know that there'd be a bullion run?' Dave decided to join in again.

'Because the bank does 'em regular,' sneered Baker.

'How did that help?' asked Dave, leaning a little closer to the prisoner.

'Rod had clocked one or two of the previous runs and thought this was a job that was worth having a pop at.'

'So why, less than two weeks before it was

157

going to come off, did someone take out Skinner?'

Baker laughed again. 'P'raps you'd better ask the blokes he grassed up, and who got twenty-five years in the nick as a result.'

'D'you think it was one of their mates?' I asked, taking the questioning back again.

'Dunno, mate. But you're the copper. Work it out for yourself.'

'How did you know that Skinner was a grass?'

'You don't think we couldn't suss that out, do you? Six guys do a heist up Wembley, and only five of them get sent down for it. And who was the one who got away? Dennis Miller, alias Rod Skinner. Don't take much to work out what happened there. Then suddenly Dennis surfaces a few years later in some swish drum down Cobham, flashing the gelt about and calling himself Skinner.'

Suddenly a motive was emerging. Rod Skinner, an accomplished robber, gathers together Metcalfe, Groves and Baker and tells them he's setting up a job. But this little team knows that he's a grass. So they wait until he's set it all up, and just before the job's pulled someone takes him out. In case he grasses again. For all that the robbers now in custody knew, he could even have set it up at the behest of the Flying Squad, but without furnishing the police with the final details. But of course I knew that that hadn't happened.

'And that's when Soapy Hudson was brought in by Eric Groves,' I mused. 'D'you trust Groves, Brian?' I asked, staring at Baker.

'Why shouldn't I?' Baker asked, but there was an edge of apprehension to his voice.

'Well, Brian, look at it like this: Skinner gets topped, Hudson's brought in by Groves who says he's got this reliable informant called Charlene Allen who's given him the low-down on the movement of the bullion van. Then it all goes pear-shaped.' I lit a cigarette and waited for Baker's reaction.

Baker shot forward in his chair. 'Are you telling me that it was Groves or Hudson what grassed us up?'

'You're the robber, Brian. You work it out,' I said, turning his earlier phrase against him. 'But why don't you wait and see which one of you *doesn't* get sent down for this job.'

'So that means that Rod must've got topped for nothing, Mr Brock,' said Baker, shaking his head in apparent disbelief. After his initial hostility, he had become much more amenable to my questions in the face of the suggestion that one of his own mates had turned informant.

'Looks like it,' I said, by no means sure. 'So who d'you reckon did him?'

'Must have been bloody Groves,' said Baker disgustedly. 'What a bastard.'

159

★ ★ ★

Unfortunately, mere speculation was not enough to put before a jury. We had to have firm evidence and so far we hadn't got any. But it was beginning to look as though it was one of the 'Heston Services Four' who'd murdered Skinner.

The other theory was my original one: that one of the Wembley robbers that Skinner had informed on was responsible, indirectly, for his murder.

I had decided early on in the enquiry that there was little point in talking to them. I'd learned that they were in five different prisons: Wormwood Scrubs, Wandsworth, Canterbury, Winson Green in Birmingham, and Parkhurst on the Isle of Wight. But unless I had something to offer, like a reduction in sentence – which was well beyond my powers – they would have no reason to say anything. In fact, mere knowledge of a plot to kill Skinner might even involve them in further charges of conspiracy to murder.

With a sigh, I decided that Dave and I would talk to Soapy Hudson.

'How come you got involved in this heist, Soapy?'

Hudson stared at Dave. 'It's what I do, boss.' He grinned, revealing several missing teeth. 'I'm a robber.'

'I know that, but you weren't supposed to

be in on it.' Dave threw a cigarette across the table at Hudson.

'Well, I heard the sad news that someone had done the business on Rod Skinner.'

'When was this?' I asked while Dave was lighting his own cigarette. I was hoping, in vain as it turned out, that Hudson had received this information *before* Skinner had been murdered.

'On the Sunday after he got hit.'

'And how did you hear about it?'

'On the news on the telly, weren't it?'

Interesting. Skinner's name hadn't been released to the media until the following Tuesday. But I let it pass. For the moment. Apart from which, anyone who had witnessed the shooting could have told him, and we knew that some of the robbers were frequent visitors to the Starlight Club.

'And then Eric Groves got in touch, did he?'

'Yeah. That was on the Tuesday. He said that this job was up and running and did I want in. To take Rod's place, like.'

'You've worked with Groves before?'

'Sure. We done a tickle or two.'

'How long have you known him?' I couldn't be bothered to enquire what jobs he and Groves had done. Right now I was only interested in who had murdered Skinner.

Hudson inspected the ceiling of the interview room for a few moments. 'About a year,

161

I s'pose,' he said eventually.

'Were you surprised that Skinner had been murdered, Soapy?'

'Nah! He was a grass.'

'How did you know that?'

'Common knowledge.'

'So someone obviously had it in for him, and when they caught up with him, they topped him. Is that it?'

'I reckon that's the strength of it, guv'nor, yeah.'

'Any idea who?' I kept repeating this question to each one of the robbers I interviewed, but without hope of getting a useful answer. 'Was there a contract out on him?'

'Maybe,' said Hudson cautiously. 'Probably a mate of one of the Wembley team he grassed up. See, it wasn't only that he put the whisper on 'em, he saw 'em off for part of the drop.'

'Meaning?'

'Well, when they done that place up Wembley, word was they had a million away that wasn't accounted for, see. They was going to split it after, along with the proceeds of the tomfoolery and the rocks they'd nicked. But then Skinner opened his big mouth. Your lot recovered most of the take and his five mates go down big time, and Skinner – he was called Miller back then – takes it on the toes with the spare. Bound to upset 'em, ain't it, guv'nor?'

Once again there was only speculation. But what interested me was that Hudson had heard about Skinner's murder before it had been released to the general public. If he had got the date right. But I wasn't too sure of that. Nevertheless I tucked it away for future reference.

Dave Poole and I got back to Curtis Green at about eight o'clock at the end of what had been a very long day.

Dave took off to see his wife Madeleine. She had a break from dancing at the moment, and it was rare for them to spend an evening together.

'Miss Sutton phoned about an hour ago, sir,' said Gavin Creasey, ferreting about on his desk. 'Ah yes, here we are. She said would you ring her at home whatever the time.'

I went into my office and telephoned Gail, somewhat concerned that there might be a problem. There had been an occasion when I'd taken my previous girlfriend, Sarah Dawson, home to her flat in Battersea only to find that it had been broken into and wrecked.

'Harry, how are you?'

'I'm fine. What's wrong?'

'Nothing, darling, but I heard about some bullion raid on the news and I wondered if you'd been involved.'

'How the hell did you come to that conclusion?' I asked. I'd mentioned nothing to Gail about the heist and even now didn't admit that I'd been there.

'Call it feminine intuition,' said Gail.

'You sound just like my mother,' I responded. For some reason or another my mother, a retired Woolworth shop assistant, always imagined that I was involved in any big job that came up. 'Anyway, why did you want me to ring?'

'Just to say that I've prepared a cold supper for you, together with a chilled bottle of Alsace. So hurry on down, as they used to say on some TV programme.'

Ten

I arrived at Gail's house in Kingston at about nine o'clock that evening.

'You look worn out, darling,' she said, handing me a large glass of whisky. 'Hard day at the office?'

I thought I detected a touch of cynicism in that question. 'You could say that,' I said, and told her briefly what I'd been doing.

'But you said you weren't involved.'

'I didn't want to worry you.'

'And these men were all armed? But you could have been shot.' Gail opened her eyes wide in a combination of surprise and fear for my safety. Well, I hoped that's what it was. Having spent all her adult life in the make-believe world of the theatre, she'd been cocooned from the harsh realities of a copper's daily routine.

I shrugged. 'It comes with the territory,' I said, using a cliché that would undoubtedly have brought a frown to Dave's face had he heard it.

What Gail described as a scratch cold meal was, by my standards, a banquet, and the Alsace was chilled to perfection. After supper we relaxed in the sitting room with the French windows open to a pleasant summer's evening.

Gail brought me a brandy and curled up on the settee with a glass of champagne.

I reflected that it was almost a fortnight ago that I'd been sitting in exactly the same place, at about the same time, when I'd received the call from Gavin Creasey telling me that Skinner had been murdered. And I had made very little progress since then.

It was certainly looking as though one of the bullion-van gang had topped him, but I was woefully short of proof. Something I'd learned many years ago was that criminals tend to close ranks when policemen come asking questions about a murder. There are, of course, exceptions to this rule. Any information that comes through the prison grapevine about child murders or terrorist outrages will be passed on to the police with alacrity.

I was once the recipient of information from a prisoner I'd been instrumental in getting sent down for ten years for armed robbery. He told me that a paedophile on remand had confessed to him the brutal child-murder with which he'd been charged. The prisoner who had told me this was not seeking a reduction in sentence or, for that matter, any sort of preferential treatment. He had only one request.

166

'When this bastard gets sent down, Mr Brock,' he had said, 'can you fix it for him to serve his time in Holloway? I reckon the girls up there'd make him very welcome.'

Unfortunately, I was unable to accede to that request. Our beloved Home Office would have held up its collective lily-white hands and wailed in horror at such a suggestion.

'Penny for them, darling,' said Gail.

'I'm sorry,' I said, breaking my reverie. 'Just thinking about the Job.'

'Well, don't,' she said, and poured me another brandy. 'I've been thinking,' she continued, waving her hand at a pile of brochures on the floor near her settee, 'that we ought to have a holiday.'

'Good idea,' I said, without a great deal of enthusiasm, 'but I've a murder to solve first.'

Gail groaned theatrically. 'You should have told me what it would be like going out with a copper when we first met,' she said.

'Would it have made a difference?'

'No.'

Although I was inclining towards one of the Heston Services team having killed Skinner, I decided, against my better instincts, that I would, after all, interview the prisoners that Skinner had grassed on. Despite having determined previously that I wouldn't do so.

I knew from the outset that it would be a

fruitless exercise. On two counts. Firstly, a prisoner serving a sentence is under no obligation to talk to the police if he doesn't want to. Most do because it affords them a break in the routine, and gives the more malicious of them a chance to settle old scores, or to set the detective on a bum steer. Just out of spite. Secondly, of course, I doubted that any one of Skinner's 'victims' would be able to shed any light on his demise. Or if they were able to, wouldn't be prepared to for fear of being implicated.

Being a lazy man, I started with the prisoner who was incarcerated nearest to Curtis Green.

On Monday morning, Dave and I journeyed to Wormwood Scrubs, being marginally closer than Wandsworth.

Ted Glass, known to police and villains alike as 'Break-in' Glass, was happy to see us and, surprisingly, equally happy to talk to us about anything.

'I'm DCI Brock and this is DS Poole,' I said by way of introduction.

'Have we met before?' enquired Glass politely, as though he'd just bumped into us at Ascot or Henley or Wimbledon.

'Not that I can recall,' I said, 'but I'm investigating the murder of Rod Skinner, who you knew as Dennis Miller.'

Glass let out a raucous laugh that ended in a coughing fit. 'Excuse me,' he said, when eventually he recovered his breath. 'A bleed-in' tragedy, Mr Brock, being cut down in his prime, and that's a fact.'

'I thought you'd be upset, Ted, but have you any idea who might have topped him?' I asked, and handed him a cigarette. A mistake; when he lit it, it provoked another coughing fit.

'Not a glimmer, guv'nor,' said Glass, once he'd recovered again, 'but if I ever meet him I'll shake him by the hand.' There was a pause. 'Any idea what the test-match score is?'

'No.' I was not a cricket enthusiast and frankly didn't care who won the Ashes. Curiously enough though, Dave, although of Caribbean descent, was an ardent England supporter. Even when England played the West Indies. Lord Tebbit would have been proud of him.

'England are fifty-two for one,' said Dave.

'See, Miller done the dirty on us,' continued Glass. 'That's why we're here. But I'll tell you this, Mr Brock, I don't think we was the first.'

'You mean he'd grassed on someone else before your job at Wembley?'

'That's what I heard, but I never heard it until after we got nicked. It was when we was on remand down Brixton, I got talking to a finger who was banged up for a whole string of long-firm frauds. And he'd got previous.

Anyhow, I told him what had happened, and he said as how he'd heard, on the grapevine like, that Miller was a grass. Well, that chuffed us up no end. If only we'd known that for starters, we'd never have had nothing to do with the bastard. But by the time we was nicked, it was too late.'Glass shook his head mournfully. 'If only we'd known.'

'Who was this LF guy, Ted?' asked Dave.

'Can't remember his name, and he's well away now. If I remember, he got a three-stretch. Out after eighteen months for good behaviour most likely. Probably well at it again by now.'

'Was he doing his time at Brixton, or was he on remand too?' said Dave.

'Nah, he went to Ford Open nick a month after he got sent down, jammy bastard. Nice place that. Down Arundel way, in Sussex. More like a holiday camp. It's where they send the toffs mainly. You know, lords and company directors an' that.'

'When was this?' Dave was busy making notes in his pocket book.

Glass thought about that. 'Five years ago, I s'pose,' he said.

I gave Ted Glass another cigarette and we left him to serve the remainder of his sentence. Which probably wouldn't amount to very much, knowing what a beneficent government we have.

'What d'you reckon, guv?' asked Dave, as

we left the urine-laden atmosphere of Worm-wood Scrubs prison.

'It's opened up the field a bit, Dave. If we can trace this long-firm fraudster, we might get another name, but like our friend "Break-in" Glass back there' – I cocked a thumb towards the huge gates – 'we'll get everything except the name of the guy who topped Skinner.'

Dave Poole was very good at what he called 'armchair detective work', and spent several hours on the telephone. Finally, he came up with a name for the LF man whom Glass had mentioned: Roy Reeves.

Making use of his contacts in the Job, and informants outside it, Dave eventually discovered an address for Mr Reeves. It was a shop in Coldharbour Lane, close to Brixton railway station, and less than two miles from Brixton prison.

'He hasn't moved far,' said Dave with a chuckle.

We surprised Mr Reeves with a visit on the Wednesday morning. And it was a surprise too. For him.

'Roy Reeves?'

Reeves looked foxily guilty. 'Who wants to know?' he asked, knowing perfectly well who we were. It's instinctive.

I suppose that two unmistakeable police officers, one of whom was black, was sufficient to put the wind up a convicted long-firm fraudster.

'We're police officers,' I said, converting his spurious doubt into certainty, and looked searchingly at his stock of television sets and other electronic gadgetry.

I'd better explain that the operators of long-firm frauds are villains who set up shop and buy in their stock for cash. They pay the bill in full on delivery. Over the succeeding weeks they increase the order and continue to pay. Once established as reliable, they secure credit. They continue to order, still paying, until finally they do a runner with their last, unpaid for, huge order. Only to start again somewhere else.

'Oh yeah? And what can I do for you, gents?' asked Reeves nervously. Dave, meanwhile, was wandering around Reeves's shop, humming quietly and closely examining various TV sets as though about to commit himself to an unsustainable hire-purchase agreement.

'When you were in Brixton on remand, about five years ago, Roy, I understand that you met another prisoner, called "Break-in" Glass.'

'Might've done.' Reeves, a worried frown on his face, looked continually over his shoulder to see what Dave was doing.

'And you discussed a mutual acquaintance whose name was Dennis Miller.'

172

'Here, what's this all about?' Reeves had the nervous demeanour of a man who was about to be arrested, and suspected that the police were just playing games with him. Well, sometimes it works like that, but when you've got a murder that's beginning to get whiskers on it, you don't have time to fool around.

'Well, did you or didn't you, Roy?' Dave returned from his wanderings and put in his two penn'orth.

'What d'you want to know for?'

'Look, pal,' said Dave menacingly, 'I've just had a look round your stock. Got accounts for it, have you? All catered for in the books? Who's your supplier?'

'I'm going straight now,' whined Reeves.

'Is that a fact?' Dave stared at Reeves, his expression one of his cynical best.

'All right, all right. Yes, I did meet Ted Glass in Brixton. What about it?'

'You told him that you knew Dennis Miller was a grass.'

'So?'

'Well, how did you know?'

'Word gets around.'

'Speak,' said Dave.

'I heard it from another bloke I was in the nick with.'

'Name?' demanded Dave.

'Eric Groves.'

Suddenly the whole Skinner murder enquiry was turned upside down. If Groves knew Skinner was a grass, why in hell's name did he allow him to get involved with the heist for which Groves and the others had been arrested? One thing was sure: there was a very strong motive for Groves murdering Skinner. And there was no doubt that we'd have to speak to Groves again, and quickly.

Dave and I returned to Curtis Green. The first thing Dave did was to telephone the CID at Brixton and tell them the glad news that Roy Reeves, convicted long-firm fraudster, had set up shop in Coldharbour Lane on their manor. 'Thought you might like to take a gander, mate,' said Dave.

Eric Groves, along with the other three, had been remanded in custody to Brixton prison, and Charlene Allen had been sent to Holloway. All were due to appear before a crown court judge in the very near future. Back we went to Brixton.

'And to what do I owe this pleasure?' asked Groves sarcastically when he was brought into the interview room. 'Thought of something else to stitch me up with?'

'We've been talking to an LF specialist called Roy Reeves,' I began.

'Never heard of him, and I've never dabbled in LF,' said Groves dismissively.

'And he tells me that when you were on

remand here about five years ago, you told him you knew Miller was a grass.'

'Oh yeah, now you come to mention it, I do remember the guy. So?'

'Well, is it true that he said this about Skinner, or Miller as you knew him then?'

'Yeah.'

'Then why did you get involved with him in the Heston Services job?'

Groves remained silent while he spent a minute or two teasing tobacco into a Rizla paper and rolling a cigarette. 'Because Dennis Miller was a bloody good planner, that's why,' he said eventually. 'He knew how to set up a job.'

'But it was a hell of a risk, taking him on, wasn't it?'

'Sure it was,' said Groves, licking the gummed edge of his Rizla paper. 'But we'd arranged to take care of that.'

'What, by topping him?'

Groves lit his cigarette. 'Look, Mr Brock, we might be into armed robbery, but we're not into topping people. Not unless it's an accident.'

'Walking into the Starlight Club and letting go with both barrels of a sawn-off doesn't sound like an accident to me. And DI Naylor found a sawn-off in your garage, carefully wrapped in sacking in an inspection pit.'

'Well, it wasn't the one that did for Skinner.'

'So what was it doing there?'

'Tools of the trade, innit? Anyway, that's not what I meant. Sometimes in a robbery someone gets shot, accidental like. And they die.' Groves shrugged his shoulders as though such an occurrence was a commonplace. 'But to stroll into a jazz club on a Saturday night and top a bloke in full view of the bloody audience ain't exactly using your loaf, is it?'

'You said you'd arranged to take care of the problem of Skinner being a grass. How were you going to do that?'

'The minute the job went down we was going to take him back to Cobham and sit on him till the heat was off. He wouldn't've been on his own for a split second.'

'And what d'you think Babs would've said about that.'

'I don't give a toss what Babs would've said. That's the way it was going to be. You see, Dennis, or Rod, or whatever he was calling hisself, had got it all worked out. Like I said just now, he was good at setting up jobs. He'd cultivated Roxy Peters and she introduced him to Charlene, and he passed her on to me. Told me where to find her in some dive down Wimbledon, and I took it from there. Well, she was a peach ... as an informant, I mean. Between you and me, I didn't rate her much as a screw, but when you have to, you have to.'

'It's a hard life,' commented Dave.

'So what about Rod screwing Charlene in the summerhouse at Cobham?'

'Yeah, well, that was well out of order, and I told him so. But it don't call for no topping. All right, we had a few words in the heat of the moment, and then it passed over. But if he'd carried on like that, he could've fucked up the entire job. You start getting a bit of needle between the blokes on a team and it could end up a bleedin' shambles. Anyway, there was plenty more fish in the sea, if you know what I mean.'

I found it very difficult to credit the tale that Groves had been telling me, and I said so.

'Well, you can believe what you like, Mr Brock, but that's the way it was. And if you think you can hang Rod's topping on me, you're welcome to try. But I'll tell you this: I've got a brief who'll take you to the cleaners up the Bailey. Stand on me.'

And Groves was right. There wasn't a shred of substantial evidence that would tie him – or any of his cohorts – to the murder of Rod Skinner. But I still had difficulty in accepting what he'd said previously about sitting on Skinner until the heat was off. I was sure that one of them had murdered him, but proving it was going to be damned hard.

'Of course, Skinner could've tipped off the law *before* the job, Eric,' I said, just to give him something to think about. But I knew it wasn't true.

Back at Curtis Green, there was a message from Brixton CID waiting for Dave.

'They turned over Reeves's shop, Dave,' said Colin Wilberforce, the day-duty incident-room manager, 'and they reckon it's all legit. They looked at his account books and everything. All in order.'

'They weren't bloody well trying,' muttered Dave disgustedly. 'Reeves'll do a runner very shortly, you mark my words, Colin.'

Dave and I settled down in my office to review the situation, and Kate Ebdon joined us.

'We're going round in circles with this enquiry,' I said gloomily.

'That is a truism, sir,' said Dave.

'So what do we do next?'

'I reckon it's time for another chat with Babs Skinner, guv,' Dave said. 'Now we know that the team knew Skinner was a grass, we may find out a bit more from her. And we may find out where Skinner and company were going to take the bullion. And we may find out a bit more about the stash he got from the Wembley job. And that, in turn, may give us another name. For all we know there may have been a seventh finger in that job that the Flying Squad knew nothing about, and who came looking for his cut. And when

178

he didn't get it, he turned nasty and topped Skinner in the hope that he'd get the lot.'

'That's a hell of a lot of theorizing, Dave,' I said, 'and you might be right. But we'll make it tomorrow morning. See if we can get to Babs before she's put too many gins down her throat. Ring and make an appointment. I don't want to go all the way down there if she's going to be out.'

Eleven

We were out of luck. Even though it was only ten o'clock in the morning, Babs Skinner opened the door with a glass in her hand. She seemed delighted to see us.

'Come in, Mr Brock, and you too, Sergeant Poole,' she said, the edges of her consonants already blunted. With a swish of her full-length silk robe, she led the way into the sitting room. 'Would you like a drink?'

I knew that she wasn't talking about coffee. 'No thanks,' I said. 'It's a bit early for me.'

'Have you come to tell me you've found out who killed poor Rod?' Babs plonked herself on the sofa still tightly clutching her gin and tonic, as though she feared it might get stolen. Some of it spilled onto her robe and she brushed absently at it with her free hand.

'Not yet, Mrs Skinner, but—'

'Do please call me Babs, darling,' she said, repeating the request she'd made the last time we were here. 'I hate all this formality.'

'Not yet, Babs, but I was hoping you may be able to help me.'

'I don't know how, but if you think I *can* help, then I'll be happy to.'

'When you were living at Hatfield—'

'Whatever makes you think we ever lived in Hatfield?' said Babs, contriving an impressive expression of bewilderment.

I smiled. 'Babs, we know all about Dennis Miller, and we know that he was involved in the safety-deposit job at Wembley. And later on the Flying Squad arrived at your house at Islington and arrested him.'

'I never understood how they found out that he was involved,' said Babs. She shook her head and then looked as though she wished she hadn't.

'No, I don't suppose you do,' I said, and I wasn't about to tell her that one of the security guards heard one of Skinner's accomplices calling him 'Dusty', and that that eventually led the Squad to him. 'Anyway, Rod decided to turn informant and shopped the other five who were with him.'

'Oh dear!' Babs rose, somewhat unsteadily, to her feet and made her way to the drinks table. With her back to us, she asked, 'How did you find out?'

'I'm a police officer,' I said.

'Mmm, I suppose so.'

I presumed she supposed that that was how I'd found out, rather than she supposed I was a police officer.

'What d'you want to know, then?' she asked as she sat down again. 'You seem to know it all already.'

'Where did all your money come from?' I waved a hand around the sitting room. 'For this house, for your two cars, and the lavish lifestyle you seem to be enjoying.' I knew the answer, of course, but I wanted to hear her version.

'There was a bit left over after Rod and the others did the Wembley job, Mr Brock. You see, the owners of the safety-deposit place checked with all their customers and found out what was missing. Of course the jewellery and diamonds that were left, and the cash the boys had made from selling the rest of it, had to be returned when the other five were arrested, and Rod had to give up his share too. But it turned out that there were some dishonest people' – Babs shot me a mischievous smile – 'who had money stashed away there that they didn't want the Inland Revenue to know about. So they lied and said they hadn't lost anything.'

'And how much was that?'

'Rod told me it was over a million pounds … in used banknotes.' Babs chortled at that, but finished up coughing. She reached out and took a cigarette from an open packet on the arm of her sofa. It didn't seem a sensible panacea to a coughing fit. 'That's what he told me, anyway, but it might have been even more. Rod was a bit vague about it, but I know it was a lot.'

'And Rod hung on to it, I suppose.'

'Yes.'

'Where did he put it?'

Babs raised her eyebrows in a parody of wide-eyed innocence. 'In a bank, of course.'

I laughed at the thought that Skinner and company had raided a safety deposit and then put the unaccounted-for proceeds in a bank.

'But once Rod had informed on the others, the police put us in this witness thing.' She was speaking quite lucidly even though the words were beginning to get quite slurred.

'Witness-protection programme,' I murmured.

'Yes, that was it. They moved us into that horrible little house in Hatfield and we had to change our names to Wright, Ann and Jimmy Wright. And we had to pretend to be poor. It was ghastly, Mr Brock. The neighbours were quite appalling.' Babs had a problem with the last word, repeating it a couple of times until she got it right. 'Not what we'd been used to at all.'

I wondered whether she was trying to convince me, or to fool herself, of her status in life. 'And how long were you there?'

'We stuck it for about three years. Rod didn't do anything. In fact, he put it about that he was on benefit because of an accident at work. That was almost true because your nice police force paid us while we were there. But Rod was bored stiff, and so was I. But we kept ourselves very much to ourselves, and spent most of the time watching telly. Believe me, Mr Brock, daytime telly is dire. But then Rod said he'd had enough. So one night, after the rest of our awful neighbours had gone to bed, we packed our belongings, got into my clapped-out Fiat and took off.'

'And you didn't tell the witness-protection people?'

'Not bloody likely, darling,' said Babs vehemently.

'Where did you go?'

'We changed our names once again, to Rod and Babs Skinner this time, and stayed in a hotel just outside Guildford for a few weeks while we looked for a house, this house. I liked the name Babs, better than the Daphne I was christened, so that's what I decided on.'

'And now you're living on the million pounds or so that was stolen.'

'Plus the interest.' Babs laughed. 'Rod got a very good rate of interest, and you'd be surprised how much you accrue when you haven't touched the capital for three years.'

All of this was more or less what we'd gleaned from DCS Drew and from talking to the Skinners' erstwhile neighbours at Hatfield.

'You do appreciate, I suppose, Babs,' said Dave, 'that you may well lose this money.'

Babs scoffed. 'Who does it belong to, then? If anyone cares to come along and prove to my solicitor's satisfaction that it's theirs, they can have it. But I'll bet you no one will.'

I had to admit that Babs Skinner had a point there. If the original losers hadn't been willing to claim ownership at the time of the robbery, I doubted that they would want to identify themselves some five years later. If for no better reason than that HM Revenue and Customs has an even longer arm than the police.

But then I had another nasty thought. Supposing one or more of the losers of this illicit stash of money had come after Skinner, seeking its return. I hastily put that from my mind. For the moment.

'But then Rod decided to get involved in another robbery,' I said.

'He did?' Babs raised her eyebrows again. 'Whatever makes you think that?'

'There was an attempted robbery at Heston Services on the M4 last Friday, Babs.'

'Yes, it was on TV. But what did that have to do with Rod?'

'You mean you didn't know that he was supposed to take part?'

'The bastard,' said Babs. 'He promised me he was going straight.'

I didn't believe that she could not have known. 'The wild party you had here a couple of months ago,' I said.

'What about it?' Babs wrinkled her nose at the very thought of it.

185

'That was when the plan was finalized. Fruity Metcalfe, Eric Groves and Brian Baker were all here, along with Roxy Peters, Charlene Allen and one or two other girls.'

'Don't remind me,' said Babs.

'Well, five of them were arrested for that job.'

'*Five?*'

'Yes. The three men I mentioned, plus a man called Soapy Hudson, and Charlene Allen. She was the one who told them where the bullion van was going to stop. But we knew about it, and when it was going to happen, and that's how they were captured.'

'The sassy little bitch,' said Babs. 'Serve her right. She was the one who went after my Charlie.'

'But it was nearly put in jeopardy because your late husband was about to have sex with Charlene in your summerhouse when Eric Groves walked in on them. Groves was annoyed because he'd brought Charlene to the party. If Metcalfe and Baker hadn't stepped in, there might've been a punch-up, or worse. And if that had happened, the whole plan could've unravelled.'

Babs gave a raucous laugh. 'Rod could never resist an available woman,' she said. 'That's why I found myself Charlie Hardy. He's good at restoring old things, is Charlie, and he's done miracles for me.' She tottered across to the drinks table again and poured herself another gin and tonic. 'So you think that Eric murdered Rod, do you?'

'I don't know, Babs. What d'you think?'

Returning to the sofa she collapsed onto it with a deep sigh. Once again she spilled some of her drink onto her robe, but seemed not to notice. 'Rod had a lot of enemies, Mr Brock, that's for sure. Starting with the five that got sent to prison because he turned informer.'

'This Wembley job,' said Dave. 'Were there only six of them in on it? Including Rod, that is.'

Babs gave Dave an incisive stare. 'D'you mean you don't know?'

At last. Was Babs about to reveal that someone else had taken part?

'No, we don't know,' said Dave patiently.

'Well, there was someone else, Sergeant darling.' Babs cast a lascivious glance at Dave. No doubt she fancied him. Most middle-aged women seemed to, lucky bastard. 'A man called Freddie Peacock was in on it, too. Rod told me everything about that job. How they were going to do it and when.'

'Why didn't Rod tell the police about him, then?' I asked.

'There was no point,' Babs said. 'Straight after the robbery, Freddie took off for Spain, or Mexico, or somewhere like that. I know it was somewhere that didn't have one of those export things.'

'Extradition treaties,' murmured Dave.

'I do believe you're right,' said Babs, slurring delightfully. 'But straight after the job was done, Freddie said he'd go abroad and lie low until it had all died down. Then he was going to come back and collect his share. Very shrewd was Freddie, much more so than the others. Anyway, Rod had done enough to get himself off the hook, and Freddie was out of the way. So why tell the law about him?' She hiccupped loudly and laughed. 'Sorry,' she said.

'Did Peacock ever come back, Babs?' I asked.

'I've no idea. I think that once he found out that the others had been arrested and sent to prison, he probably thought he'd cut his losses and stay where he was. At least for a while.'

But did he come back looking for his share? And when he found that Dennis Miller had disappeared with the loot, vowed to find him? And when he did and discovered that there was no money left – because that's what Miller, masquerading as Skinner, would've told him – he topped him. And, at the same time, exacting revenge on behalf of his imprisoned mates.

'Well, thank you for your assistance, Babs,' I said. 'I don't think there's anything else you can help us with.'

'If there is, darling, pop down any time. Gets terribly lonely here, you know, and I do love having a chat.' Babs gazed out of the window at the tranquil surface of the pool. 'I think I'll have a swim now,' she said, and laughed. 'Sober me up a bit. And then it'll be lunchtime.' She cast a longing glance at the drinks table. I had no doubt what would constitute lunch in her case.

We were now faced with one hell of a problem. If Freddie Peacock had returned to this country looking for his part of the haul from the Wembley job, and had killed Skinner, where was he now? It was almost certain that he would have changed his name and, in all probability, returned to wherever it was he had come from.

I telephoned DCS Drew and told him what we'd learned from Babs Skinner.

'There was a whisper that there'd been a seventh man, Harry,' said Drew, 'but no one was prepared to give us a name. When Dennis Miller was nicked, he denied that there was anyone else, and the five that were banged up for the job stayed shtum. Frankly I've no idea where you'd start looking for the guy.'

But we had to try because suddenly Freddie Peacock was the one man who would have had a real motive for killing Skinner. I sent for Kate Ebdon and explained the problem.

'How good are your snouts, Kate?'

'I've got one or two dinkum ones in my collection, guv. And no doubt I can lean on them.'

Knowing what I did of Kate's reputation, particularly when she was on the Flying Squad, I almost felt sorry for the countless 'faces' that would shortly be interrogated by her. When Kate's fiery Australian temper got the better of her, she had a way of persuading members of the criminal fraternity to part with information.

Ten minutes later, she was back in my office.

'Blimey,' I said, 'you haven't found him already, have you?'

Kate grinned. 'No, guv, but I have found his record. I did a search and came up with this.' She laid a printout on my desk. 'He's an armed robber with decent form, and he's done a bit of bird for it, too.'

I skimmed through the sheet of paper that outlined Peacock's criminal history. He was now forty-five, and since the age of seventeen had served eleven of those twenty-five years in prison. But he had last been released, from Pentonville, some ten months before the Wembley job occurred.

'So he could have been there,' I mused.

'I've sent for a photograph of him,' said Kate, 'but it'll be so old it won't be worth looking at. He got a handful for a betting-shop robbery and came out nearly six years ago. And if he'd heard about Skinner grassing up the five who are in the nick now, he's probably had a face job done. That's assuming he's back in this country and not wandering around the pampas of Mexico or wherever.'

'You've cheered me up no end, Kate,' I said, 'but see what your team can find out.'

'They'll be right, guv,' said Kate cheerfully, whatever that meant. She didn't seem nearly as depressed by the prospect of finding Freddie Peacock as I did.

But I didn't intend leaving it all to my DI. I too had been a Flying Squad officer a few years ago, and I had some snouts of my own. And there was one in particular who, albeit a long time ago, had always had his ear to the ground.

The square mile of Soho is a fascinating mix of races, cultures, professions, trades ... and villainy.

It is here that you can buy exotic foods and rare wines, and dine in restaurants as varied as Chinese, Cajun, Thai, Indian, Hungarian, Vietnamese and a score of others. Even basic fish and chips. And it is in its narrow, garbage-strewn streets that you will hear a dozen different languages.

It is an area frequented by the rich and famous, the open-mouthed tourist, and the naive home-grown adventurer who has come up from the sticks to see life in the raw.

And many of them are likely to get ripped off by the sharks in the shadows. Some of these predators will wait with outstretched greasy palms demanding exorbitant fees just for the sight of a naked girl performing contortions around a chromium-plated pole.

Others will be found in the back rooms of video shops selling debased hard-core pornography of every description, or who introduce men – or even women – to prostitutes of both sexes who are willing to pleasure them in ways that beggar belief, or who will fleece the innocent for admission to low dives where dissipated men and tired women will perform sexual acts in dark caverns for the gratification of spellbound punters.

One of the drawbacks – or maybe advantages – of being a plainclothes police officer is that, whatever you may think, you are immediately identified as such by the criminal classes who haunt this area. Some sixth sense warns the oleaginous pimps in sharp suits, and the scantily attired 'hostesses', of your presence, and they will disappear as if by magic the moment you approach the doorways in which they lurk.

But Dave and I knew where we were going.

'Looking for a good time, gents?' asked a muscle-bound yob who had secreted himself inside the entrance to one such establishment. 'Twenty quid each.'

Without breaking step, Dave waved his warrant card under the bouncer's nose and I was gratified to see him leap for the telephone, doubtless to inform the owner that the Old Bill had come among his clientele.

'Well, well, Mr Brock. How very nice to see you again.' The man who oiled his way towards us was called Monty. He was bald-headed, overweight, sweated profusely and his fidgeting fingers were adorned with several gold rings, one of which bore a stone of quite vulgar proportions. 'A drink, gentlemen? Scotch, if I remember correctly.' He snapped his fingers imperiously at the bartender.

'Business seems to be flourishing, Monty,' I said, glancing round at the garish decor of the subterranean cave he dignified with the term 'nightclub'. A naked girl was performing listless gyrations on a table surrounded by open-mouthed men.

Monty spread his hands and waggled his head. 'Not so good, Mr Brock. It's these terrorists. It drives away the tourists.'

'Lucky tourists,' said Dave, noisily sniffing the whisky that the barman had placed in front of him.

'It's the very best malt, Mr Poole,' commented Monty hurriedly, thinking that Dave's little pantomime was a criticism.

'I think you may be able to help me,

Monty,' I said.

'You know me, Mr Brock. Anything I can do to help the law. Only too willing.'

I knew that Monty was a bent bastard and Monty knew that I knew. That's why he wanted to help, but he wasn't prepared for my next statement.

'Somebody murdered a grass with a sawn-off shotgun, Monty. In a club, would you believe?' I said, glancing around. 'And I'm looking for the man who did it.'

There was a sharp intake of breath as Monty realized that I had just placed him between what the cliché-ridden call 'a rock and a hard place'. Or put more simply, between the police and those members of the criminal fraternity who would stop at nothing to punish any informants in their midst.

'How's the insurance business going, Monty?' I asked, just to encourage him.

'That's all behind me, Mr Brock. I learned my lesson. I'm legit now.'

'Good.' I knew that Monty had served time for a protection racket some years ago, but I was sufficient of a cynic to believe that he was still at it. 'About five years ago, Monty, a robber called Dennis Miller turned super-grass on the Wembley job. And the guys he grassed up went down for twenty-five years.'

Monty winced. 'I heard about that job, but I don't know the name,' he said. 'Miller,

194

you say?'

'Well, a fortnight ago someone topped him.'

'Dreadful, dreadful.' Monty shook his head. 'One of the hoods he fingered, I suppose.'

'No. They're all still in the nick, and their outstanding account with the Queen is in the red to the tune of least a score. Not allowing for parole, of course.'

Monty looked uncomfortable. 'Another drink, Mr Brock? Sam, another drink for the gentlemen.'

'Now it so happens, Monty, that a name's come into the frame. Freddie Peacock.'

A topless, miniskirted waitress glided past and winked at Dave. Dave blew her a kiss.

'Peacock, Peacock.' Monty frowned as he savoured the name. 'I don't think I—'

'A good robber with a lot of form behind him,' I continued. 'Rumour has it that he too was involved in the Wembley job five years ago, but did a runner to Spain or South America. In fact, you might even have met him when you were in stir.' I put that in just to remind Monty again that I knew he'd got form. 'But I've reason to believe he's back in this country now, and I need to speak to him.'

'I'd love to help, Mr Brock, but—'

'I'm sure you'll keep your ear to the ground, Monty, like the upright, honest citizen you are. If you hear anything, give me a bell.' I gave him one of my cards. 'On the other hand, I could pop in from time to time to see what you've heard.' That should encourage him, I thought. I finished my Scotch and put the glass back on the bar. 'Mind you stay on the right side of the law, now.'

But as it turned out, I never heard from him. But, as it also turned out, I didn't need to.

Twelve

'The photograph of Freddie Peacock's come through, guv,' said Kate Ebdon as she breezed into my office and laid the print on my desk. 'Like I said at the time, it's years old, and I'll put money on him not looking anything like that now.'

I glanced at the photograph of Peacock taken when he was last arrested, and decided it would be a waste of time circulating it. If he were back in this country, he would have changed his appearance beyond all recognition, especially if he thought that Skinner had grassed on him and that we were still looking for him.

'We can forget that,' I said, returning the photograph. 'Anything else?'

'I've been doing some digging around, guv.'

'Did you turn up anything useful?'

'Yes and no,' said Kate. 'D'you remember that Cyril Underwood, the trumpeter in the jazz band at the Starlight Club, said that Rod Skinner had answered an advert in the *Fulham Gazette*?'

'Yes, I do,' I said, wondering what gem Kate was about to come up with.

'Well, just for the hell of it, I paid a visit to the paper's offices. I had them go right back through their records and there wasn't any such advert.'

'Perhaps Underwood got the name of the paper wrong,' I said. 'There must be quite a few local rags that cover that area.'

'I thought of that, but I wasn't going to go round all of them. I think a better idea would be to speak to Underwood again. But apart from anything else, Skinner doesn't seem to have had any connection with Fulham, except playing in a band there. So how come he reads the *Fulham Gazette*, and finds an advert for a drummer that's not in the paper?' Kate smiled, presumably at the inescapable logic of what she had just said.

'What nights do these guys play at the Starlight?'

'Fridays and Saturdays, guv.'

'And today's Friday,' I mused. 'We shall pay the Starlight Club a visit this evening,' I said.

'I thought we might,' said Kate.

The blue-chinned bouncer appeared to have become a permanent fixture at the Starlight Club; a classic example of providing security after the need for it had passed.

'We're not open until eight o'clock, sir,' he said.

'Is Mrs Leech here yet?' I asked, waving my warrant card at him.

'In her office, guv'nor,' said the bouncer, apparently deciding that it had been a mistake to call a visiting police officer 'sir'.

We walked through the deserted public area of the club to the office in the corner near the bar.

'Oh, not again.' Erica Leech looked irritated, to say the least, at our arrival.

'I'm afraid that one of the penalties of having people murdered in your club, Erica, is that you'll get quite a few visits from the police until the murderer is arrested.'

'Well, I don't see how I can help you any more than I have done.'

'Tell me about Cyril Underwood.'

'Who?'

'The trumpeter in the same band as your late boyfriend Rod Skinner,' I said.

'I don't know anything about him,' said Erica. 'He just comes here with the band and plays jazz.'

'Where do they keep their instruments?' asked Kate, suddenly deciding to take an interest.

'Er, I'm not sure. I think they sometimes leave them in the storeroom at the back,' said Erica. 'But there again, they sometimes take them. Usually if they've got another gig some place. Why?'

'So, they don't only play here. Is that what you're saying?'

I wasn't quite sure what Kate was driving

at, but was prepared to let her pursue her line of enquiry. She usually had a good reason for going off at a tangent and, no doubt, she'd explain later on. Unless it became evident in the next few minutes.

'Yes. I've just said they have other gigs.' Erica was obviously mystified by Kate's line of questioning. But so was I.

'Any idea what these guys do for a living?' Kate took out her pocket book, and rested it on her knee. 'They obviously haven't given up the day job if they only play here twice a week, and do the occasional session somewhere else. And I don't suppose that pays them enough to live on.'

'I really don't know,' said Erica. 'It's not my business. All I want is a band here every night to keep the customers happy.'

'When will Underwood be here?'

'He usually gets here at about half-past seven.' Erica glanced at her watch. 'About now, in fact.'

'So they've found another drummer, have they?'

'Yes, but before you ask, I don't know where he came from.' Erica was becoming increasingly irritated by Kate's questioning.

The door opened and the head of Les Roper, the bass player, appeared round it. 'We're ready to go as soon as you open, Erica,' he said. Then he caught sight of Kate and me. 'Oh, you're back,' he said.

'Yes,' I said. 'Is Cyril Underwood out there?'

'Sure.'

We followed Roper out to the main area of the club. The band was setting up, and the two briefly clad waitresses were arranging tables and chairs and lighting candles.

'That's a fire risk,' commented Dave, but no one took any notice.

'Are those two waitresses the two who were here the night of the shooting, Kate?' I asked.

'That's them, guv. Two of the doziest sheilas I've ever come across. Couldn't add anything to our tiny pile of evidence.'

We crossed to the stage.

'Mr Underwood,' I said to the trumpeter, who by now was playing a few scales to warm his instrument.

'Oh, hello.' Underwood rested his trumpet on his knee.

'I'd like a word.' I said. 'Perhaps you'd come over here.' I gestured at a table in the corner.

Carefully placing his trumpet on the seat of his chair, Underwood followed us across the room, away from the flapping ears of the other members of the band. 'What's the problem?'

'This advert you put in the *Fulham Gazette*, Cyril,' said Kate. 'When did you insert it?'

'About six weeks ago,' said Underwood after a moment's thought. But he was beginning to look shifty.

'Did you keep a copy of it?' asked Kate.

'No. I chucked it away as soon as Rod turned up.'

'There wasn't an advert at all, Cyril, was there?' said Kate. 'I checked with the paper. They've never published an advert for you, and they haven't published an advert for a drummer for over a year.'

'They must've made a mistake,' said Underwood lamely.

'No, mate, you're the one who made the mistake. Now, Cyril, I'm going to have the fingerprint boys take your dabs because I—' But that was as far as she got.

Underwood shot off his chair and ran for the exit.

Kate was after him instantly. But the speed with which he'd taken flight took both of us by surprise. Kate shouted at the doorman to stop him, but in vain. Underwood legged it rapidly up the stairs, pushed the bouncer violently to one side and ran into the street. The last we saw of him was hopping on a bus that, fortunately for him, happened to be right outside with its doors open.

'Sod it,' said Kate, standing with arms akimbo and staring at the disappearing bus. Parking being what it is, we'd had to leave our car a street away from the club. Kate looked round for a taxi, but there was none in sight. Like policemen, there's never one when you want one. 'The bastard's shot through, guv,' she said disgustedly.

We returned to the club to find Erica Leech talking to what remained of the band.

'What's happened?' she demanded.

'You're short of a trumpeter, Erica. Looks like he's given up jazz for a while.'

Les Roper joined us. 'What did you say to him?' he asked, obviously blaming us for the loss of the brass section.

Kate countered Roper's question by asking one of her own. 'When you took Rod Skinner on as a drummer, Cyril Underwood said he'd answered an advert in the *Fulham Gazette*,' she said. 'Did you see that advert?'

'No,' said Roper. 'When the last drummer left, Cyril said he'd find a new one. He said that he'd put an ad in the local paper. We left it to him, and a couple of weeks later Rod turned up, complete with his kit. He was bloody good, was Rod, and we took him on.'

'How long have you known Underwood, Les?'

Roper pursed his lips. 'About a year, I suppose.' He glanced at the other musicians for confirmation and they mumbled agreement.

'Where did he come from?'

'No idea,' said Roper.

'Well, how did you meet up?'

'He was busking in the Underground at Embankment Station. I listened to him for a while and decided he was good. So I asked him if he'd like to join us for a few sessions. And that's how he became a member of the band.'

'Where does Underwood live?' demanded Kate.

'No idea,' said Roper. 'I think he said something about being down Catford way.'

'What happened if you had a cancellation, or a last-minute booking for a gig, or one of your guys took a sickie? How did you get in touch?'

'I've got a phone number for him,' said Roper.

'Then why the hell didn't you say so?' demanded Kate impatiently. 'Let's have it.'

Roper mounted the stage and took a diary from his jacket pocket. 'There you are,' he said, pointing to an entry.

Kate copied it into her pocket book, and then punched a number into her mobile phone. Seconds later she was asking Gavin Creasey for a subscriber check on the telephone number Roper had given her.

'We might get lucky, guv,' she said, 'but there again he might have decided against going home.'

'What are we going to do without a trumpet player?' wailed Roper.

'I reckon you'll just have to hum those bits,' said Kate.

We took possession of Cyril Underwood's trumpet. One of the useful aspects of a brass

204

instrument like that is that it often yields an excellent set of fingerprints. And right now, Kate and I were not convinced that Cyril Underwood was, in reality, Cyril Underwood.

'What made you suspect him, Kate?' I asked.

'Copper's nose,' said Kate mysteriously. 'But when I checked out the address he gave me the night Skinner got topped it turned out to be duff.'

'But what did you suspect him of?'

'No idea, guv.'

The location of Underwood's telephone number went out to a guy called Henry Smith, who lived not in Catford but at 13 Yardgate Street in Lewisham, a Victorian terraced house that had yet to be gentrified in the manner of many of its neighbours. For what difference any of that made.

In answer to Kate's sustained hammering, the door was eventually opened an inch or two and a black face peered round the edge.

'Yes?'

'We're police officers.'

'How do I know?' It was obvious that this man had difficulty in accepting that a red-headed Australian woman in shirt and jeans was a copper.

Kate produced her warrant card. 'I'm Detective Inspector Ebdon,' she said.

'Drugs Squad?' asked the black face.

'No. Why, do they come here often?'

'No, miss, not at all.'

'Right. Now we've been through that palaver, we want to talk to Mr Underwood.'

'Cyril's not here.' At last the man relented and admitted us to the narrow hallway. 'You better come in, I s'pose.' Edging sideways, he led us past a couple of bicycles and into the front room. 'What's Cyril done wrong?'

'I didn't say he'd done anything wrong,' said Kate. 'We think he may be able to help us with our enquiries. Who are you, anyway?'

'Henry Smith, Inspector.'

These days almost everyone, thanks to television, knows that 'helping the police with their enquiries' means that they have been, or are about to be, arrested. It fools no one and, judging from his expression, it hadn't fooled Mr Smith either.

'And d'you own this place, Mr Smith?'

'Yes, miss.'

'And you rent out rooms, including one to Mr Underwood, is that right?'

'Yes, but all the tax and everything is properly paid for.'

Kate sighed audibly. 'I'm a police officer, not a tax collector,' she said.

'Cyril's not here,' said Mr Smith again.

'So where is he?'

'Playing in a jazz band. He's a very good trumpeter.'

'Yeah, we've heard him,' said Kate, even though all we'd heard was him warming his instrument earlier that evening.

'He won't be back until about one in the morning,' contributed the helpful landlord.

'With any luck he'll be back a bit earlier than that,' said Kate, 'so we'll wait and see. If that's all right with you, Mr Smith.'

Henry Smith shrugged. 'If you want to wait here, that's OK with me.'

'One other thing,' said Kate. 'When he turns up, don't tell him we're here. We want it to be a nice surprise.'

'OK, boss.' Henry Smith had obviously weighed up the pros and cons of the situation and decided, rapidly I imagine, that it would be safer to offend Cyril Underwood than to upset Kate.

It is one of the facts of criminal investigation that there are some very wily villains about. But there are also some rather dim ones. Perhaps Cyril Underwood fell into the latter category, or perhaps he thought that we weren't smart enough to have obtained his phone number *and* traced it to where he lived. And that we managed to get there before London's inadequate public-transport system had conveyed him from Fulham to Lewisham.

Whatever the reason, about a quarter of an hour later, we heard a key in the front door. This was followed by the noise of a bicycle falling over and an oath.

'Hello, Cyril,' said the voice of Mr Smith. 'You're home early tonight.'

There was no reply, but we heard someone racing up the stairs, followed by a frantic opening and slamming of drawers and cupboard doors. Cyril Underwood, I thought, was about to terminate his tenancy agreement.

Having learned from Mr Smith which room Underwood occupied, we mounted the stairs as quietly as we could.

Kate gently pushed open the door with her foot. 'I don't understand it, Cyril,' she said. 'There we were in the middle of having a cosy little chat with you when you ran away.' Her expression was one of feigned innocence at such extraordinary behaviour. 'Now why should you have done that?'

Underwood, in the act of throwing clothing into a grip, gave up and sat down on the bed, a resigned look on his face.

'We've got your trumpet in the car outside and we're going to get the fingerprint guys to give it a going over,' continued Kate. The car wasn't outside, of course. It was four houses down on the other side of the road. We're not that daft.

'Don't bother,' said Underwood. 'You know bloody well I'm Freddie Peacock. That's why you've come after me.'

Well, he said it, not me.

'Really?' I said. 'In that case, Freddie, you're nicked for being concerned with others, deceased or in custody, for the robbery at a safety-deposit company in Wembley some five years ago.' I turned to Kate. 'Caution him, Inspector.' I had to let her do it because I have this problem with the caution. I knew the old one, but ever since they introduced the later, and quite unnecessary, version, I could never remember it. And I'd lost the little card with it written on. I must try and get a new one.

As Freddie Peacock was under arrest, I deemed it politic to remove him to Lewisham police station in Ladywell Road. The Crown Prosecution Service, to say nothing of Her Majesty's judges, tends to look askance at any admission made other than in the presence of a recording machine. It is an inviolable rule of British justice that we must protect the accused and to hell with the victim.

But we needn't have worried. In the car, Peacock said nothing. But then he probably knows more about the Police and Criminal Evidence Act than I do.

The custody sergeant eventually completed the plethora of paper that is the inevitable consequence of any knock-off, and we sat down in one of the interview rooms.

I got Kate to caution him again, just to be on the safe side, and was about to pose my

209

first question when Peacock started talking.

'I know what you're thinking, Mr Brock,' he said.

'And what am I thinking?' I asked.

'You think I topped Miller.'

I laughed. 'I know you didn't, Freddie. We have witnesses to say that a masked man with a sawn-off entered the club and shot Miller, or Skinner as he was calling himself then. You were playing trumpet at the time and were still there when we arrived. In fact, you were lucky you didn't get topped yourself.'

'Yeah, well, I meant to top him.'

'Really?'

'Yeah.' Peacock lit a cigarette, moved his position so that he was sitting sideways on to the table and crossed his legs. 'See, after we done the Wembley job, I took it on the toes to Mexico. The others thought they was well clear, but I decided I'd play it a bit shrewd.' He tapped the side of his nose and then laughed, but there was no humour in it. 'I reckoned we'd've scored about eight hundred grand each, after the gear had been knocked out like, plus what wasn't accounted for. And the unaccounted-for should have added up to at least a million, probably more. So all up I reckoned we was standing in for not much short of a million quid apiece. We'd agreed that we'd lie low for about a year before we started spending. My mistake was I trusted the others, and I

210

certainly never reckoned on Miller grassing us up.'

'Why did you come back from Mexico, then, Freddie?' I asked.

'I read what had happened in a local English newspaper over there. Read that five of my mates had been nicked by the Flying Squad and all went down big time. But one name was missing: *Dusty Miller!* So I was pretty bloody sure that he'd ratted on us, and I was determined to come back and sort him. And collect my share of the leftover. So I had a face job done in Mexico City.'

'That must have cost,' I said.

'Yeah, it did. So did the duff passport. But I'd taken some of my share of the gelt with me, and left the rest with the lads. Well, the up and down of it was that when they was nicked they all had their cut of the take seized by the Old Bill. Well, you'd know that, Mr Brock. But there was still the unaccounted-for million or so. It seemed to make sense to me that as there wasn't nothing in the papers about it, Miller had to have it stashed away. So, Freddie, I says to meself, get back home and claim your slice of the cake.'

'But then you found that Miller had disappeared.'

'Yeah, the bastard. But then I had a bit of luck. I was clubbing up West and renewing old friendships, as you might say, when I bumped into this geezer who I'd done a job with in the dim and distant.'

'Name?' I asked.

'Leave it out, Mr Brock,' said Peacock with a grin. 'Anyhow, I got chatting to him about Miller and he told me as how he'd grassed, which I'd worked out anyway, and had been put in witness protection. But then this mate said he'd ducked out of that, changed his name to Rod Skinner and was living the high life down some place called Cobham. Right, I thought, time for your comeuppance, Dennis Miller. But not before I'd had me money off of him.'

'What happened next?'

'I set him up. Years ago, he'd told me that he'd played drums, so I give him a bell, introduced meself as Cyril Underwood and asked him if he wanted in on our combo. Simple as that.'

'And he fell for it?'

'Couldn't resist it.' Peacock scoffed. 'I don't think you understand about jazz, Mr Brock,' he said. 'Like I told you the night Skinner got shot, it gets in your blood. It's not the money, it's the playing. It's like a drug, see. You just want to go on playing it. Anyway, along he comes. And he never recognized me because of the face job.' He lifted his chin and ran a hand round it. He was obviously pleased with the work the Mexican plastic surgeon had done.

'But what was the point?'

'I wanted to find out where he'd stashed the money, and I was going to have it. And I wanted to find out where he went, and what he did, so's I could top him. After I'd got me money, of course. See, he owed me, but more to the point he owed the poor five bastards what he'd put away. And that's a topping job, Mr Brock. See, that's something we can't stand for. It wasn't as if they'd got a rap over the knuckles, was it? I mean to say, twenty-five years' porridge is serious birdlime. It's the code, see. You don't turn your mates over to the law and then walk away. It's not on.'

'But you didn't get your money and you didn't top him, did you?' I said.

'No. I never had time. Before I could set it up proper, some bastard got there before me. I wanted to pick somewhere to do the job so's no one'd be able to pin it on me. One of them quiet lanes round Cobham would have been spot on. And in my professional opinion the Starlight Club wasn't the place to do it. You'd have to be a raving nutter to do him in front of all those people. You could've knocked me over with a feather when that went down.'

'Which brings us to our next point, Freddie,' said Kate. 'Who did top him?'

Peacock spread his hands. 'I dunno, miss. Still, whoever it was done me a favour. But if he's grassed on anyone else, he'll've accumulated quite a few enemies, and that's a fact.

Could've been anyone.'

'And did he grass on anyone else?'

'Not that I know of, miss.' Peacock paused. 'But the worst part of it is I'll never get my cut now.'

And that was that. We handed Freddie Peacock over to the Flying Squad so that they could have a go at getting him convicted of the Wembley job.

And we went back to the drawing board.

Thirteen

I sat in my office on Saturday morning gloomily contemplating the calendar. It was three weeks to the day since Rod Skinner had been shot dead in the Starlight Club. Between us, Dave and I, and Kate Ebdon and her team, had interviewed countless people. But one by one the promising leads had fizzled out.

'D'you remember the two parking tickets we found in Skinner's car, guv?' said Dave.

'Don't tell me, it's a blow-out.'

'Yeah. Both go out to streets around Kingston on a Saturday morning. Probably went there shopping.'

'We'll never know now,' I said, 'but I don't suppose it matters.'

'One of the people we haven't interviewed,' said Dave, abandoning the subject of parking tickets, 'is Howard Leech.'

'Yes, I suppose we ought to eliminate him,' I said, but without much enthusiasm. Furthermore, if we didn't do it the commander would undoubtedly notice. Very hot on trivia, is the commander.

'I don't know about eliminate him,' said

Dave. 'He might well be in the frame.' He opened his nylon excuse for a briefcase and took out an orange. I hate the smell of oranges, but Dave's wife Madeleine says they're good for him. And who am I to argue with the gorgeous Madeleine?

'How so, Dave?'

'We've only got Erica Leech's word for it that they've separated. For all we know, Howard might have gone screaming up the wall when he found out that she'd spent three weeks in the South of France with Rod Skinner. We don't know what sort of guy Leech is, but if he found out she was over the side, he might just have topped Skinner. We don't even know what he does for a living. Could be a bank clerk or a professional hitman,' he added, tossing orange peel into the wastepaper basket. 'And with a name like Leech he might even be a tax collector.'

'And that reminds me that there's something else that's been bothering me,' I said. 'Erica met Skinner over a year ago, when he took her to the South of France. And yet he only started playing at the Starlight Club about six weeks ago, at the behest of Freddie Peacock. A coincidence, or what? We must ask Erica next time we call in at the club. Anyway, in the meantime, we'll go and have a word with *Mr* Leech.'

The residents of World's End like to think

they live in Chelsea, but – whatever the local council tells them – geographically they're in Fulham, which, apparently, does not have the same cachet.

I don't know why they bother. As far as the police are concerned there's no great difference. The lawlessness that now prevails in the capital makes no exception of the sham-genteel, would-be, has-been, or never-were people who live in Chelsea. Just like all the others, they will be blatantly robbed in broad daylight, have their cars vandalized or stolen, become the victims of con artists, and be threatened by bogus beggars who are probably making more than those from whom they aggressively solicit.

There is a plus side for the residents, however: drugs of all descriptions are plentifully available; it's a snorter's paradise.

The main artery of this area is the King's Road. It runs, in one form or another, all the way from Sloane Square to Putney Bridge – by which time it's become *New* King's Road – and is a haven for those seeking anything and everything from the bizarre to the banal. Under-funded boutiques, over-priced antique shops, quirky restaurants and purveyors of 'ethnic' merchandise abound. But they are often here today and gone tomorrow.

The only constancy is to be found in the pubs, the landlords of which gaze on the passing, changing scene with cynical stoicism.

Howard Leech seemed to fit perfectly into the arty-crafty scene to which so many Chelsea-ites aspire.

He was in his late forties and, when we called on him that evening, was dressed in a colourful shirt, moleskin trousers and sandals with no socks, and was smoking a meerschaum pipe with a curved stem. On his left wrist, just above his gold Rolex, was a coloured band that doubtless implied his temporary unwavering support for some underprivileged, unheard-of protest group. And he was agitated.

'I've been expecting you,' he said nervously when we told him that we were police officers. 'I suppose it's about this murder at Erica's club.' Leech spoke over his shoulder as he led Dave and me up the stairs to the top flat of the house he shared with his estranged wife. And just to confirm it, he added, 'Erica and I don't live together any more.'

The sitting room was a shambles. Worn armchairs were set on an equally worn carpet, and there were books, magazines and newspapers – the *Guardian* principally – spread about in profusion on every available surface. He didn't look like a man who had plenty of money, but you can never tell. Some people enjoy living in a tip.

'Why's that?' I asked, using his last statement as a useful hook on which to hang the question.

'We just didn't get on,' said Leech blithely. 'But we're still good friends.'

Funny the way separated couples always say that. Believe me, Helga and I aren't good friends. Come to that I don't think we ever were.

'It had nothing to with the affair that she had with Rod Skinner, or rather Jimmy Wright as she knew him then?'

'Do take a seat, Mr ... ?'

'Brock. Detective Chief Inspector Brock, and this is Detective Sergeant Poole.'

Leech nodded an acknowledgement in Dave's direction. 'That happened after we'd split up. She went her way and I went mine.'

'But she still lives here.'

Leech smiled. 'Pure economics, Chief Inspector,' he said. 'We neither of us wanted to leave Chelsea, and these days moving costs a fortune.'

Dave smirked but said nothing. He knew it was Fulham.

'So you didn't mind Skinner taking your wife to the South of France for three weeks.'

'Not at all. As I said, we'd decided to go our separate ways.'

'Did you know Skinner? Ever meet him?' I asked.

'No. I suppose I might have seen him. I call

into the club occasionally.'

'What's your profession, Mr Leech?' asked Dave.

It clearly crossed Leech's mind that this had nothing to do with the murder of Skinner, but he answered nevertheless. 'Antiques.'

That covered a wide range of activity, genuine and bogus. 'What are you into then, house clearance?' Dave could be very perverse when he wanted to, and it was one of his quirks to burst the bubble of those he saw as pretentious.

But it washed over Leech. 'No, not at all. I run an antiques business. I travel around the country buying up good-quality pieces. Brighton's a very good place to go for auctions.'

'What d'you know about Frank Seaton?' I asked.

'Seaton, Seaton? Ah yes. He was one of Erica's boyfriends. Dabbles in art, so she told me.'

'Your wife said that it was her affair with Frank Seaton that caused the break-up between you.'

Leech smiled condescendingly. 'That might have been the reason she gave,' he said, 'but we'd decided that we were incompatible long before that. Her relationship with Seaton was the consequence of our separation, not the cause of it.'

'Did your wife have any other men friends?'

220

I asked.

'Possibly. I think there was one chap called Jolyon. Silly name.' Leech paused in thought. 'Yes, it was Jolyon. Can't recall his surname. Something to do with racehorses, I think. Has stables down Newbury way, I believe. Or it might have been Hampshire. Didn't last long, anyway. Don't think he had what it takes.'

'What, money?' asked Dave.

'No, sex. Erica's a very demanding lady.' Leech crossed his legs and put his hands behind his head. 'She's very keen on that sort of thing; in fact she's insatiable. She'll run after anything in trousers or, better still, not in them. And the rougher they are the more she likes them. I think that even other women take her fancy from time to time. Changes her lovers about as often as I change my shirt.'

But I dismissed that as a spiteful comment, even though she did appear to have had a string of admirers.

'Saturday the sixth of July, Mr Leech,' I said.

'What about it?'

'It was the night that Skinner was murdered. In your wife's jazz club.'

'Oh yes, of course.'

'Where were you?'

'With a friend. We spent the evening together.' Leech smiled. 'And the night.'

221

'And her name?'

'It was a he, not a she,' said Leech with no trace of embarrassment at his admission.

'I see.'

'Perhaps we could have his name, Mr Leech,' said Dave.

Without asking, Leech took Dave's pocket book and scribbled down a name and address. 'I'm sure he'll be happy to vouch for me,' he said.

All of which readily explained why Erica had gone in search of other men.

Another one off the list. Provided, of course, Leech's alibi checked out. But I had no doubt it would.

Nevertheless, Erica Leech's promiscuity warranted further investigation. It is one of life's little ironies that a woman as free with her favours as the jazz-club owner appeared to be often attracted jealous men. And a man who thought he was on to a good thing would sometimes get violent if, suddenly, he was deprived of those favours.

It was about nine o'clock by the time we got to the Starlight Club, and it was throbbing. I suppose the notoriety of having had its drummer murdered in front of a paying audience guaranteed a good gate, as they say in the football world.

The Jazz Kittens were performing as usual, although without the services of Cyril

Underwood, alias Freddie Peacock, some-time trumpeter and armed robber. They had, however, summoned up a spare horn-player from somewhere, and were managing to play some quite decent jazz numbers. So Dave told me. Something else I learned about Dave was that he was very keen on jazz, and muttered names like Chris Barber and Dave Brubeck and Jellyroll Morton, all of which were meaningless to me. I have heard of Louis Armstrong, though.

I may have mentioned before that some-where in the Metropolitan Police District there is a huge kaleidoscope that some vin-dictive hand takes a delight in shaking. And it happened tonight.

We crossed the floor to the office and I pushed open the door.

Erica was seated behind the desk in her leather office chair. But it was turned away from us and her short blonde hair was only just visible above the chair's high back.

'It's us again, Erica,' I said, but there was no reply.

I walked round to face her and there it was.

A small entry wound in her left temple that had all the signs of a pistol shot discharged at close range.

I went through the standard first-aid rou-tine of applying a finger to her carotid artery, but there was no sign of a pulse.

'Topping weather we're having,' said Dave,

and then leaped into action. Pulling out his mobile and calling 999 as he ran, he sped towards the entrance, intent on not letting anyone in or out until the cavalry arrived to take over.

I looked around the office. There was no sign of a handgun, so that ruled out suicide. Nor was there any indication that there might have been a struggle. On her own admission, Erica could take care of herself, and Frank Seaton's statement that she'd once kneed him painfully in the crotch, and then chinned him, supported that. It appeared that she had been taken by surprise.

'The feet have arrived, guv,' said Dave, reappearing ten minutes later – he always referred to the Uniform Branch as 'the feet' – 'and I've got Gavin Creasey to send for the usual back-up.'

A uniformed inspector appeared in the office doorway. 'I've got tapes up round the premises, sir,' he said. 'Getting to be a habit.' He was the same inspector who'd been the incident officer the night Rod Skinner was murdered.

'Good. Get some of your chaps to start taking names and addresses, but no one's to leave. OK?'

'Right, sir.'

Within thirty minutes, Henry Mortlock – on call yet again – was on the scene, and moments later Linda Mitchell and her team of forensic practitioners had arrived.

Henry opened his ghoulish box of tricks and began the task of determining cause and time of death, although I knew he wouldn't tell me either until after the post-mortem.

But I had to try. 'Prepared to take a cock-shy, Henry?' I asked hopefully.

'At a guess, Harry dear boy, I'd say dead not more than two hours, possibly less, but that's subject to my findings at—'

'I know,' I said. 'Wait for the PM.'

'Howard Leech could have had time to do it and get back to World's End before we got there, guv.' Dave made this thoughtful observation while leaning against the doorpost with his hands in his pockets.

'Possibly,' I agreed. 'Dave, get round the staff and find out if and when any of them came in here. There's the bar staff, the band, those two daft waitresses, and anyone else you come across. And find out if anyone saw Howard Leech in here this evening.'

As Dave departed, Kate Ebdon came through the door. 'I've got some of the team with me, guv, and I've called the rest out. They should be here as soon as they can make it.'

There was no doubt that I was lumbered with this latest murder. It would be no good appealing to the commander for help; he thought that two murders could be solved as easily as one. Which reminded me. Reluc-

225

tantly I pulled out my mobile and punched in his home number.

Fortunately the commander is a great social climber, and Mrs Commander even more so, or so I've heard. And tonight, being a Saturday, they were probably dining with someone they perceived to be of influence. Whatever, there was no reply; just his wife's plummy tones on his answering machine telling me that she and her husband were 'unavailable to take your call'. I decided not to leave a message. Instead I rang Gavin Creasey and asked him to try contacting the commander from time to time. I'd enough on my plate without the big white chief offering advice down the phone from his detached residence in Orpington.

Kate Ebdon's team began to report back. No one had seen Howard Leech in the club that evening, but that didn't mean he hadn't been there because most of those questioned had said they didn't know him anyway.

The last person to have seen Erica Leech alive seemed to be the barman who told DC Sheila Armitage that he had gone into Erica's office at about eight o'clock. He had wanted the keys to the cellar, which she had given him. She was still working on the accounts for the tax people, she'd told him, and didn't want to be disturbed again until she'd finished. She told him to hold on to the keys in case he needed them again.

All of which meant that Henry Mortlock's assessment of death occurring within the previous two hours could now be shortened to an hour or less.

And that let Howard Leech off the hook; we had been talking to him an hour ago, and had come straight here from World's End.

Each member of Kate's 'legwork' team had asked whether anyone had heard a pistol shot. No one had. But given that the Jazz Kittens were blasting out their own particular brand of trad jazz, that came as no surprise.

Eventually Linda Mitchell and her assistants finished photographing the scene and examining surfaces for fingerprints. They had gone over the carpet in Erica's office with their E-vac machine, a device guaranteed to pick up the most minute of fibres and other deposits left by anyone who had been there. I'm sure that Gladys Gurney, my cleaning lady, would have loved to own one of those machines.

So far, everything we had was negative. No one had seen anyone going into Erica's office, no one had heard anything unusual – if you ignore the few bum notes played by the stand-in horn-player – and there were no overt signs to point us in the direction of either a motive or a murderer.

Kate Ebdon said that she'd run the barman's particulars through CRO, just in case.

'Just in case what, Kate?' I asked.

'Just in case he was the one who topped her, guv,' said Kate. 'Might be a mate of the Wembley Five.'

I groaned, but then Dave put in his two-penn'orth.

'We'll never be able to ask her now, guv,' he said.

'Ask her what?'

'How she came to meet Rod Skinner a year before he started to play drums here.'

It was midnight and there was nothing further to do right now. Erica Leech's murder had opened up the unpalatable vista of more countless useless statements to be taken and read through, and reports from Henry Mortlock and Linda Mitchell to be studied, analysed and acted upon.

I pondered the proposition that the same killer was responsible for both Erica's murder and Skinner's, something that may narrow the field a bit. But if that were the case, he must have possessed a positive arsenal of weapons. Well, certainly a sawn-off shotgun and a handgun. And that pointed to the criminal community. Normally God-fearing, law-abiding citizens do not arm themselves to that extent, even though the government's limp-wristed approach to crime may just tempt them to get tooled up.

Most television viewers are led to believe that

it needs only two CID officers to investigate a murder, the detective chief inspector and his sidekick. And half the time the TV chief inspector never knows whether he's a chief inspector or an inspector. He really ought to find out because the difference in pay can be as much as eight grand a year.

The reality is that there are at least twenty officers at work solving a killing, sometimes many more. The DCI is certainly the officer in charge of the case, and was once likened, by some academic copper at the Police College, to the conductor of a vast orchestra. Well, you can forget that. There are times when I'm convinced he's a one-man band.

But fortunately I have Dave Poole and Kate Ebdon and her team.

Sunday was not a day of rest for them. Names and addresses of the Saturday-night patrons of the Starlight Club had been taken, and lists of them had been allocated to Kate's detectives. They were now out and about taking statements that I knew would be largely useless. But every once in a while there comes a glimmer of light that enables further enquiries to lead to something valuable.

But not in this case. Remarkable though it might seem, no one had seen anyone enter Erica Leech's office and shoot her dead. And then disappear.

On Monday morning, I received Henry Mortlock's report of the post-mortem.

Erica had been shot at close range with a nine-millimetre-calibre handgun. Death had been instantaneous. Well, it would be, wouldn't it?

Linda Mitchell's scientific examination of the scene was similarly unhelpful. No cartridge case had been found, ergo the killer had either taken it with him – if he'd used an automatic – or he'd used a revolver, which wouldn't have ejected the shell case anyway.

Later that morning, however, there came a handy, and at once confusing, snippet of information. The ballistics examiner had compared the round taken from Erica's cranium with other rounds found at various scenes of crime.

And the round that had killed Erica Leech tallied with a round recovered at the Wembley safety-deposit job five years ago.

One of the robbers had discharged a handgun into the ceiling, just to put the frighteners on the security guards, but none of the guards knew which villain had done it. Probably on account of them all wearing masks at the time.

Erica's killer certainly wasn't Freddie Peacock, known musically as Cyril Underwood. Last Saturday morning, the district judge at West London court had banged him up in Brixton prison, and there he remained. The

'Wembley Five' were doing time, doubtless playing volleyball, weight training and watching television, and Rod Skinner was dead. And the Heston Services lot were also banged up.

However, it is a fact that villains tend to hand their weapons around. Indeed there are 'faces' in the underworld who specialize as armourers, hiring out weapons for a job. Usually there is a heavy additional fee if the weapon was used because that necessitates its destruction. Unless of course the aforementioned armourer wants to work off a grudge by hiring out a suspect weapon to a 'foe'. Like a grass. Thus rendering him liable to prosecution for a crime he did not commit. If he's unlucky enough to get nicked in possession of the weapon, that is. The life of a villain can be very hard at times.

However, given the time lapse between the commission of the Wembley job and the apprehension of those convicted of it, it is likely that they would have unloaded their shooters. In more ways than one.

The inescapable conclusion was that the weapon used to kill Erica Leech could have passed through numerous felonious hands in the past five years.

And that made my job bloody difficult. If not impossible.

'Ah, Mr Brock, a moment of your time. You too, Sergeant Poole.'

231

Bloody hell! The commander had come among us.

'Yes, sir.' We followed *el supremo* into his office.

'Tell me about this homicide at the, er...' The commander paused and fingered a single sheet of paper across his otherwise virgin desktop. 'The Starlight Club.' He never called them murders, just in case the jury found them to be manslaughter. Bit of a pedant, is the commander.

'I tried to contact you on Saturday evening, sir, but there was no answer. In the interests of security, I didn't leave a message on your answering machine.'

'Quite right and proper, Mr Brock. As a matter of fact the lady wife and I were dining with friends in Bromley. He's something big in the City, you know.'

'Very pleasant, sir,' I said. The commander's problem was that the pedestal upon which he'd placed himself wasn't quite as high as he thought it was. I knew very well that the moment he ceased to be a high-ranking copper and became a civilian he'd be of no further use to his 'influential' acquaintances, and they'd drop him like a stone.

'Now then, how are you getting on, Mr Brock?'

I'm not getting on at all, sport.

'We're making progress, sir,' I said, and told him that the round that killed Erica had come from the same gun that had been used at Wembley.

'An early arrest, then, would you say?' The commander primped his pocket handkerchief and adjusted the half-moon spectacles he believed gave him an air of gravitas.

'I'm afraid it's not that easy, sir,' I said. 'There's still a lot to be done.'

'However, sir,' put in Dave, *'labor omnia vincit.'*

'Quite so, Sergeant Poole,' murmured the commander as though he'd understood what Dave was talking about.

'What the hell did that mean, Dave?' I asked once we were back in the incident room.

'Work conquers all things, sir,' said Dave smugly.

Fourteen

'We're going to have to speak to Dick Norton, Dave. See if he can throw any light on this firearm that was used to murder Erica.'

I remembered 'Flash' Norton from my years on the Flying Squad when I was a sergeant. He was a sharp, switched-on, typical Flying Squad DI with dark, slightly greying wavy hair. It was rumoured that he had an East End *schneider* under his thumb because he was always nattily dressed, and never seemed to wear the same suit more than three or four times. He had an eye for the women, and they for him, and it was well known that he had a bird on the side, if not two or three. And he was renowned for the number of villains he knew and the prodigious stable of informants he ran.

'Who's Dick Norton, guv?'

'He was the guy who nicked the Wembley Five. See if you can find out where he's stationed now.'

Dave returned to my office some ten minutes later. 'He retired three years ago, guv.'

'Brilliant,' I said. 'Don't tell me, he now

lives in Australia or America or somewhere that's equally inaccessible.'

'No, as a matter of fact he lives in Saltdean, just along the coast from Brighton. Looks like a day at the seaside, guv. Want me to look up the train times?'

'I reckon so,' I said. 'I don't fancy going all that way by road. Give him a bell and ask if it's OK to pop down and see him on Monday.'

We arrived at Brighton railway station at about three o'clock on the Monday afternoon, and took an expensive taxi ride along the coast to Saltdean. God knows what the commander will say when he gets my claim for expenses. It was just as well that I hadn't asked for permission to go to Australia or America on the off-chance of finding out something useful.

Norton's bungalow in Donahue Drive was a typical white-stuccoed retirement property, similar in every particular to all the others in the road. I often wondered why blokes like him leave the frenetic life of London's Flying Squad to settle in places like that. I suspected that his neighbours were also pensioners whose only topic of conversation was how well, or how badly, their dahlias were doing this year.

'Dick Norton?' I hardly recognized the stooped, bald-headed man in an old green cardigan who opened the door. He was wearing glasses and a hearing aid, and bore little resemblance to the man I remembered. Clearly 'Flash' Norton had gone to seed.

'Harry! Long time no see.'

'Hello, Dick,' I said. 'This is DS Dave Poole.'

Norton shook hands with me and nodded in Dave's direction. 'Come in, Harry. The missus has just made a cup of tea.' He gave me a crooked grin. 'Unless you'd prefer a drop of the hard stuff. You never used to say no to a bevvy as I recall.'

'Wouldn't go amiss,' I said, as Norton shuffled ahead of Dave and me into a fussily furnished sitting room on the front of the house. Among other things there was a Flying Squad wall plaque, a row of inscribed tankards on the mantelpiece and, horror of horrors, a small purpose-made display case containing his Long Service and Good Conduct Medal. He opened a small cabinet, took out a half-bottle of supermarket whisky and poured substantial measures into three cheap tumblers.

A grey-haired woman in a flowered apron appeared in the doorway with a tray of tea, and stared crossly at the whisky. 'I wish you'd told me you were going to have that *before* I made the tea, Dick,' she said.

'This is the wife,' said Norton ignoring her protest. 'Meet Harry Brock, Doreen. He's a

DCI now. Done well for himself, hasn't he?'

We shook hands with Mrs Norton and then sat down.

'I'll leave you to it, then,' said Doreen Norton. 'I know what you coppers are like when you start talking about the Job. And I've heard it all before,' she added with a derisive lift of her eyebrows. 'I'll be in the kitchen if you want anything, Dick.' And she left the room taking the tea tray with her.

'Huh! Women!' muttered Norton.

'Nice little place you've got here, Dick,' I said without meaning a word of it. It struck me as a crummy sort of house in which to finish out one's days, but I was still coming to terms with the change in Norton that the years had wrought.

'Yeah, smashing, Harry. And you can see the sea if you stand on the fucking roof.'

'You're enjoying your retirement, then.' I intended the comment to sound sarcastic.

But Norton thought it was a serious observation. 'More or less.' He handed round the glasses of whisky. 'Trouble is, I left it too late.'

'Too late?'

'Yeah. I was daft really, but I stayed on till the age limit – plus extensions – hoping I might make the next rank. But then they started cutting back on promotion. Said it had to do with budgets and all that crap. As if you can budget for a bloody murder. I ask you! Plus the guv'nor we had at the time had it in for me. When I packed the Job in, I tried to get something in security, but when you're sixty they look down their noses at you, give you a torch and offer you night duty on a building site. Me, an ex-DI on the Flying Squad. Bloody insulting I call it. Still, only another two years and I get the old-age pension.'

Norton had become a typical whingeing old copper, always blaming someone else for his own inadequacies, and I was beginning to doubt whether he'd be able to help me track down the errant firearm that had been used in the Wembley heist. He certainly seemed to have lost some of the sharpness for which he'd been renowned when he was a Squad DI. But now that I was here, I had to try.

I explained about the murder of Erica Leech, and how the gun used to kill her had featured in the Wembley heist. And I asked Norton about the arrests of Ted 'Break-in' Glass and the other four.

'That was a good knock-off, Harry, although I say it myself.' A sparkle came into Norton's eyes as he recalled what doubtless he would call 'the good old days'. He then went on to tell us what we knew already, about the robber called Dusty and how they'd eventually tracked him down to his house in Islington and turned him into a supergrass. 'Bit of luck that was: one of the team calling him "Dusty".' He leaned back with a satisfied smile on his face.

'I was told that one of the villains fired a shot into the ceiling of the safety deposit, Dick,' I said. 'Any idea who he was?'

Norton topped up our glasses from his dwindling bottle of Scotch and sat down again. 'We heard about that from one of the guards,' he said, 'and I asked Miller if he knew who it was. For what it's worth, he told me it was a bloke called Watson. Lenny Watson. In fact, Miller was bloody annoyed about it. Reckoned that loosing off a round like that could have alerted the Old Bill.' He scoffed at the very thought. 'Certainly wouldn't've done these days. Hardly ever see a copper on the streets now. Wouldn't have happened when you and I were PCs on the street.' There seemed no end to Norton's catalogue of continuous complaints.

It was just my bloody luck that Lenny Watson happened to be in the nick furthest from London: Winson Green in Birmingham.

'Was the weapon ever found, Dick?' I hoped that it hadn't been seized after the raid because that would imply some police malpractice. The disappearance of a firearm from a police property store would be the sort of complication I could well do without.

'No. By the time we got around to feeling Miller's collar and scurfed up the rest of the team, they'd unloaded any incriminating evidence they might have had.' Norton gave a savage laugh. 'Except the cash and the sparklers, of course. But once Miller started singing, and we'd nicked his mates, we had that off them. Well, most of it. There were a few whispers about some extra gelt that the losers didn't own up to – probably villains themselves – but I don't know about that. Generally speaking, though, I suppose our little team had done the usual stupid things like pissing it up against the wall, and flashing it about up the West End. They never bloody learn, you know, Harry. But no, we didn't find any shooters. I s'pose they'd hired 'em, but we couldn't find the armourer. If Miller knew who it was, and he must have done, he certainly wasn't saying.'

'Were there any sawn-off shotguns used in that heist, Dick?' asked Dave.

'Not that I know of,' said Norton curtly, and turned back to me. I got the impression that he didn't care much for black detectives. 'The security guards reckoned they only saw handguns. Might have had some sawn-offs stashed in their getaway car, I suppose. Why d'you ask?'

'Because Miller was blown away with a sawn-off in the Starlight Club.' I'd thought that Norton would have known why we'd posed the question. That he'd queried it was further proof that he'd lost his edge.

'Yes, of course. Saw it on the box.' Norton waved at a small television set in the corner of the room. 'Well, Harry, I wish you luck. Sounds a tricky one. None of your snouts singing?'

'Not a peep, Dick,' I said.

Norton nodded. 'Yeah, a tricky one,' he said again.

I stood up before Norton could embark on the usual litany of reminiscences that are characteristic of many retired policemen. 'Thanks for your help, Dick,' I said, and meant it. I'd come for a name and I'd got one. But whether Lenny Watson would talk to me was another matter. I took a bottle of Famous Grouse whisky from my briefcase and put it on the coffee table.

Norton laughed. 'I see you haven't forgotten the traditional tribute, Harry. I hope it's on incidentals.'

'Of course it is, Dick.' 'Incidentals' is the general heading detectives use to claim small expenses that aren't covered by other allowances. And sure as hell a bottle of whisky as a gift for a retired DI is not catered for in the regulations.

'Ah,' sighed Norton, 'those were the days.'

An expert at short-circuiting problems, Dave spent half an hour on the phone as soon as we returned to Curtis Green. Minutes later, he gave me the result of his efforts.

'I spoke to the prison liaison officer at West Midlands Police, guv. He rang back to say that Lenny Watson is willing to see us tomorrow. I suggested that we'd get there at about eleven o'clock, and the PLO said he'd meet us at New Street railway station and take us direct to the prison.'

'Great. So what time do we have to leave here, Dave?'

'The nine-ten from Euston arriving at New Street at ten-forty-one,' said Dave.

'Bloody hell! An early start, then?' I said, thinking that I would have to get to Waterloo from Surbiton, and then across to Euston. In the rush hour.

'I reckon so, guv.'

'I'll meet you at Euston.'

'DI Charlie Gardner, boss,' said the prison liaison officer, and waved a hand at a marked police car. 'Hope you don't mind travelling in that,' he said, 'but the traffic's bloody awful, even at this time of day, and it helps to have blues and twos.'

I suppose the West Midlands police driver was intent on showing us that he was every bit as good as his Metropolitan counterparts. Whatever the reason, he carved a priority passage through the west of the city to Winson Green Road, depositing us at the prison gates within what seemed like minutes of our arrival in Birmingham.

'This guy Watson is not the man he used to be, boss,' warned Gardner as we waited in reception for an escort. 'He's lost weight and keeps himself very much to himself. Refuses to take part in association or any of the activities in the prison. Frankly I don't think he'll live long enough to see the end of his sentence.'

'Is he suffering from something, sir?' asked Dave.

'I would think so, Sarge, but patient confidentiality operates here as well as outside,' said Gardner and turning to me as a prison officer arrived, added, 'I'll leave you to it, boss. I'll be with the governor, so perhaps you'd get one of the POs to ring for me when you're done.'

It was blatantly obvious that prison life did not agree with Lenny Watson. Looking much older than his forty-five years, he shuffled into the interview room. His wispy grey hair was over his ears and collar, and he looked desperately thin. A grey-bearded grey face matched the grey jogging trousers and singlet he was wearing, and which hung on him as though they'd been intended for someone three sizes bigger.

'What d'you want to talk about, then?' asked Watson listlessly, once I'd introduced Dave and me.

'The Wembley heist.'

'Yeah, I s'pose so. Long time ago now.'

243

'You heard that Dennis Miller was murdered, I suppose.'

'Yeah. Bloody good job too.'

'Any idea who topped him, Lenny?' I asked, throwing Watson a cigarette.

But Watson leaned forward and flicked the cigarette back in my direction. 'I've got cancer,' he said. 'And it's what you'll get if you keep on smoking them coffin nails. No, I've no idea who topped the bastard, but I wish someone had done it about six years ago.'

'I heard that you were the guy who fired a shot into the ceiling at the safety-deposit place, Lenny.'

Watson gave a throaty chuckle that quickly degenerated into an almost uncontrollable cough. 'You going to do me for that, are you?' he asked, once he'd recovered. 'Could tack it on the end, I s'pose, but I got sent down for twenty-five and I ain't going to finish it. The only way I'm leaving here is in a wooden box. Yeah, I let one off at the ceiling, just to put the frighteners on one stupid sod who wanted to argue. I dunno why. It wasn't their bleedin' gear we was nicking.'

'What happened to that firearm, Lenny?' I asked.

For a moment or two, I thought that Watson wasn't going to answer, but it seemed he was having trouble remembering. 'I give it to Dusty Miller straight after the job.'

'Were you the one who used his name during the heist?'

'Probably. Why? What's that got to do with anything?'

'It was because of that you were captured, Lenny. The Flying Squad did a trawl through records and found that the only robber capable of doing a job like the Wembley one, and who wasn't in stir, was Dennis Miller, known as Dusty. And the moment he was nicked, he started singing.'

'Well I'm buggered,' said Watson. 'I never knew that. I mean I never knew that's how you lot found Miller.'

'Any idea what Miller did with the shooter?' asked Dave.

'No, mate.'

'What was it?'

'A Walther nine-mill,' said Watson without hesitation. It seemed his memory was still good when it came to talking about the tools of his trade.

'Did you have any sawn-off shotguns in your armoury when you did that job, Lenny?' I asked.

'Yeah, a couple, but we never took 'em up Wembley. Couldn't see as how we'd need 'em. Why d'you wanna know that?'

'Because Miller was blown away with a sawn-off,' said Dave.

Watson laughed again, a rattling laugh that died in his throat. 'How's Daph?' he asked, suddenly changing the subject. 'I s'pose you must've seen her if you're doing Miller's topping.'

'Daph?' I queried.

Dave leaned across and whispered in my ear. 'Daphne Miller, sir, now known as Babs Skinner.'

'Of course.' I turned back to Watson. 'She's fine, Lenny. Enjoying herself and drinking to excess. Why are you interested in her?'

'We had a fling once, Daph and me. A bit of all right, she was.'

'Oh? When was this?'

'Before the Wembley job, obviously. Well, it would've been, wouldn't it?' Watson tried a careful laugh. 'That Miller was a bastard, always cheating on his missus. I never knew why we trusted him. Half the time he'd be up West shagging some bird. Didn't give a fuck about Daph. Well, one night, after we'd had a bit of a drink-up down Miller's place in Islington, and he'd got hisself as pissed as a fart, Daph poured her heart out to me. So one thing led to another and while her old man was lying arseholed on the kitchen floor we had it off there and then. And we done it quite regular after that. If we'd pulled a stroke and was a bit flush I'd take Daph to a posh hotel down Chislehurst way and fuck the arse off her. About once a week. And if we was short of the readies, we'd go to a pub her sister-in-law kept down Bermondsey and we'd have it off in one of the upstairs rooms.'

'She had a sister-in-law, did she?' queried Dave.

'Yeah, married to Daph's brother. But he got hisself killed in some car accident, about the time we was nicked, and his missus married again and pushed off to Canada. So that was the end of that. In more ways than one.'

'Didn't Dennis object?' I asked.

'I don't think he knew, but I couldn't've given a toss if he did. After all, he was having it off some other place. Daph shouldn't never have got wed to that stupid sod. Too good for him, she was. Didn't know how to treat a good woman, didn't Miller. Anyhow, give her my best if you happen to bump into her.'

'Well, thanks for your help, Lenny,' I said, as Dave and I stood up.

'Help? I never said nuffink. Wotcha fink I am, a bleedin' grass?'

And with that, Lenny Watson shuffled out of the interview room. Two months later he was dead. But by then, I'd discovered who had killed Rod Skinner, formerly Dennis Miller, and sometime James Wright. And I'd arrested his killer and Erica Leech's.

We returned to Curtis Green at five o'clock that afternoon, and started to struggle with our dilemma. Lenny Watson had given his Walther nine-millimetre to Rod Skinner after the raid on the Wembley safety deposit. Skinner had almost certainly disposed of it because the police who arrested him searched his house at Islington and found nothing. Except a substantial quantity of cash and what was left of the jewellery. So where the bloody hell had the Walther gone?

There remained only one thing to do: interview the other prisoners who had been involved in the heist. I knew from the outset that it would be a futile exercise. They probably didn't know what had happened to the pistol, and even if they did they probably wouldn't tell me.

That, of course, is the problem with prisoners serving a long sentence. They don't have to talk to the police, and if they do, they don't have to tell them anything.

'Why don't we have a word with Freddie Peacock first, guv?' suggested Dave.

'Why him?'

'He's on remand in Brixton and he might know something about this missing shooter. Apart from anything else he might think that we could use a bit of influence with the CPS to get him a lesser sentence.'

'We couldn't tell him that, Dave,' I said. 'That would be dishonest.'

'Who said anything about telling him, guv,' said Dave as he extracted a banana from his makeshift briefcase. 'There is such a thing as insinuation.'

'You're a devious bastard, Dave.'
'Yes, sir.'

I decided that we should have an early night. Dave went home to Madeleine – who wasn't due to appear in a new ballet until next week – and I went home to Surbiton.

I let myself into my flat and was surprised to see a vase of fresh flowers on the table in the hall. This was a mystery. Gladys Gurney, my faithful 'lady who did', was many things, but a provider of fresh flowers she was not. Apart from anything else, Gladys did not clean my flat on a Tuesday.

I walked into the kitchen, intent upon getting a cold beer from the fridge. The crockery from the hurried breakfast I'd had before setting off for Birmingham that morning had been washed up and put away.

Then I realized what had happened. Some time ago I'd given a key to Gail, but she'd never used it before, other than when I was already at home.

I went into the sitting room and there she was, reclining on the sofa.

'Hi!' She stood up and smiled.

I smiled too because as she walked towards me, she abandoned her robe to leave it in a little cloud on the carpet.

'You're very playful this evening, darling,' I said, admiring her figure.

'And I've only just started, buster,' she said.

249

Fifteen

I was beginning to get sick of the inside of Her Majesty's prisons. I seemed to be spending more time in such places than in my own office.

'Do I need to have a brief here, Mr Brock?' was Freddie Peacock's opening question when we met in one of Brixton prison's interview rooms.

'Shouldn't think so, Freddie,' I said. 'I was hoping you'd be able to help me.'

Peacock laughed. 'Anything in it for me?' he asked.

'You know my guv'nor can't answer a question like that, Freddie,' said Dave, 'but, well, you never can tell.'

Nice one, Dave. I had made no promises, and even the hint of a promise made by my sergeant ostensibly on my behalf would carry no weight whatsoever. Certainly not with the Crown Prosecution Service, and even less with a judge.

'When the raid took place at Wembley, Freddie, who fired a round into the ceiling of the safety depository?' I asked, seeking to confirm what Dick Norton had told us.

250

'I don't know, Mr Brock. I wasn't there.'

That was inevitable, I suppose. Peacock had yet to stand trial for his part in the Wembley heist, and he obviously feared that anything he said to me now would be trotted out at the Old Bailey. But he seemed to have forgotten that when we arrested him, he'd admitted his involvement.

'I haven't cautioned you, Freddie,' I said, 'so nothing you say can be used in evidence. Apart from which, as a shrewd operator like you will have noticed, there isn't a tape recorder in here either.'

'Got a fag, Mr Brock?'

I gave him one of my Marlboros and waited while he considered his position, as politicians are wont to say when they're in deep mire.

'It was Lenny Watson, the stupid sod. Made enough noise to wake the dead. Didn't half get up Dusty Miller's nose.'

'Not half as much as it would have done if he'd known Watson was giving his missus a seeing-to,' said Dave quietly.

'Do what?' Peacock's face registered astonishment and then annoyance.

'You heard,' said Dave.

'Bloody hell!' Peacock sat back and mulled over what Dave had just said. 'The saucy bitch,' he said eventually. 'So was I.'

'Where did this go on?' I asked.

'Up her place at Islington. Whenever Miller

251

went out of an evening – and that was most nights – she'd give me a bell and I'd go round and give her one. I didn't live far away then.'

'Well, she was obviously fitting you in when she wasn't fitting Lenny in,' said Dave. 'To coin a phrase.'

'The saucy cow,' muttered Peacock again, and shook his head. But then he laughed. 'Still, she was worth it. Bit of a goer in her younger days, was that Daphne. Give her my regards if you see her again.'

'Anyway, Freddie, I haven't come here to talk about your love life. D'you know what happened to Watson's shooter after you split?'

'Not a clue, Mr Brock. I'd help you if I could, but I dunno what happened to it. Why? What's it got to do with anything? After all that job's nigh-on six years old now.'

'That shooter was used to murder Erica Leech.'

'Christ, I never knew she'd been topped. When did that go down, then?' Peacock's face expressed profound shock at this piece of news, and I wondered why he should have been so upset. It wasn't long before I found out.

'Last Saturday night. At the Starlight Club.'

'Who the bleedin' hell'd want to top a lovely girl like Erica?' Peacock shook his head and looked down at the table, a sad expression on his face.

'I've no idea, Freddie. That's why I'm asking questions.'

'What a bloody turn up,' continued Peacock mournfully, still shaking his head. 'The poor cow. She was a bit of all right, was Erica.'

'Don't tell me you had a fling with her as well,' I said, recalling what Erica's estranged husband had said about her obsession with sex and her frequent change of lovers.

'Only the once,' admitted Peacock. 'It was while we were setting up one evening, about half an hour before the club opened. The barman came across and said that Erica had rung through and asked if I'd go and see her in her office. I thought she must want to discuss something about the band or the music we were playing, and so I just barged in. Well, you would, wouldn't you? But she was getting changed, and there she was in her Eddies and—'

'Her *what*?' interrupted Dave, to whom some elements of criminal argot were a mystery even to him.

'Eddie Grundies: undies,' said Peacock. 'You know, B-and-Bs: bra and briefs. Anyhow, there was no messing about. It was obvious what she wanted. She locked the door and come on to me straight away. The next thing was that we were across that big desk of hers and I was giving it what for. But the next time I went in, a week later – hoping for an action replay, like – she give me the cold shoulder and told me to piss off.' He sighed, apparently at opportunities lost and never to be repeated.

I regret to say that our chat with Freddie Peacock set the pattern for all the others. Dave and I spent the remainder of the week interviewing the rest of the Wembley Five. On the Thursday, we spoke to John 'Spike' Hughes in Wandsworth and Steve Noble in Canterbury, and on Friday we saw Peter Briggs in Parkhurst and visited Ted Glass again in Wormwood Scrubs. None of them knew anything about the missing handgun, or if they did they weren't saying. All we achieved was confirmation of what we had been told by ex-DI Dick Norton and Freddie Peacock, and the admission by Lenny Watson that it was he who'd fired the round into the ceiling.

That left just one other person who may know what had happened to Lenny Watson's Walther nine-millimetre. And that was Babs Skinner.

It was with a marked lack of enthusiasm that Dave and I drove down to Cobham on Saturday morning.

It was another sweltering hot day, and by the time we arrived at The Gables at eleven thirty, the sun was high in the sky. I had worked on the principle that Babs Skinner was, in all probability, someone who did not rise too early. Particularly if she was suffering from a hangover, which, given her prodigious intake of gin, she almost certainly would be.

On the drive of the Skinner house was a new Mercedes open-topped sports car that I'd not seen before. Dave took the number.

I was not too surprised therefore when, after some considerable delay, the front door was opened by Charlie Hardy, antiques restorer and Babs's on-demand toyboy. Neither was I too surprised that he was wearing an open towelling wrap over a pair of boxer swimming shorts.

'Oh, hello,' he said, as ingenuous as ever. 'You'll be wanting Babs, I suppose. Come on through. She's in the pool.'

We followed Hardy out to the patio just as Babs emerged from the water. I have to say that there are not too many women in their mid-forties who can get away with wearing a micro-bikini, but Babs was one of them.

'Mr Brock darling, what a pleasant surprise. And you too, Sergeant darling.' She squeezed the water from her peroxide-blonde hair and sat down in one of the half-dozen or so aluminium chairs that were dotted around the pool area. 'Charlie, be a love and get these wonderful policemen a drink.' Little droplets of water clung to her body, but she made no attempt to dry herself.

255

I noticed with some apprehension that there was a gin and tonic on the table, and that her speech was already slurred.

'Just something soft for us, please, Mr Hardy,' I said. I had no intention of getting into a G & T race with Mrs Skinner.

'Coca-Cola all right?' asked Hardy.

'Fine,' I said.

'Well, it's nice to see you again, Mr Brock,' said Babs, crossing her legs and waggling a foot. Her toenails were painted bright red and there was a gold chain around her left ankle. 'But I suppose you're here on business.' She reached across and picked up her drink.

'Yes, I'm afraid so.'

'Oh, what a shame. Never mind. So what can I do for you?' Babs took a long draught of her gin and tonic, let out a sigh of satisfaction and leaned back in her chair.

Charlie Hardy returned with two tins of Coke and two glasses on a tray. And a beer for himself. 'It's all right,' he said, following my glance, 'it's alcohol-free.'

'I take it that's your car outside, then,' I said.

'Nice, isn't it? Babs bought it for me.'

Obviously a reward for services rendered.

'Yes, very nice.' I took a sip of Coke and turned to Babs. 'I went to see Lenny Watson on Tuesday,' I said.

'Lenny Watson. Well, well. God, that brings

back memories. How is the dear man?' Babs turned to Hardy. 'Lenny was one of my lovers, Charlie. He used to take me to a hotel down near Chislehurst at least once a week.' She looked dreamily across the pool, he was bloody good.'

Charlie Hardy didn't seem at all put out by this revelation, but then I recalled that he'd told me his arrangement with Babs was purely a sexual one.

'He's dying of cancer, Babs,' I said. 'I don't think he's got long to live.'

'Oh, how awful.' Babs looked sad. 'And you can blame Rod for that,' she said. 'He'd never have been sent to prison if it hadn't been for Rod turning informer.'

'We also saw Freddie Peacock. In Brixton. He and Lenny both asked to be remembered to you.'

'Really?' Babs looked sharply at me. 'Have you been checking up on all my lovers, Mr Brock darling?' She didn't seem at all surprised that Peacock was back in England, and I wondered, briefly, if she'd known all along.

'How many lovers did you have, Babs?' asked Hardy with a wide grin.

'You mind your own business, Charlie my sweet. Just be satisfied that you're the one who shares my bed now,' said Babs, and laughed. 'My Charlie's a very good performer, you know, Mr Brock. He's very inventive.

Wonderful what he does with his hands,' she added as the dreamy expression returned. 'Wears a girl out, he does.'

'I do my best.' Hardy didn't seem at all embarrassed that his sexual prowess was being described to two comparative strangers.

'And your best is very good, lover,' Babs said to Hardy. 'Anyway, Mr Brock, you didn't tell me why you went to see Lenny and Freddie.'

'When the Wembley job was pulled,' I began, 'Lenny Watson fired a round into the ceiling of the safety depository.'

'I'm not surprised. Those boys were like that,' said Babs with a giggle. 'But they *were* robbers.' She finished her gin and tonic and handed her glass to Hardy. Without a word, he disappeared indoors. 'But why are you interested in all that? I thought you were trying to find out who'd killed Rod.'

'We are. But we're also trying to find out who murdered Erica Leech.'

'Erica Leech?'

'Yes. I mentioned her on one of the occasions I came to see you. I think I told you that she owned the jazz club where your late husband played drums with a group. She was having an affair with him, and about a year ago he took her on a three-week holiday to the South of France.'

'Well, that's bloody charming, that is,' said

Babs with a sudden show of spirit. 'The sod never took *me* to the South of France. A weekend in Paris was the most I ever got out of him. And then he didn't come with me.' She shot me an arch smile. 'So I went with someone else ... but Rod paid for it.' Without a word of thanks, she took her recharged glass from Charlie, who appeared to double as her faithful slave, responding to her every whim. I suppose she was worth it, and looking at her, I thought she probably was, coarse tart though she clearly was. 'So who murdered this Erica woman?' she asked.

'I don't know. That's what I'm trying to find out.'

'I'm afraid you're confusing me terribly, Mr Brock darling. First you tell me that you visit my ex-lovers in prison, and then you start talking about this Leech person. I really don't understand the connection.' Babs's words were now becoming quite slurred, but her concentration appeared not to have suffered too much as a result of her gin consumption.

'The handgun that was used to kill Mrs Leech was also used at Wembley, and it was the weapon that Lenny Watson fired into the ceiling.'

'Good heavens!' Babs took a large mouthful of her drink. 'But why are you telling me all this? I really don't understand.'

'Because, Babs, Lenny Watson said that

after the Wembley job he gave the handgun to Rod.'

'Whatever for?'

'For safekeeping, I suppose. But the reason I'm here is to ask whether you know anything about it.'

'Well, it's no good asking me what happened to it. After the raid at Wembley, when your people eventually caught up with Rod, they went through our house at Islington with a fine-tooth comb. There was a very nasty man from the Flying Squad called Merton or Norton, or something like that. A very rude man, he was. They stripped the beds, turned out all the cupboards and all the drawers of chests...' Babs paused and hiccupped. 'No, that's not right,' she slurred. 'It's chests of drawers, isn't it?' She enunciated each of the words slowly. 'Yes, that's it. And they pulled up the floorboards. I tell you, Mr Brock darling, they made a terrible mess, and I had to clear it all up after they arrested Rod.'

'So you've no idea what happened to this gun.'

'No idea at all. I didn't know anything about it. Didn't see it and don't know what happened to it. I didn't know anything about it.' Babs had started to repeat herself. By now it was obvious that the gin was getting to her, and I decided that nothing would be gained by questioning her any further. If she was as gin-sodden five years ago as she was now, I reckoned that she wouldn't have noticed the wretched pistol if someone had tucked it in her bra.

But then Dave, who had been listening patiently to our exchange, came to life. 'My guv'nor told you just now, Babs, that Rod had taken Erica Leech to the South of France for three weeks about a year ago. What reason did he give you for disappearing for that length of time?'

'He said someone had told him there was a … oh, what d'you call that, when someone's going to kill you?'

'A contract,' said Dave.

'I do believe you're right, Sergeant darling. He said he was worried that someone connected with the people he'd informed on would catch up with him. Anyway he said he had to get away until he found out who it was, and that he'd buy them off. I told him not to be stupid and that he should tell the police. But he said he couldn't do that because we'd run away from that witness thing we were in at Hatfield.'

I didn't bother to ask if Rod Skinner had told his wife the name of this potential assassin, because I knew damned well that it was the excuse that Skinner had used to cover his holiday with Erica. Either that or Babs knew what he was up to and didn't care.

'And you believed that?' asked Dave.

Babs smiled foolishly. 'Don't be a silly boy, Sergeant darling. Of course I didn't,' she said and belched. 'Whoops! Sorry.' By now her words were running into each other and it was becoming increasingly difficult to understand what she was saying. 'I was certain he was with some tart, and you've just told me he was. Anyway, I didn't waste that fortnight—'

'Three weeks,' interjected Dave.

'Well, whatever it was. So I rang up a very special friend of mine' – Babs touched the side of her nose with a forefinger – 'and suggested he took care of me for a while. And he did, bless him. We went to a hotel in Brighton and only got up for meals.' And with that admission she hiccupped again. 'But he wasn't as good as you, lover,' she said to Charlie, reaching out and touching his hand.

'Well, Babs, we'll leave you to enjoy your swim,' I said, as Dave and I stood up.

Babs stood up too, but lurched and had she not clutched the table would undoubtedly have fallen over. 'Do come again, Mr Brock darling,' she said, and giggled. 'You too, Sergeant dear.' Still holding on to the table, she addressed the loyal Hardy. 'Charlie, darling, see these lovely policemen out and then come back here and take me to bed.'

Hardy raised his eyebrows and shook his

head. 'Sit down, Babs, before you fall down,' he said. 'I'll be back in a moment.'

'Is she always like that, Mr Hardy?' I asked as we reached the front door.

'I'm afraid so, Mr Brock. She once told me that Rod neglected her and was always out with his friends or with other women. She was very lonely and I think she turned to alcohol to cheer herself up. I've tried to get her to ease up on what she drinks, but it doesn't seem to be working. She's still a fantastic lover, though, even when she's drunk. Which is most of the time.'

I wondered briefly why on earth a well-built and good-looking young fellow like Hardy stayed with a lush like Babs Skinner. He must have had the pick of available and attractive women of his own age. But then I remembered the Mercedes sports car on the drive and knew why he stayed.

'Well, I don't know, Dave,' I said on the journey back to London. 'A gun that was used at Wembley disappears and no one knows where the bloody thing went. Until it turns up killing Erica Leech.'

'I've been thinking, guv,' said Dave, braking hard to avoid an idiot motorcyclist who had overtaken and cut in, 'that Charlie Hardy is a touch too innocent for my liking. Look at it like this. When we interviewed him at Esher, he reckoned that he first met Babs a year ago, at some dance in Cobham. Now, suppose he and Rod Skinner weren't as chummy as Hardy claimed. Skinner takes objection to Hardy screwing his missus, and threatens to sort him out. But Hardy's got his eye on the main chance, like the money. He follows Skinner and finds that he's in a band at the Starlight Club. So one Saturday, he goes up there and blows him away.'

'But where did he get the weapon from?' I asked, warming to Dave's theory.

'Either he found it at The Gables, because I can't believe that Rod Skinner would have left himself completely without some form of armament, just in case there *was* a contract out on him. Or, on the other hand, Hardy bought a shotgun, legit, and shortened the barrel himself. After all, he's got all the equipment to do it in that workshop of his.'

'You might just have hit on it, Dave,' I said, trying hard not to get too excited. I've been disappointed before. Many times. 'But you can't buy a shotgun without a certificate. So do a check.'

It wasn't until Monday morning that Dave was able to get hold of anyone in the department at the Yard that deals with shotgun certificates, but the result was worth waiting for.

'Hardy obtained a shotgun certificate about ten months ago, guv. The reason he gave was that he'd been invited to join a shoot in Guildford.'

'But did he actually buy a shotgun, Dave?'

'That I don't know, guv, and neither does licensing branch. The local nick should have done the occasional check, though, but there's a quicker way of finding out.'

'Which is?'

'We'll ask him ... sir.'

Charlie Hardy was working at a lathe when we arrived at his workshop later that morning. A radio on the bench was playing pop music. Loudly.

'Good morning,' I said.

Hardy turned. 'Oh hello.' He evinced no surprise that we had come to see him again only two days later, but there again it had been pure chance that he'd been at The Gables on Saturday morning. He turned off the radio. 'What can I do for you?'

'I understand you own a shotgun,' said Dave, making it a positive statement rather than a query.

'How did you know that?' asked Hardy, posing the question with his usual open-faced innocence.

'Because you have to be licensed by the police in order to possess a shotgun, and I belong to the police,' said Dave patiently, as though explaining a simple problem to a child.

'Oh, I see.'

'Where is the weapon?'

'Over there.' Hardy pointed to a steel cabinet in the corner of his workshop. 'It's locked and it's screwed to the wall, like it says in the regulations.' Despite his artless attitude, he obviously knew a thing or two about the law regarding firearms.

'May we see it?'

'Sure.' Hardy took a bunch of keys from a clip on the belt of his jeans and crossed to the cabinet. Unlocking it, he took out a new double-barrelled shotgun, broke it and laid it on the bench. 'There you are. A beauty, isn't it? Unfortunately I've never used it.'

'Oh? Why not?' Dave picked up the shotgun and examined it closely. Not that he had to do so to see that the barrel hadn't been reduced in length.

'Well,' said Hardy, 'when I was at the dance in Cobham – the one where I met Babs – I also met this guy who owned an estate just outside Guildford. We got talking and I said I'd always wanted to do some rough shooting. He said he couldn't offer me that, but he did have some pheasant on his estate and I was welcome to go down during the season.'

'So why didn't you?' I asked.

'It was rotten luck really, but he died about a fortnight later and the estate was sold to a company that was going to set up a conference centre. Still, I might be lucky enough to find somewhere, I suppose.' Hardy ran a hand over the shotgun and sighed. 'If not I'll sell it.'

'Where d'you live, Mr Hardy?' I asked.

'Here of course, Mr Brock. I've got a room at the back of the workshop. It's not much, just a bed, an armchair and a TV.'

'And when are you moving in with Babs Skinner?' asked Dave suddenly, taking a wild guess.

'How did you know about that?' For the first time since we'd interviewed Hardy, just over three weeks ago, he showed signs of being disconcerted.

'I didn't, but I do now,' said Dave. 'When was that arranged?'

'The day before yesterday.'

'So that would have been on the Saturday when we came down. Did this discussion take place before or after our visit?'

'After.'

It looked as though, at last, a motive was starting to emerge.

First of all Babs Skinner acquires herself a youthful stud in the shape of Charlie Hardy. Then her husband is murdered in Fulham, and within weeks, Hardy has acquired a top-of-the-range Mercedes convertible. And now he's about to shack up with Rod Skinner's widow, into accommodation that would far surpass the workshop he was living in at present. And Babs Skinner had money. Lots of money.

There were two points about that that worried me.

We only had Hardy's word for it that it was Babs who'd propositioned him at the dance in Cobham, rather than the other way round. Perhaps he had set his sights on a moneyed woman with a strong sexual appetite, and decided to ingratiate himself with her. And having learned something of Babs Skinner's past, I know that she would not have turned down the opportunity of being bedded by the much younger Hardy. To coin an apt phrase, she must've thought her luck had changed.

And secondly, it was he who told us that he was moving in to The Gables. Had Babs invited him in, or had he taken advantage of a drink-befuddled woman who seemed not to know what she was doing half the time? Or even all the time.

'One other thing, Mr Hardy,' I said. 'I've asked everyone else, but I forgot to ask you the routine question. Where were you the night that Rod Skinner was murdered?'

Again Hardy afforded us his familiar ingenuous grin. 'With Babs,' he said. 'In bed.'

Now I knew that we'd have to see Babs Skinner again. But somehow I doubted that we'd get any more sense out of her than we had done previously.

Sixteen

I didn't intend to waste any more time on Babs Skinner than I had to. I was determined this morning there would be no sitting around on the patio while she disported herself in the pool or got even more drunk.

'Mr Brock, darling. How nice.' When Babs appeared at the door, somewhat belatedly, her hair was tousled and she was wearing a full-length pink satin robe. 'Sorry I was so long, but I was in bed.'

I thought it impolitic to ask with whom she'd been in bed; I knew it wasn't Charlie Hardy because we'd just left him. But, taking the generous view, perhaps she'd been alone.

Babs showed us into the sitting room and opened the curtains before disappearing again. Moments later she returned with a glass of water to which she added a couple of large white tablets that fizzed up.

'Got a bit of a head, darlings,' she said, drinking the contents of the glass at a single swallow. 'Can I get you a drink?'

'No thanks, and we won't keep you long.'

She sat down, crossed her suntanned legs, and deliberately allowed the skirt of her robe to part so that they were exposed.

'We were speaking to Mr Hardy earlier this morning,' I said, 'and we asked him the question we've been asking everyone.'

'Whatever could that be?' asked Babs with a conjured air of innocence.

'Where he was the night your husband was murdered.'

'Good heavens, you surely don't think he had anything to do with that awful business, do you?' she asked, shock apparent on her face.

'No,' I said blithely. 'As I said, it's a question I have to ask everyone.'

'Well, you haven't asked me where I was,' said Babs.

'We didn't have to,' volunteered Dave. 'When you rang the police at Esher, you told them that you were worried because Mr Skinner had not returned home the previous evening. In order to know that he hadn't come home, you must have been here.'

'How very clever of you, Sergeant darling,' said Babs, her glance lingering on Dave. 'And what did the lovely Charlie say?'

'He told us he was with you,' said Dave.

Babs appeared to give that some thought. But then she said, 'Well, I'm sure that's right. Yes, of course he was. He was in bed with me. All night.' She sighed and shot me a guilty smile.

But I was by no means convinced that that

was the truth. Given her addiction to alcohol, I didn't think she could be sure which nights – or days for that matter – Charlie Hardy had been in her bed and which he had not. As far as I was concerned, Babs's claim that Hardy had been with her on the night of the murder didn't necessarily let the Esher antiques restorer off the hook.

'What time is it?' asked Babs.

I looked at my watch. 'Just after midday,' I said.

'Splendid. Well, I need a drink. Are you absolutely sure I can't tempt you, Mr Brock darling?'

The question was accompanied by a suggestive smile.

'No thanks, Babs,' I said. Looking at her shapely legs, she might well have tempted me to something other than alcohol had the situation been different, particularly in her present sober state. But she was the widow of the murder victim whose death I was investigating. Even so, I could think of one or two of my colleagues who would have taken advantage of her veiled offer, even in those circumstances. And I could also think of one or two of them whose careers had been abruptly terminated because they had been compromised in that way.

'Oh well, you won't mind if I do, will you?'

'Not at all.' I couldn't imagine that any objection on my part would have kept her

271

from her gin bottle. 'Mr Hardy also told us this morning that he was moving in with you. Is that right?'

'Is that what he said?' Babs turned from dispensing what I presumed was her first gin and tonic of the day. I wondered briefly how many bottles she got through in a week.

'But have you discussed this arrangement with him?'

'I might've done. I don't really remember.' Babs looked vaguely mystified. 'But he's more than welcome. It would save me sending for him, wouldn't it?' she added with a girlish giggle. 'I'd have him on tap,' she said, and giggled again.

It appeared to me very much as though Charlie Hardy was inveigling his way in, but whether he'd discussed it with Babs was another matter. Perhaps she *had* invited him to make their relationship more permanent and, because of her constant drunken stupor, had forgotten she'd done so. On the other hand, that might be the story Hardy would tell her when he turned up on her doorstep with all his belongings. And she wouldn't know one way or the other.

'Well, we must be going, Babs.'

'Do call in again, Mr Brock darling. You too, Sergeant darling. It gets rather lonely here, you know.'

'What d'you reckon, guv?' asked Dave once

we were back at Curtis Green.

'I don't think Babs has got any idea which days and nights Hardy was there with her, Dave,' I said, putting my previous thoughts into words. 'I suspect it all passes in an alcoholic haze.'

'Yeah, I don't think it holds up for an alibi. Anyway that guy is far too goody-goody for my liking. All that bloody innocence makes me think he's as guilty as hell. And I think he's decided to shack up with the sexy widow whether she asked him to or not. There's money there, and I reckon he wants some of it. And the one sure way of getting his hands on it was to top Rod Skinner.'

'Possibly,' I said cautiously. There were times when Dave's theories were a touch impulsive, but there were also as many occasions when his suppositions eventually came to be supported by hard evidence.

'I think we ought to have him in the nick and dust him with the frightening powder,' said Dave as he peeled an orange. 'See what he's made of.'

And that is exactly what we did.

It was obvious that Hardy hadn't started work yet. The doors to his workshop were closed and when eventually he opened one of them, he was holding an electric razor.

'Good morning, Mr Hardy.' It was eight o'clock on the Tuesday morning. The day after we'd last spoken to Babs Skinner.

'Hello again.'

'I would like you to come with us to the police station, Mr Hardy.'

Most people confronted with a request like that will bristle with indignation and ask if they are being arrested. But not Hardy. Well, not quite.

'Why?' He inclined his head and grinned, as though it were all a huge joke.

'Because there are certain aspects of the matter of Rod Skinner's murder that require clarification, and it's in your interests that your answers to our questions are recorded,' said Dave, a master of gobbledegook when the necessity arose.

What Dave didn't say was that we could have interviewed Hardy there and then. In the circumstances, there was no need for all the recording paraphernalia that exists at police stations. But interviews in police stations often have the effect of concentrating people's minds.

'Oh, all right then.' Hardy did not seem either to understand what Dave was talking about – which was what Dave had intended – or to be too concerned that we were carting him off to the nick. 'Is it all right if I finish shaving?'

'By all means,' I said, following him into his cramped living quarters.

I'm afraid our arrival rather alarmed the custody sergeant at Esher police station when we swept in with Charlie Hardy. Perhaps because it was early in the morning and he was conditioned to receiving prisoners in the late evening or during the night.

'Is this an arrest, sir?' asked the sergeant, peering at me over his spectacles.

'No, it's an interview,' I said.

'Oh well, that's all right, sir. It's just a case of which forms I have to fill in.'

I don't know why that puzzled him. Ever since the introduction of the Police and Criminal Evidence Act, the same forms – more or less – have been used to document persons brought to a police station whichever constabulary area we were in. I didn't think the Surrey Police was any different. Personally I always leave it to the custody sergeants. They usually seem to know what they're doing.

'I must emphasize, Mr Hardy,' I began, 'that you are not under arrest and you are free to leave at any time.'

'Right,' said Hardy with a grin. But he appeared to be wondering why he was here at all if that were the case.

'Now then, you say that on the night of Rod Skinner's murder – that was Saturday the sixth of July – you were with Mrs Skinner.'

'That's right. I was.'

275

'Where?'

'At her place at Cobham.'

'What time did you arrive?'

Hardy reflected on that question. 'Must have been about half-past six, I suppose. Why don't you ask Babs?'

'I did, but she didn't seem very certain that you *were* there. How long did you stay with her?'

'All night.'

'Did she mention anything about being concerned that her husband had not returned home?'

'No. In fact, she said she wasn't expecting him.'

'Had you any idea where Mr Skinner was that night?'

'No.'

'Did Mrs Skinner telephone the police about her husband's absence while you were there?'

'No. I didn't know she had phoned them.'

'What time did you leave on the Sunday morning?'

'After breakfast. We had it by the pool and then I went home.'

'And did you spend the whole time in bed with Mrs Skinner, apart from breakfast?'

'No. We had a few drinks on the patio on the Saturday evening, and then we spent about an hour skinny-dipping in the pool.'

That came as no surprise. 'And then?'

'We had some supper and went to bed around ten. Got up again at about half-past nine. Then, like I said, we had breakfast on the patio and I went home.'

'And you're absolutely certain that this all took place on the night that Mrs Skinner's husband was murdered?' I asked.

'Yes, positive.'

'I shall now ask you to make a written statement to that effect, Mr Hardy,' I said, and decided to get a bit heavy. 'But I must warn you that if that statement is tendered in evidence you would be open to prosecution if you wilfully state in it anything which you believed to be false or did not believe to be true. Now then, are you happy with what you've told Detective Sergeant Poole and me?'

That did it.

'Well, I'm *pretty* sure.'

'In that case, what exactly is it that you're *not* sure about?' I asked.

'Well, I think it was that weekend. You see, I tend to spend lots of weekends with Babs.'

'And when did you hear about Mr Skinner's murder?' asked Dave.

'Er, it was the Sunday after it happened.'

'Morning or afternoon?'

'Afternoon, I think. Yes, it was the afternoon.'

'In other words, only hours after you'd left Mrs Skinner.'

'I think so.' By now, Hardy was beginning to look nervous and unsure of himself. 'Yes, I remember Babs telephoning me at about four that afternoon.'

'So the truth of the matter,' said Dave, 'is that you don't know whether you spent that weekend with Mrs Skinner or not.'

'I thought I had, but now I can't be sure,' said Hardy, clearly unhappy that I'd talked about the possibility of prosecution. Mind you, that can have a negative effect. Even when witnesses are sure of something, any suggestion that they may get done for perjury tends to make them jumpy.

And that was just what I wanted.

'In that case, Mr Hardy, it might be better if we don't take a statement this morning, and that you go away and think about that weekend. And if you come to the conclusion that you weren't with Mrs Skinner, you'd better remember where you really were.' I gave him one of my cards. 'My telephone number's on there. Give me a ring when you've made up your mind.'

Hardy shoved the card into the back pocket of his jeans and nodded. We'd put him in a quandary: if he didn't get in touch, he knew we'd come looking for him. If he was Skinner's murderer, he'd made the mistake of relying on a woman with a serious drink problem to provide him with an alibi. If Babs were ever sober enough to make it to the Old

Bailey to give evidence in Hardy's defence, prosecuting counsel would destroy her credibility within minutes of her stepping into the witness box.

The one thing that puzzled me about Hardy was that he didn't ask why any statement he made might be put in evidence. Which was just as well, because I wouldn't have known the answer.

We took Charlie Hardy back to his workshop, leaving him to ponder the problem with which we'd presented him, and returned to Curtis Green.

'I think we should have nicked him there and then, guv,' said Dave, throwing me one of his Silk Cut cigarettes.

'On what evidence?' I asked. 'The fact that he says he now can't remember whether he was with Babs Skinner or not doesn't make him Rod Skinner's killer. It's up to us to prove he wasn't there; he doesn't have to prove he was. But I'll put money on what he's doing right now.'

'Yeah. On the blower to the Cobham coquette pleading with her to give him an alibi. And if he's as good a stud as she says he is, she'll do it.'

'Even so,' I said, 'the evidence of a drunk like Babs would get him nowhere.'

'Be interesting to hear what he comes up with next, then.'

What Charlie Hardy came up with next didn't help us a great deal. Two days after we'd interviewed him at Esher police station, I received a telephone call from him, asking if he could see us.

I contemplated requesting him to come to London, but then decided that we'd see him at his workshop in Little David Street. It was possible, that as a result of what he was going to tell us, we may have to see Babs Skinner yet again, God forbid. And to go on to Cobham from Esher would save us time.

'I reckon this bloody car could find its own way down the Portsmouth Road now, guv,' said the complaining Dave as we pulled into Little David Street.

Hardy had arranged three chairs around a table in his workshop.

'They look good quality,' said Dave, running a hand over the back of one of the chairs.

It was obvious from what Hardy said next that he knew his way around the esoteric world of antique furniture. 'The chairs are George the Third in the style of Chippendale,' he said, 'and the table's a Victorian walnut pedestal. Altogether that little lot's worth about seven thousand pounds. I'm restoring them for an earl.'

I doubted that the anonymous peer would

be greatly impressed if he knew that his precious antiques were being used for the purpose of taking a statement. And I was sure that we would be taking one.

'What is it you wish to tell us, Mr Hardy?' I asked by way of openers.

'After our chat at the police station, Mr Brock, I remembered what happened the night Rod was murdered.'

'Good,' I said. 'Go on.'

'That night, Babs rang me and asked me to go down to The Gables later on. At about eight, she said.'

'What time did she ring you?'

'About six, I suppose.'

'Did she say why she wanted to see you?' asked Dave impishly.

'The usual,' said Hardy in a matter-of-fact way. He ran a finger over the surface of the table, tutting irritably as he discovered a blemish. 'She said she wanted servicing.' He glanced up and gave another of his naive smiles.

'And so you went,' said Dave.

'Yes.'

Dave let out an exasperated sigh at Hardy's apparent inability to expand on what he was saying without being prompted. 'And when did you get there?'

'It must have been about eight o'clock, as Babs had suggested, but when I arrived I couldn't get an answer.'

'Why d'you think that was, Mr Hardy?' I asked.

'I thought she must've fallen asleep. She sounded pretty drunk when she rang, and it's happened before.'

'What has?' asked Dave.

'That she's sent for me, but been too drunk to perform. She'd often fall asleep even before I'd got undressed.'

'How frustrating for you,' commented Dave. 'Was her car on the drive?'

'No, but that didn't mean anything. She usually keeps it in the garage. I've warned her, over and over again, that she should stop using the car. I'm sure the police will catch her for drunk-driving one day.'

'Apart from the minor matter that she may kill someone,' said Dave acidly. 'Not that I think that'd worry her too much. She probably wouldn't know she'd done it.'

Most policemen, in their days in uniform, have come across a comatose driver, slumped over the wheel of a car, who was so drunk that he – or she – hadn't got a clue what they were doing or where they were.

'Did you look in the garage, Mr Hardy?' I asked.

'You can't see in. The doors are solid. They're one of those electronic up-and-over jobs. You aim a thing like a television zapper, and the door opens automatically.'

I hoped, at this crucial stage of the

interview, that Dave wouldn't choose to point out that if you operated a garage door with a remote control it wasn't opening automatically.

Fortunately, Dave had abandoned his English-language purism, at least for the moment. 'So you didn't see her at all that weekend.'

'Oh, but I did,' said Hardy. 'I was worried about her, so I went down on the Sunday morning.'

'What time?'

'I suppose it must've been about ten. She'd got a hell of a hangover, and I'd obviously got her out of bed to answer the door. I asked her what had happened the previous evening, and she said that she'd got drunk and gone to bed. She apologized for not hearing me when I arrived, but said she'd make it up to me.' Hardy grinned innocently. 'So we spent about twenty minutes in the pool. That usually clears her head for her. Then we had a few drinks on the patio, and I took her back to bed.'

'To sleep?'

Hardy grinned again. 'No, of course not.'

'What time did you leave?'

'Before lunch. It must've been about twelve.'

'Why?'

'Why?' repeated Hardy.

'Yes. Why didn't you stay for the rest of the

day?'

'Babs said she was in no fit state to have what she sometimes calls adult fun.'

'So you were dismissed,' said Dave.

Hardy smiled ruefully. 'Yes,' he said. 'It sometimes happens.'

Dave leaned back in his chair and gazed thoughtfully at the young man opposite him. Then he turned to me. 'Do we actually need a statement from Mr Hardy, sir?' he asked.

'I don't think so,' I said. 'That seems to clear up everything we need to know.'

In fact it was far from satisfactory, and it was certain that we'd need to interview Babs Skinner once more. Preferably at a time when she was sufficiently sober to understand what we were talking to her about.

'It seems to me that you do all sorts of things for Mrs Skinner,' said Dave. 'Apart from your primary *raison d'être*.'

'I help out with little jobs here and there,' said Hardy, clearly not understanding what Dave meant by *raison d'être*. 'More so now that Rod's dead.'

'Pop out to buy her gin for her, do you? Dave asked the question in an offhand sort of way, as though it were of no importance. Frankly I didn't know why he was asking it, but it became clear later on. Much later on.

'Yes, I do, but only occasionally,' said Hardy. 'But she also has it delivered. And the tonic water and the lemons,' he added. 'She has an account.'

'I thought she might have,' said Dave with a grin. 'Where is this place? Off-licence, supermarket, or what?'

'It's a wine merchants in Dudley Street, in Cobham. I can't remember the name, but it's the only one in the street.'

Seventeen

One of the beauties of having Kate Ebdon working for me is that like Frank Mead, the DI she'd replaced, she could be relied upon to do her own thing. That of course is what DIs are supposed to do, but I'm always grateful when they do it. And this time Kate had come up with something intriguing.

She had read and reread all the statements that had been taken, including the ones made by Dave Poole following each of our meetings with Babs Skinner. She then set her team to making further enquiries in order to clear up anything that didn't quite gel, or to clarify what had been written.

On the Monday morning following our latest interview with Charlie Hardy, she came into my office clutching a sheaf of papers, a puzzled frown on her face.

'What is it, Kate?' I asked, waving her towards a chair.

'Babs Skinner, guv.'

'What about her?'

'In Dave Poole's statement about the first interview you and he had with her, she said that Skinner's first wife was called something like Sharon or Tracey.' Kate was reading through Dave's statement as she spoke. 'It says here that she described it as a soap-opera name. She then went on to say she'd been married to Rod Skinner for eight years, but that it wasn't going to make nine.' She looked up and grinned. 'Well, she was right about that. But I had young Appleby do some checking with the General Register Office at Stockport and it ain't true.'

'You mean they weren't actually married?' This would be nothing new. It seemed to me that these days most people were, to use my mother's expression, 'living in sin'. Perhaps it has something to do with tax.

'Oh, they were married all right. Twenty years ago. And the marriage certificate shows Dennis Miller as a bachelor and Daphne Fuller as a spinster. So, for some reason best known to herself, Babs Skinner was lying. Neither she nor Rod Skinner had been married before.'

'I wonder why she should have said that,' I mused. 'Was there any reference to their occupations on the certificate?'

'Oh yes. You're going to love this, guv. Dennis Miller was shown as a musician, and Daphne Fuller as an actress.'

'A musician, eh? But when I—'

'Exactly. When you asked if she knew he played drums, she said it was news to her. But I suppose he might have played something else. Like the piccolo.'

'So what's her bloody game?'

'You did say she was a drunk,' said Kate with a laugh. 'Perhaps her brain's pickled.'

'Maybe,' I said, 'but I wonder why she should have said that. It's not as if it made any difference.'

'Unless she didn't want us to find the record of her marriage. In case it gave the game away.'

'Possibly, Kate,' I said, although I wasn't sure which particular game Kate was talking about.

'And one other thing. Appleby did a trawl through the birth records and found that they had a son, Chester, but he died at the age of four. Fell off a swing at the local kids' playground and fractured his skull.'

I felt a measure of sympathy at that. I knew what it was like to lose a four-year-old son.

While I was digesting the implications of Babs Skinner's lie, Dave came up with some more fascinating information.

'I sent Sheila Armitage down to Cobham on Saturday morning, guv, to this wine merchant in Dudley Street that supplies Babs Skinner. In the last month, she's purchased one bottle of gin and one case of red wine. And that's about average. Sheila said that the guy who runs the place looked up her account for the last year, and there was hardly any variation, month on month.'

'Very interesting,' I said. But I didn't know why. Perhaps she went elsewhere for her gin, or maybe Charlie Hardy supplied her with it out of gratitude and bought it at a supermarket. But somehow I couldn't see him affording to keep her in gin.

'What caused you to have that enquiry made, Dave?' I asked.

'I had my doubts about her, guv. This performance she puts on every time we see her is too good to be true. And now that Appleby's discovered that she was an actress it all comes together. I think Babs Skinner is guilty of over-acting.'

I'd been puzzled when Dave had asked Charlie Hardy where Babs bought her alcohol. Now I knew.

I walked out to the incident room only to bump into the commander.

'Ah, Mr Brock. How are the homicides of Rod Skinner and Erica Leech coming along? The Skinner death is over a month old now, is it not? And Leech? That was on the twenty-seventh of last month, I believe.'

'Yes, sir.' Trust the commander to know the exact dates, and use them to have a dig at me.

'Mmm! Any progress? At all?'

'I think we're on the verge of a breakthrough, sir,' I said, hoping that we were. 'I'll let you know as soon as there's a development.'

'Yes, good, good.' For a few moments the commander studied the enlarged photographs of the deceased and the numerous suspects that were exhibited on a large board. Then he nodded intelligently and wandered back to his office.

'How do I find out about actors, Colin?' I asked.

'Best place to start is Equity, sir, the actors' trade union. I've found them to be very helpful in the past.' As usual, Colin Wilberforce had come up with an immediate answer.

I gave Equity a ring and ran a few names past them, like Daphne Fuller, Daphne Miller, Ann Wright and Babs Skinner. The woman I spoke to promised to call me back. And did.

'I put those names through our index, Chief Inspector, but drew a blank,' she said, 'but then I tried combinations of them.' She sounded rather pleased with herself. 'The only name I can come up with that might help is that of a Babs Fuller. I have the name of her agent if you'd like it.'

I thanked her and promptly rang the agent who, fortunately, was not only still in business but had been for the past thirty years. He promised to return my call. Ten minutes later he was back on the line.

'This Babs Fuller was a bit-part actress about twenty years ago, Mr Brock. Never got her name up in lights, but I heard she was quite good at character parts. I suppose she gave up the profession when she got married. I certainly didn't hear anything from her again.'

'Have you any idea who she was married to?' I asked, even though I knew the answer. Well, I did if she was now called Babs Skinner.

There was a rustling of pages being turned. 'No, I'm afraid not. All I've got here is that she married one of the musicians in the orchestra at one of the theatres where she was appearing. I don't really know why I made a note of that.'

Thank God I'd come across a theatrical agent who kept records, even apparently irrelevant ones. But although this all sounded very promising, there was no proof that Babs Skinner was the Babs Fuller who'd been on the agent's books twenty years ago. The only thing that pointed to it was Babs Skinner's statement that she liked the name Babs better than the Daphne she was christened. It was possible therefore that she had used Babs as a stage name.

I called Kate Ebdon and Dave Poole into my office and told them what I had found out.

Dave nodded sagely. 'Like I said, guv. I'm sure this drunkenness of hers is all a big act,' he said.

'Well, there's one sure way of finding out. We'll get a warrant and spin The Gables.'

With the help of Dave and Kate, I managed to cobble together sufficient of an 'information' to convince the Bow Street district judge that we weren't just going to Cobham on a fishing expedition.

On the morning of Tuesday the thirteenth of August we struck. As the commander had somewhat sneakily reminded me, it was just over five weeks since the death of Rod Skinner and very nearly three weeks since Erica Leech had been murdered.

At ten o'clock, Dave and I arrived at The Gables. I saw no reason for arriving at five in the morning, the usual time for doing a search; we were not dealing with a gang of hardened villains. I had also brought along Kate Ebdon and three of her team, and Linda Mitchell and her forensic practitioners, but I left all of them in their vehicles, out of sight of the house. For the time being. Apart from Kate Ebdon, who, I decided, it would be prudent to have with me on this occasion.

It was a while before Babs answered the door, but I had now reached that level of cynicism to believe that the delay was deliberate. When she appeared, she was clutching a glass in her hand, and I thought she had probably seen us arrive, and had got herself a drink before greeting us.

'What a lovely surprise, Mr Brock darling. I hope this is a social visit. Oh, and you've brought a lady policeman with you. How nice to meet you, my dear.'

'This is Detective Inspector Ebdon, Babs, and no, it's not a social visit.'

'Oh, that's a pity. Well, you'd better come in, I suppose,' said Babs, a touch sharply. She sounded a little put out, and I suppose I must have sounded rather brusque. Either that or it was her perceived role as a sexual enchantress that was being cramped by Kate's presence. 'I was just going for a swim.' This was borne out by the towelling wrap she was wearing, beneath which there may – or may not – have been a swimsuit. 'Come out onto the patio.'

'This will do,' I said when we reached the large, airy sitting room.

'You are sounding terribly serious this morning, Mr Brock darling,' said Babs. 'Do let me get you all a drink.'

I ignored the invitation. 'When did you give up the stage, Babs?' I asked.

It struck home. She turned to face me. 'What do you mean?'

'I've been talking to your former agent, and he told me you were a quite good character actress in your time. As Babs Fuller.'

But Babs Skinner didn't react to the mention of that name in the way I'd hoped.

'We're all called actors now,' she said with an air of defiance. 'It's the sex-equality thing, you know.' Then, realizing that she had made what might be construed as a damaging admission, lapsed into silence.

'Dave.' I nodded to my sergeant. He knew what to do next.

'Barbara Skinner, you are not obliged to say anything, but it may harm your defence...' Dave, clever bugger that he is, reeled off the caution without even referring to the little card that the Police Federation had kindly given us years ago. I'd lost mine, but I think I might have mentioned that before.

Babs Skinner went white in the face and suddenly sat down on one of her sexy black leather settees. 'What on earth are you talking about?' she demanded.

'A week ago, we interviewed Charlie Hardy at Esher police station—'

'I know. He told me.'

'And we interviewed him again on Friday last.'

'He told me that too, but I don't know why you keep picking on Charlie.'

'He now tells us that he *wasn't* with you on the night of your husband's murder. He went on to say that you telephoned him at about six o'clock on that Saturday evening and asked him to come down here. But when he arrived, at about eight, there was no answer. He then returned the following morning and you told him that you'd gone to bed the night before because you were too drunk to entertain him.'

'Perfectly true.' Recovering something of her confidence, Babs rose and crossed to the drinks table. 'Are you sure you won't join me?' she asked. 'Ah, no ice. Shan't be a mo.' She walked towards the door.

'Go with her, Kate,' I said. The last thing I wanted was for Babs Skinner to escape or, worse still, take a bottleful of barbiturates and collapse dead on the floor. That really would give the commander a field day.

'I do know where my own kitchen is,' said Babs haughtily as she strode from the room. I think she knew what we were now strongly suspecting.

Dave moved rapidly to the drinks table and poured a measure from the gin bottle. He tasted it and laughed. 'Water, guv,' he said, before sitting down again.

Babs returned and poured herself a drink from the same 'gin' bottle that Dave had sampled, added tonic, a slice of lemon and a couple of cubes of ice.

'You really should put the ice in first,' said Dave. 'Tastes much better that way. Of course it tastes even better if you use gin.'

'What on earth are you talking about, young man?' snapped Babs. Suddenly the 'Sergeant darling' she had used previously had disappeared. She may have fancied

Dave's black body, but I got the distinct impression that she was averse to accepting sarcastic advice from it.

'That bottle you've just poured your drink from contains water,' said Dave. 'And according to your wine merchant in Dudley Street, you only buy one bottle of gin a month. Nowhere near enough to maintain your act as a soak.'

I don't know whether Babs intended to reply, but I decided that I'd had enough. 'I have a warrant to search these premises, Babs,' I said, 'and I intend to do so now.'

Kate took out her mobile phone and summoned the rest of her team, and Linda Mitchell and her scientists.

Babs stood up, a little unsteadily, but I attributed that to shock. She made for a cupboard in the corner of the room, took out a bottle of gin and poured a substantial amount into another glass. 'I hope you don't mind if I have a real drink now, Mr Brock,' she said sarcastically. I too had lost the suffix 'darling'. Oh well!

The search took several hours because Linda was a thorough forensic practitioner. Sorry, *senior* forensic practitioner. But it proved to be worthwhile.

The first discovery her team had made was in a stable block at the far end of the huge grounds. 'We found some interesting gear in there, Mr Brock,' she said.

'Like what?'

'Smelting equipment. It's fairly obvious that that's where Metcalfe and Co. were going to melt down the gold from the Heston Services job.'

'Well done, Linda,' I said, and tucked that item of information away for future use.

At one o'clock, Linda appeared again, a triumphant smile on her begrimed face. This time with splendid news.

'We've found a sawn-off shotgun and a Walther nine-millimetre pistol, Mr Brock,' she said. 'They were both in the loft, hidden under the fibreglass insulation between the rafters. There was a pile of suitcases on top, and that's what aroused my suspicion.' It had obviously not been sufficient of a hiding place to prevent its discovery by a dedicated search team like Linda's.

I had little doubt that the Walther would prove to be the weapon that Lenny Watson had given to Dennis Miller alias Rod Skinner after the Wembley safety deposit heist. Or that it had been used to murder Erica Leech. What surprised me was that it should still be there after Charlie Hardy had telephoned Babs Skinner with the distressing news that the wicked police had twice interviewed him. And asked him some very searching questions.

At that point, Babs must have realized that her alibi had fallen apart. So why didn't she get rid of these incriminating weapons? Maybe Hardy *hadn't* telephoned her and told her of his interview.

Then a nasty thought occurred to me.

Perhaps she didn't know they were there.

Had Hardy murdered Rod Skinner and then put the weapons in the loft at The Gables unbeknown to Babs? The question that wasn't answered, however, was why Hardy should have murdered Erica Leech. Had he had an affair with her too? An affair we'd heard nothing about, and which had come to an end when Erica had summarily discarded the handsome Charlie. We knew she had a penchant for such behaviour; Freddie Peacock had told us.

But then one of Linda Mitchell's team found a leg that had been cut from a pair of tights, and carelessly abandoned at the bottom of Babs Skinner's wardrobe.

'There are traces of what appears to be head hair inside, Mr Brock,' said Linda.

Interesting. In fact, very interesting. Why should there be hair inside the severed leg of a pair of tights unless it had been worn over the head? *As a mask.*

'Can you run a DNA test, Linda?' If the hair proved to be that of Babs Skinner, then we were home and dry. Perhaps.

'Only if we're lucky enough to find a hair with the root intact, Mr Brock,' said Linda. 'But there's no need for that. We can compare the hairs in the stocking with those I found on Mrs Skinner's hairbrush. You don't need DNA.'

That's you put in your place, Brock. Leave the science to the scientists in future.

'I can do it straight away,' continued Linda. 'I've got a microscope in the van. You'll need a hair taken from her head under evidential conditions to make sure it satisfies the court, but we can do that later.'

'Yes, I know,' I said, but I couldn't be too curt; Linda had such an enchanting smile.

I don't know how these forensic practitioners go about the more arcane aspects of their work, but a few minutes later Linda returned.

'It's a match, Mr Brock,' she said.

Here we go, then, I thought.

After the first and only real gin and tonic Babs had consumed, she had remained in the sitting room drinking tea and talking to Kate Ebdon. But even Kate's subtle interrogation techniques hadn't managed to extract anything incriminating.

'Mrs Barbara Skinner,' I said when Dave and I entered the sitting room, 'I am arresting you on suspicion of having murdered Rod Skinner on Saturday the sixth of July this year, and Erica Leech on Saturday the twenty-seventh of July this year, both at the Starlight Club, Fulham Palace Road, London.' I glanced at Dave and he reeled off the caution yet again.

Babs Skinner stared at me listlessly. 'I don't know what you're talking about,' she said. 'I was here all the time. I never go out.'

Dave wrote it all down in his pocket book.

I decided that in so serious a case as this, I wouldn't take Babs Skinner to the local police station. Complications always seem to arise when you start off by taking a murder suspect to a police station in another constabulary's area, and from which they later have to be transferred. Apart from anything else there's always some sort of procedural mumbo-jumbo about the interview clock beginning to tick. Usually Dave explains it to me.

'I shall now take you to Charing Cross police station,' I said.

'I suppose it's all right for me to get dressed first, is it?' asked Babs caustically. 'Or perhaps the boys in blue up there would prefer to see me like this.' Shrugging off her towelling robe to reveal a yellow bikini that could best be described as affording minimal coverage, she pushed one leg forward and placed her hands on her hips in a classic pose.

'Detective Inspector Ebdon will come upstairs with you,' I said, dragging my gaze away from her alluring figure.

Ten minutes later, Babs Skinner returned to the sitting room. But this was a new Babs

Skinner: sophisticated and well dressed. Gone was the tart's ankle chain. Gone were the 'raddled features' of the provocative tipsy tart of previous interviews; her make-up was now immaculate, and she was wearing a smart Chanel suit in pearl grey over a white silk blouse, black tights and black high-heeled court shoes.

But then she was an actress.

'I'm ready,' she said.

Eighteen

It was four o'clock on that Tuesday afternoon by the time we arrived at Charing Cross police station, just off Trafalgar Square.

There was not a lot I wanted to say to Babs Skinner. The evidence we had found at The Gables in Cobham was damning enough, but I felt I had to give her the opportunity to put her side of it. And if she made a voluntary confession, so much the better.

She sat down in the interview room, crossed her legs and arranged her skirt decorously over her knees. There was none of the flirtatiousness to which Dave and I had become accustomed over the weeks since Rod Skinner's murder.

I offered her a cigarette. There was a pause before she took one and another while she waited for Dave to produce his lighter.

'Is there anything you want to say to me before I charge you with your husband's murder and the murder of Erica Leech, Babs?' I saw no reason to start calling her Mrs Skinner just because this was a formal, recorded interview. 'You don't have to say anything if you don't want to, and you may have a solicitor present if you would like to have one here.'

'No, I don't want a solicitor. As a matter of fact, I'd like to tell you all about it.' Babs looked around the austere room. 'Is there any chance of a cup of tea before we start, Mr Brock?'

I broke off the interview, rang the custody sergeant and asked him to arrange for some tea. Five minutes later, a constable appeared with a tin tray on which were three cups of canteen tea.

'I'm afraid that's the best we can offer, Babs,' said Dave, who was familiar with the quality of canteen tea.

'If it's wet and warm it'll do,' said Babs, taking a mouthful and grimacing. 'I'm not sorry I killed him, Mr Brock,' she began. 'I stuck with that man through thick and thin. I kept things going when he was in prison, and I shared the dangers with him when we were put into the witness-protection scheme. We never knew whether someone he'd informed on, or one of their friends, would find him and kill him. We had to pretend we were on our beam-ends up in Hatfield, waiting for the fuss to die down so we could start spending the proceeds of what he'd stolen from the safety deposit. The money that wasn't accounted for, I mean. Then at last we moved down to Cobham and could start to have a bit of the high life.'

'What went wrong?' I asked.

'He did,' said Babs bitterly. 'He promised me faithfully that he was going straight, but then he let slip that he was planning another job, the bullion van that was attacked at Heston Services.'

'When did he and the others start planning that?' I asked.

'I really don't know, but I think they put the finishing touches to it at that dreadful party I told you about. In fact, I think you said as much. I can tell you, Mr Brock, I was furious when I found out what he was up to. I didn't fancy being a prisoner's wife again and I told him so, but he just laughed and said they wouldn't be caught. But I wasn't so sure. You see, I'd been through it all before: traipsing backwards and forwards to Parkhurst or wherever, and having the screws treat me as though I was the one doing the time. And how did he repay me for my loyalty? I'll tell you. By screwing any good-looking young brass he came across. Amateur whores, all of them. Took them abroad for expensive holidays, some of them. He even took that bitch Erica Leech to the South of France. That must've cost an arm and a leg. I was very bitter about that.'

'How did you know it was Erica he took?'

'I guessed it was her, at first anyway. As a matter of fact, I did a bit of detective work.' Babs gave me a shy smile. 'Or at least I got

Charlie to. Do anything for me, will Charlie.' She paused and smiled again. 'I even convinced him that I was a hopeless drunk. Anyway, I got him to follow Rod one Friday night and he found out that he was in a jazz band at the Starlight Club. So I went up there myself the following week and watched him leave arm in arm with that brazen hussy. They went back to her place at World's End and I suppose he stayed the night. Anyway, he didn't come home till the following morning. So I went back a few days later – one of the nights when Rod wasn't playing in the band – and stormed into Erica's office. When I challenged her about the affair she was having with Rod, she laughed in my face and had the audacity to say that if I couldn't hold on to a man, there must be something wrong with me. And as if that wasn't enough, she had the cheek to suggest I couldn't satisfy him in bed. You ask Charlie whether I'm a good lover, Mr Brock. See what he says. And finally she boasted that last year Rod had taken her to the South of France for a holiday. Threw it in my face, she did. That really was the last straw.'

'When did this confrontation with Erica take place, Babs?' I asked.

'A few days before I went up and blasted him.' Babs took another sip of her tea, grimaced again and pushed the cup and saucer away. 'But before that, as if that sort of humiliation wasn't enough, Rod had organized that party I told you about. I enjoy fun and games of that sort, and why not? Having a different man every now and then does me the world of good. And you know I'd had affairs with Lenny Watson, dear man, and Freddie Peacock.' She laughed without embarrassment. 'And quite a few others that you *don't* know about.'

'So you didn't object to this party as much as you said you did,' I put in.

Babs smiled mischievously. 'Of course not. Except that it was a bit one-sided. Rod had the pick of the available talent – and there was a lot of it – but I didn't fancy any of the men. Thank God I had Charlie there. Rod indulged himself a few times on the patio with me watching, and not giving a damn what I thought.'

'And that annoyed you?'

'Only that he was so blatant about it. After all, I knew what he was like, but there is such a thing as a bit of discretion. I knew he was cheating on me, but he could've had the decency to pretend he wasn't. It was just as well that Charlie was there and taking care of me, if you know what I mean, but at least we did it in private. As a matter of fact, I love doing it in the open air, especially if it's raining, but only when there's just the two of us.' Babs broke off, momentarily lost in thought at the memory. 'No, it was what happened about an hour later. I noticed that Rod had disappeared, so I went looking for him and found him screwing some tart of a girl. *in our bedroom.* Well, that *really* annoyed me. There were plenty of other rooms he could have used, but to use my bedroom was bloody insulting.' She paused to accept another of Dave's cigarettes. 'That little bitch couldn't've been more than twenty. And d'you know what the saucy cow did? She rolled off the bed – my bed – stark naked and stood in front of me. "This is what he likes," she said, and put her hands under her boobs and held them up, flaunting herself. And Rod laughed. Would you believe it, he damn well laughed at me. I tell you, Mr Brock, if he hadn't got between me and that little slut, there'd've been the mother and father of all catfights. Is it any wonder I did for him?'

'D'you want to tell me how you pulled off his murder, Babs?' I asked.

Babs laughed. 'It was easy. I knew he was playing at the Starlight Club on Fridays and Saturdays, so I drove up there and killed him with his own shotgun.'

'Where did that shotgun come from, Babs?' asked Dave.

'No idea. All I can tell you is that he got hold of it about six months before the Heston Services job – for protection, he said – and hid it in the loft where you found it. And he told me where it was. So I used it to kill him, and then put it back in the loft after I got home. That's irony for you, isn't it, Mr Brock?'

'As a matter of interest, Babs, what were you wearing that night?' asked Dave.

'Apart from the stocking mask, you mean?' she asked and laughed. 'A black sweater, black jeans and a three-quarter-length black leather coat. I'd fixed up a sort of hook arrangement inside the coat to take the shotgun. Funnily enough it was Rod who showed me how he used to do it,' she added with a sadistic chuckle.

So much for the descriptions we'd obtained from the so-called witnesses, not one of whom had accurately described Babs Skinner's clothing. But there was nothing new about that.

'I knew that the police would come and see me, and that's why I rang Esher police station to say that I was worried about Rod. So that you'd find me quickly.'

That wasn't very clever, I thought, because if she hadn't telephoned we might not have found her. But then Babs didn't know that Rod Skinner's record had been taken out of the general index after he was put into the witness-protection programme. But for her phone call, Rod's death might well have remained unsolved. I've never understood why she didn't disappear again and emerge somewhere else with a different identity.

'I'd thought it all out, and decided how I'd behave right from the start. I used to be quite a good character actor in my youth, and whenever you called there was always a delay in my answering the door.' Babs smiled at the recollection. 'That was to give myself time to put on my tart's make-up and get into the part. I pretended to be a lush, but I hardly drink. What you thought was G & T was just water and tonic with ice and lemon, but Sergeant Poole worked out what I was really up to.' Babs glanced at Dave and smiled. 'Didn't you, you clever sergeant?' she said, and turned to me again. 'I didn't think you'd ever suspect me, Mr Brock. I mean to say, who would ever think that a drunk like me could stroll into a Fulham jazz club and murder the drummer? Well, I did, and I'm not sorry either.'

'But what about the murder of Erica Leech, Babs?' I asked. 'How did you manage to walk into the club, shoot her, and then walk out again?'

Babs smiled. 'Easy when you've been an actor,' she said. 'I put on a black full-length wig, jeans and a sweater, the horn-rimmed specs with plain glass that I'd kept from my acting days, and different make-up. And in I went. No one challenged me. Well, it is a club, isn't it, so they wouldn't've done. I just paid the entrance fee and that was it. I went straight into Erica's office and shot her.

Simple as that. The pity of it was that she probably didn't know it was me who'd killed her. Shame that.' She laughed at the thought. 'Then I walked out again, got a cab to Waterloo and came home.'

It was breathtaking, but I could see how easy it would have been for an actress accustomed to treading the boards. To her it must've been just like another play.

'And the pistol? Where did that come from?'

'You were right about that, Mr Brock. Lenny Watson gave it to Rod after the Wembley job. God knows why. I told Rod he was a bloody fool to hang on to it, but he said it might come in useful. He was always worried that someone would turn up intent on killing him for having grassed. Anyway he bunged it in the loft along with the shotgun. And told me where it was.'

'Why did you tell me you'd only been married for eight years, Babs?' I was still puzzled by that deception.

'I thought that if I told you that, you'd never find our marriage details in Somerset House, so I gave you the wrong cue, as we used to say in the theatre. I didn't want you to find out that Rod had been a musician and, more importantly, that I'd been an actor.'

It was a naive sort of reason, and proved that despite having lived with a convicted robber for years, Babs was still none too familiar with police investigative techniques. What was more, she didn't even know that the General Register Office had moved a hundred and eighty miles away to Stockport in Cheshire.

'What about the smelting equipment my officers found in the stable block, Babs?'

'That was set up by Rod, to melt down the gold from the bullion job. But after I'd murdered him, I told Fruity and the boys that they could use it.' Babs smiled. 'So long as I got a cut.'

And that was it. I was amazed at the ingenuity of the woman. Although she'd made mistakes, she'd made less than many professional killers that I'd come across.

I stood up. 'You'll be taken through to the custody sergeant now, Babs, and in a minute or two I'll come and charge you with the murders of Rod Skinner and Erica Leech,' I said. I opened the door of the interview room and summoned a uniformed policewoman to conduct her to the custody suite.

Babs Skinner stood up too, and carefully smoothed her skirt. 'I suppose you have to do what you have to do, Mr Brock darling,' she said and smiled. 'You too, Sergeant darling,' she added, giving Dave a cheeky wink. 'I really could've fancied you, you know, Dave. You don't mind me calling you Dave, just this once, do you?' She sighed. 'Another

311

time, another place.' And with that she went.

'Hell hath no fury like a woman scorned,' I said, unwisely as it happened.

'"*Nor Hell* a fury, like a woman scorned" is what William Congreve actually wrote ... sir,' said Dave, somewhat smugly.

'Smart-arse,' I said.

The Crown Prosecution Service declined to include a count of conspiracy to rob when they drew up the indictment against Babs. They decided that her constructive possession of the smelting equipment and her desire to have some of the proceeds of the bullion job were too tenuous to put before the court.

The CPS also decided that Charlie Hardy had no case to answer. Counsel's opinion was that although Hardy had followed Rod Skinner, and then told Babs where her husband was playing in a jazz band, such acts did not amount to conspiracy to murder because he didn't know why she'd asked him to do it. And for once I agreed with them.

Consequently, Babs Skinner stood alone in the dock of Number Four Court at the Old Bailey to answer the two counts on the indictment of murdering Rod Skinner and Erica Leech.

Thanks to her substantial means, she had been able to engage the services of a leading silk. But there didn't seem to be much point.

She pleaded guilty to both murders.

But it was her counsel's plea in mitigation that proved he was worth every penny. With an eloquent delivery that would have done credit to the finest Shakespearian actor, he outlined all that Babs had had to put up with in her married life. He emphasized her loyalty during Rod Skinner's frequent periods of incarceration, and made great play of his extramarital affairs, flagrant affairs that had no regard for his wife's feelings. He described in detail the goings-on at the infamous party at The Gables – slanted very much in Babs's favour – and what took place at the confrontation between her and Erica Leech. He even mentioned Babs's affair with Charlie Hardy and, with open hands, pleaded with the jury not to blame her for 'a little bit of innocent fun'.

But at the end of it all, the judge had no alternative in law but to sentence her to two terms of life imprisonment. I thought it significant, however, that His Lordship pointedly imposed an incredibly lenient tariff, and went on to say that he would expect her to be paroled at a quite early stage in her sentence.

'I don't think the Lord Chief Justice will like that very much,' said prosecuting counsel, leaning back to speak to me.

As the two prison officers took her down, Babs paused and waved to Dave and me, and smiled that lascivious smile that we'd got to know so well.

Dave and I adjourned to the Magpie and Stump, the pub immediately opposite the Old Bailey, and sank a couple of pints of best bitter.

'Hello, Mr Brock. You've got another one sent down, then. Bit juicy by all accounts.'

I knew the voice. It was that of a crime reporter known universally as Fat Danny, an odious creep who worked for possibly the worst tabloid in Fleet Street.

I didn't even bother to turn. But Dave did, and using a well-known expletive, invited Danny to indulge in what, euphemistically, is known as sex and travel.

That evening Dave and I took Madeleine and Gail out to dinner. Not to celebrate the successful conclusion of the case; there was no cause for celebration in seeing Babs Skinner being sent to prison. The reason was that this was the first guaranteed free evening we'd both had since the start of the investigation. I'd even turned off my mobile phone.

It was towards the end of the evening, after we'd told the girls about the case, that Gail made a statement that took my breath away.

'I wish you'd told me about Babs earlier, darling,' she said. 'Years ago, when I first started in the theatre, I heard about this Babs

Fuller of yours. She'd left the stage by then, of course, but she was always mentioned whenever there was talk of character actors. Everyone said that she'd rise to the top of the profession, but she suddenly quit. The rumour was that she'd run away with a sessions drummer from the orchestra at a theatre where she was appearing. Mind you, the same rumours suggested that no man was safe when she was around. She broke up one or two marriages, so it was said.'

MAR

- 9 JUL 2011   2 9 JUL 2014

2 6 MAR 2010   - 7 APR 2015

2 2 NOV 2010   1 4 SEP 2011

3 0 DEC 2010   25·4 2012

20TH JAN

1 5 FEB 2011   1 2 JAN 2013

2 5 MAR 2011   1 7 JAN 2013

2 8 APR 2011   2 7 JUL 2013

1 8 MAY 2011

1 6 JUN 2011   - 6 DEC 2013

2 3 APR 2015

1 8 AUG 2015